THE (

N. Head

First published in 2022 by Blossom Spring Publishing
The City © 2022 N. Head
ISBN 978-1-7391561-7-6
E: admin@blossomspringpublishing.com
W: www.blossomspringpublishing.com

Acknowledgements

Thank you to my parents, who encouraged my reading and writing as a child, and who supported me through my education.
Thank you to Jorgen and Lina, who cheered me on to believe in myself and pursue my dreams.

Chapter One

It always surprised me how many people wanted to get drunk on a Wednesday night. Despite having worked at the bar for almost four months, and having adapted to the nocturnal lifestyle, I was still taken aback when businessmen and women stumbled out of the door at 3am on a weeknight, with seemingly no thought to the following morning commute. Personally, I couldn't face the thought of handling a hangover at a desk. But then, I'd never really done the nine to five thing.

Tonight was particularly busy, with a hen party in one corner making so much noise that even the heavy thump of the speakers was virtually drowned out. Of course, it was part of my job to tolerate the loudness — encourage it, even if it meant the liquor sales increased, but this particular group of young women were especially irritating. As I watched the bride-to-be fall over and reveal that she had chosen to forego underwear this evening, all I could think was *she's getting married, and I can't get a date?*

Maybe I was jealous, since my line of work didn't really permit a social life, let alone any romantic prospects. Obviously, the bar gig presented me with regular opportunities; it was the other job that kept me away from such frivolities.

Luckily for me, the hen party left a little after midnight, but my hopes of an early night were shattered when, ten minutes before closing, two men pushed through the heavy glass door and into the bar. I started to roll my eyes, until I recognized their faces. They hopped onto stools at the end of the bar, and nodded vaguely in my direction. Without a word between us, I set about pouring their usual orders — two double vodkas and added it to their seemingly limitless tabs. I guessed being friends with the owner of the bar had its advantages.

Come to think of it, *being* the owner of the bar seemed to have its advantages too — my boss, Jono, rarely emerged from the office upstairs. Not for one second did I believe that he spent all that time doing paperwork while I ran the bar for him, but I didn't mind working alone, so I never brought it up.

I approached the two men, sliding the tumblers of cool, clear liquid over the surface of the bar towards them. The older man smiled, and I returned the familiar expression. Doro and I had been friends for years, though throughout most of that time I had addressed him by his real name and dealt with him in his real occupation. He'd been undercover here in the City for almost two years now, so he was a lifer compared to my four months. But my observation and assimilation period was over now; it was time to introduce my character to the game.

'How are you?' I asked Doro, leaning over the bar and giving a wide smile.

'I'm good, hon. It's good to see you,' Doro replied, the secret familiarity twinkling behind his dark eyes, and creating a hidden softness to his tough appearance. In his forties, with hardened facial features and silver streaks through his hair, Doro could have looked just like any other weary city-dweller, if it weren't for his hulking size and the dark ink of the gang tattoos curling around his arms and peeking out beneath the neck of his shirt. Combined, his appearance was one of absolute intimidation.

My gaze travelled to the man next to Doro, who was ignoring our conversation entirely and focusing instead on his drink. He was younger than Doro, in his early thirties. That meant he was likely only a couple years older than me, but that fact did not make him easier to relate to. The cold, hard exterior of his mental shield sent shivers over my skin even from this distance. Menacing was not a strong enough word to describe him.

Before I'd moved to the City to begin my time undercover, I had gone through a process of intensive preparatory training with the police. During this training, the man before me had been identified to me as Dimitri Savchenko, a very dangerous player in the gang that we were trying to infiltrate. My superiors would never have sent me into the City if they didn't believe that I was ready for this, but in this moment, faced with this man, a little doubt about their decision started to creep into the corner of my mind.

Since Dimitri seemed determined to avoid all human interaction, Doro had to make a move to bring him into the conversation. Doro had gained the gang's trust soon after his time undercover began, and he'd undergone their initiation several years ago. He was officially in, so Dimitri listened when Doro spoke.

'This is Mari,' Doro introduced me by my undercover name. I'd been using it since I moved here, but it was still an adjustment. 'She's my favourite barmaid.'

I smiled, and Dimitri finally looked at me. He didn't return my expression, settling instead for a half-hearted nod.

'Nice to formally meet you. I've seen you in here a bunch of times.' I commented in an attempt to extend our interaction, resting my elbows on the bar and dipping my head to make eye contact with him.

He didn't seem particularly receptive to that plan. 'Yeah.' Well, one word was better than nothing.

Doro jumped to my rescue. 'Doesn't she look familiar?' he asked Dimitri, gesturing to me with his thumb.

Dimitri raised his gaze again to reluctantly look me over again. 'No.' His voice was so monotone and uninterested it actually surprised me. I'm not sure what I'd expected from my first meeting with Dimitri, but this definitely wasn't it. Men in general usually had a slightly more positive reaction to me, and in keeping with this establishment, I always dressed in more revealing clothes than usual when I was working. Still, as far as he was concerned, I might as well have been a blank wall.

Doro smirked. 'She's Max's kid — one of them, anyway. Hell knows he had near a hundred.'

Max Peters had been a very powerful man within the rankings of this particular gang until he had been killed last year by a rival organisation. He wasn't really my father, obviously, but he was known for his womanising (alongside his horrific violent behaviour, of course) and he'd had illegitimate children of his turn up before looking for daddy — or money.

My superiors had worked hard and researched rigorously to come up with a convincing and irrefutable backstory for my undercover persona, and since he was now dead, Max himself couldn't exactly argue. So he had become my cover story, and hopefully my primary way of gaining the gang's trust.

Finally, Dimitri showed some interest — a flicker of surprise passed over his icy features, though it lasted for only a fleeting moment before he composed himself once more. His eyes narrowed, and he spoke in a suspicious tone. 'I don't remember you being at the funeral.'

I shrugged, easily. 'He might have been my father, but he wasn't my dad. Once I found out who he was, I was hardly gonna go running into his arms, you know?'

After a second, Dimitri nodded, apparently convinced. I let go of a breath I hadn't realised I was holding in.

I glanced up at the clock behind the bar. It was after one. 'Closing time, guys. Time to get outta here.'

Doro downed his drink, and leaned over the bar to kiss

my cheek goodbye. Dimitri nodded in my direction, before following Doro out of the door. I locked it behind them and set about the closing duties, reflecting on my first face to face interaction with a member of the gang. It had felt a lot more natural than I'd expected, which was both positive and a little unnerving. I was pleased, but meeting Dimitri really highlighted how difficult it was going to be to earn his trust. He was cold and hard. I supposed that one had to develop those traits in order to survive this world. But Doro had wormed his way in all by himself, and now I would benefit from his established position, and the years of knowledge he'd gathered. Of course, after that length of time, Doro could provide enough evidence and information to make arrests on a dozen men, if not more. But we were going after bigger fish.

After I finished washing the last of the glasses and deposited the till money into the safe, I locked up and headed out into the night. The fifteen-minute walk back to my flat took me through a neighbourhood I would usually have avoided, but I was already starting to feel at home here. I wasn't sure if that was a good thing or not.

As I turned onto my street and my building came into view, I noticed two men stood outside. The glow of the nearby streetlight silhouetted their figures, but didn't allow me to see their faces. Automatically, my muscle tension increased, and I felt my hands brace into fists, ready to fly. Despite my physical reaction, I forced myself to walk calmly past them, and I thought I'd made it to the door without any trouble, when a clammy hand grabbed my wrist.

I spun on my heel and came face to face with a man in his forties, gazing at me through heavy-lidded eyes, a cigarette between his cracked white lips. When he spoke, it didn't fall.

'You are here to see Dimitri?' His voice was low and gruff, from too much smoking and drinking.

'No. Get off me.' I tried to yank my arm away, but he held on tightly. Too tightly.

'You're here to see Dimitri,' the man repeated, this time not a question. 'You're just his type. No wonder he won't answer my damn calls.'

What was he talking about? Dimitri from the bar? It couldn't be the same Dimitri — I would have been informed if one of the gang members was living in the same building as me. In fact, I doubt I would have been placed in the building at all if that were the case. Not to mention that I probably would have crossed paths with him at some point in the past four months since I'd moved here, yet the only place I'd ever seen him was at the bar.

'Since he is apparently ignoring me in favour of spending some...*quality time* with you...' The man pulled me closer, and I could smell vodka and cigarette smoke on his breath. 'You can go tell him I'm waiting to speak to him.'

'I'm not your errand runner,' I snapped, trying in vain to loosen his grip on my aching wrist.

His expression darkened, and his free hand encircled my neck, though not hard enough to hurt. He was just trying to scare me. 'Don't push me,' he growled, his face just millimetres from mine. 'I could always get Dimitri down here with the sound of your screams.'

My irritation flared into anger. I leaned into him and hissed, 'I wouldn't scream for you.'

The man pulled back from me, releasing his hold on my neck and raising his hand as if to hit me, but he was interrupted by a chuckle to our left. It was the second man, who I'd almost forgotten about until now. He was apparently amused by my fighting spirit.

As I turned to look at him, he surprised me by lunging forward and grabbing my small leather purse from my shoulder. It took him seconds to fish out my keys. I'm not sure how he managed that, because it always seemed to take forever to find anything in there.

This second guy was younger, and he even dared to flash me a grin as he unlocked the building door and let himself inside. The man holding my arm smirked at me, pulling me viciously through the door. He made the mistake of turning his back on me, and I took the opportunity to land a solid punch to the back of his head. It landed pretty hard, despite the fact that it was left-handed. It surprised him enough that he loosened his grip on my wrist finally, and I was able to break free. Angrily, he turned and swore venomously. I landed another blow, to his face using my stronger hand, and he cursed again.

This time, he moved faster, as his open-handed slap burned my cheek. He shoved me back into the wall of the stairwell, and my head slammed back against the cold hard concrete. My head span and my vision momentarily clouded over. When I was able to focus again, the face in front of me was not the one I'd been expecting. Instead of the random man who'd been trying to beat on me, I saw Dimitri. His eyes were such a deep brown that they looked almost black under the harsh strip lights of the stairwell.

His hand touched my shoulder gently, and he directed me towards the stairs. With the two strange men leading the way, and Dimitri behind me, I climbed the three flights of stairs to my apartment on autopilot. I was tremendously aware that I was the *filling* in a gang member sandwich.

At my front door, I realised that I didn't have my keys. 'My bag,' I said, turning to see Dimitri standing right behind me.

'They have it?' he asked, nodding towards the two men who had carried on up the next flight of stairs.

'Yeah, they took it.'

'Stay here.' Dimitri ran up the next flight of stairs, and I heard shouting, before Dimitri returned with my handbag in one hand, and my keys in the other.

I took both from him — unlocked my door and was surprised when Dimitri followed me inside. Dropping my bag onto the couch, I headed straight for the fridge and pulled out a beer, cracking it open against the side of the counter.

Dimitri followed, leaning against the wall and watching me, one dark eyebrow raised.

I took a deep breath. Dimitri was in my apartment, but there was no reason to panic. Right?

'What?' I asked, taking a long sip of the cold fizz.

He shook his head, his expression carefully blank. 'You okay?'

'Sure.' I shrugged. 'Thanks for that, I guess.' I didn't like the idea of him coming to my defence, since I could have handled the situation myself, but nevertheless he had helped me out, and I wasn't going to gain his trust by being ungrateful.

Dimitri nodded.

'I didn't know you lived in my building,' I said, in complete honesty. I'd had no idea. And it was kind of a problem. 'I've been in this flat for months and haven't seen you around here.'

Dimitri shrugged. 'Moved in last week.' The coolness in his eyes was making me feel uncomfortable and unwelcome in my own home. I wished he hadn't come in, but I also couldn't help but see the positive side of this encounter — he'd definitely remember me now.

'Oh, right.' I took a sip of my beer.

Dimitri pushed away from the wall against which he'd

been leaning, and headed for the door. 'I'll tell them not to bother you again.'

I nodded by way of reply.

He left without another word, or even another glance, and I locked the door behind him immediately. I finished my beer and grabbed another on my way to the bedroom, where I went straight for the bottom drawer of my bedside cabinet. Underneath a pile of socks, the drawer was fitted with a false bottom, under which was a handgun and a mobile phone. Switching it on took only seconds, and I hit the first number on my speed dial.

My supervisor answered after barely one ring. No surprise — he knew I'd been introduced officially tonight. 'Hello?' Taylor's voice was crisp and alert, despite the late hour.

'It's me,' I said.

'You've got a problem already?'

I rolled my eyes. 'You have such faith in me. No, just an update. Dimitri lives above me.'

Pause. 'What?'

'Dimitri Savchenko lives in the flat above mine,' I repeated, unsure of what exactly was unclear about that statement. A long drink of beer helped placate my annoyance.

Taylor sighed and cursed softly. 'How did we miss that?'

'You're asking me?' I replied, but to be fair... 'He said he moved in last week.'

'We'll get you out of there, find you somewhere else tomorrow,' Taylor said, as I heard papers ruffle on the desk, I knew he was sitting behind. He didn't have much of a social life. Then again, neither did I.

'No, don't do that,' I argued. 'He was just in my kitchen; he knows I'm here. He didn't see any boxes or anything, so it would look strange if I just moved out tomorrow. Besides, it might be a good thing.'

'This is not a good thing,' Taylor warned.

'Relax,' I rolled my eyes again. I tended to do that a lot when I spoke to Taylor. 'I have things under control. I think this can work in my favour. Being neighbours is gonna get me a lot closer to him a lot faster. I can run into him in the hallway, I'll become part of his everyday life.' There was a pause, during which my supervisor's doubt was obvious. 'Trust me.'

Taylor sighed. 'Okay. For now. But the first hint of trouble and you're out of there. Keep me posted, okay?'

'Sure.' I hung up.

I undressed and got into bed with my beer. Pressing the cold bottle against my stinging cheek, I inspected my wrist. It was definitely going to bruise, and it hurt like a bitch, but I'd definitely had worse, and I was sure I would again. I was a little annoyed with myself — I'd had total self-defence training, and I'd been slow to use it when that man got in my face. Next time, I promised myself, I wouldn't hesitate.

Chapter Two

The next day, I was in the middle of a workout when Dimitri knocked on my door. When I opened the door, he stepped inside without waiting for invitation, and it occurred to me that I was a sweaty mess. Stupid, I know, but luckily, Dimitri didn't seem concerned about my appearance, since the first thing he focused on was my wrist. As expected, the bruises had come up lovely. He gently lifted my arm to examine my bruises more closely; I had to fight the immediate urge to pull away from his touch.

'Does it hurt?' he asked.

'Hello to you too,' I said dryly.

He ignored me.

'Not much,' I answered his question with a lie. Pain shot through my wrist every time I turned it the wrong way, but I didn't need him to know that, and I sure as hell didn't need him here checking up on me. The only reason I let him get away with touching me was because I needed to get in his good books. I had to keep reminding myself that this wasn't a normal situation, and I couldn't act like my normal self. I wasn't Harper Hallowell anymore, I was Marianna Harris, and they were two very different people.

Dimitri finally looked up at my face, gently releasing my wrist, and he met my eyes with his own dark pair. 'For what it's worth, I am sorry about last night.'

I blinked. That was the most words I'd ever heard him say, in all my months of observing him in the bar. Shaking off my surprise, I shrugged in an effort to appear casual. 'Not your fault.'

He nodded and turned to leave, and my mind desperately searched for something to say in order to extend our contact.

'You've been ignoring me in the bar for weeks and now you've been in my kitchen twice in twenty four hours,' I noted, trying for a joke. 'Who knew you could get a guy's attention just by getting a little beat up?'

He didn't even crack a smile, and he didn't bother responding. His hand was on the door, and I panicked.

'Who were those men?' my question blurted out, and I instantly worried that I'd gone too far.

Dimitri's hesitation caused my heart rate to race. He stood with one hand on the latch, looking like there was nothing he'd rather do than run out the door that second. But after a few moments, he turned back to face me, meeting my gaze with a heavy expression.

'You're Max's daughter,' he said. 'You know what he did, right? What Doro does? Their jobs?'

Job was a debatable term, but I nodded.

'Well, those guys last night were just some more associates. Don't worry. I told them not to come by here anymore.'

'I wasn't worried,' I told him. 'Don't you have an office or whatever?'

'An office?' Dimitri raised one eyebrow, bemused.

'You know, somewhere you go to *do business*, or whatever.' I was asking questions I already knew the answers to. The gang headquarters was based at the Beach, an area of the City on the coast, where there was a large amalgamation of cultures. The gang — or more specifically, their boss Mikhail Ivanov — owned a lot of businesses there, but their crimes extended all over the City and the surrounding areas.

'Yeah we do.' Dimitri didn't elaborate. 'Those guys were just being assholes coming over here like that.'

I smirked. 'Isn't that quality listed in the job description?'

Dimitri looked surprised by my familiar comment, and

I could have sworn that I saw the beginning of a smile turn up one side of his mouth, but it was gone again before I could be sure. This time when Dimitri opened the door to leave, I didn't try to stop him. Interacting with him was surprisingly exhausting. He wasn't like any other man I'd ever met, and despite my thorough preparation and training, I wasn't sure how to act around him to best gain his trust. Besides that, he was for sure the scariest man I'd ever met, and realistically, that probably had a little something to do with my discomfort around him.

Returning to the lounge, I forwent the rest of my work out in favour of the sofa. While I hadn't got anything of any use out of Dimitri — we already knew about their dealings at the Beach — I at least knew that he was willing to interact with me. Even if he had avoided my questions, he had listened to them. That was something, because it meant that he believed my cover story, and we had established a basic understanding of my knowledge of the gang. Progress was progress, no matter how small.

***

That evening, I started work at seven, though the bar never picked up much until a few hours later. It was nearing midnight when Dimitri arrived, followed through the door by another man and a girl, both of whom I recognised as semi-regular customers. The second man was tall, broad, and blonde, with stunning blue eyes and biceps that looked about the same circumference as my upper thigh. The girl looked younger than me, in her early or mid-twenties, maybe. Her frame was delicate and dwarfed further by the intimidating size of Dimitri and his friend. She was pretty in an elfin way, with delicate features and a platinum blonde pixie cut.

They ordered a round of drinks and headed over to their usual booth in the corner. I took several refills to their table, but otherwise barely had the time to notice them as the bar became increasingly busy. A little while later, when I finally had a minute to myself and was taking the opportunity to tidy up the bottles scattered across the bar, the young blonde woman approached me. She hopped up onto a barstool and pushed her empty glass towards me, while Dimitri and the other guy went outside, presumably for a cigarette. I think she'd had more to drink than both men together.

She ordered a vodka coke, and I made it quickly, adding it to Dimitri's tab.

'I'm Nina,' she introduced, taking a quick sip through a thin straw.

'Mari,' I replied with a smile. I hadn't heard about this woman during my training, but from her easy demeanour around Dimitri and his friend, I knew she could be useful to me. There were, of course, many women who were involved with the business in some way or other, working at the clubs at so on, but they were very unlikely to be out socialising with the men like this. When Nina spoke some more, I knew that she definitely wasn't one of the working girls. She was too upbeat, too self-assured. She wasn't worried about talking to strangers, and she was privy to at least some information.

'I know who you are. Dimitri told us what Tony and Fabio did to you last night. Said you handled it pretty well.'

'Oh, yeah,' I replied, a little surprised that Dimitri had divulged information about the men at our building last night, but glad that she'd given me their names. 'It wasn't a big deal.'

'Heard you landed some good punches on Tony.' Nina grinned.

'Oh, yeah, I took some self-defence classes at the gym last year,' I lied.

Nina nodded and leaned in closer to speak. 'I guess it's in your blood, too, right? Dimitri told us about that, too. You know, Max.'

I raised my eyebrows. For a man in a business based almost entirely on discretion and secrecy, Dimitri didn't seem to respect other people's privacy. Not that I minded — in fact, it would probably work in my favour if this particular piece of information was heard by all the right people.

Nina looked me up and down. 'Damn, girl, you lucky you don't look more like your dad, huh? Max was...' she cleared her throat. 'Sorry. Don't talk bad of the dead and all that.'

I blinked. She talked so fast. 'No worries, we weren't close.' I noticed she'd finished her drink already. 'Can I get you another?'

She grinned. 'I'll have the same again.'

When Dimitri and his friend came back inside, Nina had once again downed her drink. No wonder she was wasted already. The two men approached the bar, and the blonde guy's arm wrapped around Nina's waist while he whispered something into her ear that made her giggle.

Dimitri met my eyes, gave me a small nod.

'Last orders,' I said, indicating towards the clock, which showed fifteen minutes until closing.

'What are we doing after?' Nina asked the two men. 'Drinks at D's place?'

Dimitri gave her an unimpressed look, and I had to fight a smile at his expression.

'Come on,' Nina cajoled. 'Please? I haven't got work tomorrow and I wanna party!'

'We can all go to mine instead?' the blonde man offered, his voice deep and pleasant. He looked at me,

'You can come, too. It's Mari, right? I'm Valentin. But call me Val.'

He winked, and I smiled. He was charming, and he knew it.

Before I could respond, Dimitri spoke. 'Not tonight.'

'How about it?' Val turned his attention back to me, ignoring Dimitri's short response.

'Oh, I've got to tidy up here. But next time, for sure,' I smiled.

I wanted to accept the offer of course, but, as Mikhail's right hand man, Dimitri was my main target right now. He'd declined the offer, so I did too. I wanted to align myself with him, earn his trust. Or at least his interest.

Nina looked disappointed, until Val pointed out that it meant they would be alone, and a mischievous grin spread over her face. While the two of them flirted in a sickeningly sweet way, Dimitri sat in stoic silence, his face blank and unreadable. I didn't understand why he chose to hang around with this couple when their enthusiasm and excitability simply seemed to irritate him. But he also didn't strike me like the kind of person who'd do something he didn't want to do. I never usually had this much trouble figuring people out. It was infuriating.

The three of them ordered one more drink each, and I set about cleaning the bar area. When the clock struck one, I dimmed the lights, and the few remaining customers trickled out into the night. Nina and Val left with a wave in my direction, and Dimitri took a seat at the bar while I tidied tables.

I looked at him. 'You waiting for something?'

He raised one shoulder, in a half-bothered shrug. 'We're going the same way.'

I frowned, but didn't question him. I knew he probably thought he was doing me a favour, given what happened last time I walked home alone, but it was the kind of behaviour that always annoyed me. Something about my appearance — or maybe just my gender — gave the impression that I needed looking after, but I never had. People always learned that the hard way.

The walk home was silent. It was a strange feeling, being alone in the dark with this man. He was close, we were alone, and it made my skin prickle. The only time I'd been this close to murderers before was when they'd been behind bars or in cuffs. And I didn't think that any of their criminal records could compare to Dimitri's. I tried not to think about that.

I knew I should take the opportunity, so I tried to start a conversation. 'How come you told Nina and Val about me?'

He glanced over at me. Since he was over a foot taller than me, he had to look down to meet my eyes. Most people did. 'They asked. I saw no reason to lie.'

I raised an eyebrow, sceptically. 'They asked you if Max Peters was my biological father?'

Dimitri rolled his eyes. 'You said hello to me when we walked into the bar, and they asked how I knew you. I just told them what Doro told me.' He shrugged with one shoulder again, his hands in his pockets. 'Is that a problem?'

'No,' I replied, mirroring his shrug.

We reached the building, and at my front door, Dimitri paused while I fumbled for my keys. I gave him a look. 'Thanks for walking me back, but you don't need to hang around. There's no one here to get me.'

He didn't seem to appreciate my sarcasm, and he ignored it. 'How is your wrist?'

I found my keys and unlocked the door. 'It's fine. Same as it was this morning.' I gave him a small smile over my shoulder as I stepped inside. 'Have a good night.'

He was already heading up the stairs.

Inside, I headed straight to bed. This undercover business sure was tiring. Or maybe that was just the bar work. The past twenty four hours had been a fairly successful introduction to Dimitri and his crew, but I knew I couldn't be too forward, and that now I had to wait for the opportunities to come to me.

***

Such an opportunity came a week later. It was a Friday shift at the bar; at weekends, I worked with another member of staff, so it was a little more interesting. That member of staff was Leigh, a vibrant young woman with purple hair and so many piercings that I always wondered how she ever got through an airport. She was easy enough to get along with, and we spent a lot of time chatting when we worked together, especially when it was quiet.

As Leigh was telling me a story about her cat, Nina walked past the bar, and gave me a wave through the window. Seeing this, Leigh rolled her eyes, and I shot her a questioning glance.

'How do you know Nina?' Leigh asked.

'She comes in here a lot,' I replied. 'You don't like her?'

'We went to school together,' Leigh explained. Two women approached the bar and ordered tequila shots. Leigh poured them expertly, continuing our conversation in a low voice. 'She was such a loser. She dropped out when we were fifteen. She was pregnant, but apparently she was forced to give up the baby for adoption or something.'

'Seriously?' I asked, shocked. 'Forced by who?'

Leigh counted change out of the till and handed it to the women before turning back to me with a shrug. 'I'm not sure. It was like ten years ago, man. Anyway, Nina didn't come back to school, and now apparently all she does is get drunk in dive bars with gang bangers.' Leigh flipped her hair over her shoulder and smirked. 'Good life choices, right?'

'How do you know they're in a gang?' I asked her.

She gave me a look, as if I was the most stupid person she'd ever encountered. 'It's obvious, and even if it wasn't, you can tell by the tattoos,' Leigh explained.

Of course, I knew the tattoos were gang tags, symbolising an individual's affiliation, and also the crimes they had apparently committed, with different images representing different attitudes and actions. It was an old-school tradition for certain organised crime syndicates, which the boss apparently felt it was important to uphold, and it had formed another part of my training.

'You seem to know a lot about the gang,' I commented, keeping my tone light.

She shrugged. 'I went to school with a bunch of guys who were involved. And Nina, of course. She's one of those desperate girls who think hanging around with a gang makes them more attractive, or safe, or something, when really it just does the opposite.'

I raised my eyebrows at the level of venom in Leigh's words, but didn't pursue it further. She clearly had a chip on her shoulder about the gang, and I could understand why; the whole City was aware of this particular criminal syndicate, and pretty much everyone was under their influence, whether it was actually working for them, being a victim of their crimes, or living in fear. It affected everyone's life in some way, and I was sure that Leigh was no different.

We locked up and said goodbye at the door, going our separate ways. When I reached my building, my throat tightened when I saw three men blocking my way to the door. Approaching warily, I relaxed only minimally when I could make out the outline of Dimitri's face in the glow of the nearby streetlight. I walked past the small group in what I hoped was a confident manner, and only when I reached the door did Dimitri seem to notice me. He split away from the others and followed me inside.

'What's up?' I asked once we were in the foyer.

'They're just some associates,' Dimitri replied, referring to the men outside.

It amused me when he spoke about his gang as if it were a legitimate business. 'So?'

'Just making sure you weren't freaking out.'

I rolled my eyes. That really wasn't how I wanted him to think of me, like some girl who needed rescuing and reassuring. Frustration bubbled beneath my skin. 'Really? Get the hint, Dimitri, I can take care of myself.' Sarcasm was heavy in my voice, but I couldn't help it. I was always defensive when people underestimated me.

Dimitri raised an eyebrow at me, clearly unimpressed. I guessed people didn't usually talk to him in such a disrespectful way, and it occurred to me that maybe I should watch myself around him. He was, after all, a murderer — when he needed to be. In fact, I knew exactly the number of murders he was suspected to be involved with. The look in his eyes made it impossible to think of anything else in that moment.

Despite my increasing heart rate, I maintained eye contact until he spoke.

'I was just going to warn you that there will be more joining us, and coming up to my apartment,' Dimitri nearly growled.

I swallowed. He was definitely pissed at me. That

made me a little nervous. Maybe I shouldn't have reacted quite so strongly. 'Uh… Well, thanks.' My mind stilled, as an idea came to me. 'Is Nina gonna be coming over?'

Dimitri hesitated, unsure of my question, and simply shook his head by way of answering. He turned on his heel, and started back towards the door.

'Hey. Do you think you could do me a favour?' I called after him.

Dimitri looked back at me over his shoulder. 'What?' His voice was suspicious, and low.

I shrugged, feigning awkwardness. 'I was just wondering if you could pass my number on to Nina. I only ask because she seemed nice, and I don't have a lot of friends here. If you think she'd want to hang out, that is.'

Dimitri blinked, and looked at me with a strange, indecipherable expression. He had clearly not been expecting that. To be fair, neither had I. After a moment, Dimitri surprised me by handing me his phone. I keyed in my number before holding it back out to him. He took it gently from my hand and slid it back into his pocket. Putting my number into his phone felt like a mini triumph.

'Thanks,' I smiled.

'No problem.' His voice was still low, but he didn't sound angry anymore, and he'd returned to his usual, unreadable self. With not another word, he left the building, and I stood on the stairs for a moment to gather myself. That particular interaction had been an unwelcome reminder of exactly who I was dealing with, and how I needed to be way more careful in how I spoke to and acted towards these people. But it had also provided me with the chance to get in touch with Nina, because after what Leigh had said about her, I had a feeling she might be the weak link I was looking for.

Chapter Three

Nina called me the following week, as I was making my morning coffee extra strong to combat the rainy Friday. In my real life, I never answered unknown numbers, but now I never knew who would be trying to make contact, so I'd started to pick up the strange calls. Until now, it had just been sales and wrong numbers.

'Is this Mari?' a soft, high-pitched voice asked.

'Yeah.' I accidentally poured too much milk into my mug, and cursed myself silently.

'It's Nina,' the voice revealed, and my attention instantly peaked. 'D gave me your number.'

'Oh, hey. What's up?' I tried to sound casual, despite the triumphant smile on my face. I was surprised not only that she had called, but that Dimitri had actually passed on my number to her. I hadn't expected him to.

Nina hesitated. 'Well, I kind of need your help.'

'Oh? What's wrong?' Exciting possibilities swirled in my imaginative mind, only to be disappointed by her answer.

'I have no clothes to wear to a club opening tonight. I don't really have any girlfriends, and men are so rubbish at this stuff. Will you come shopping with me? If you're not busy today, that is.'

I rolled my eyes, but kept my tone light and interested. Acting was one of the skills I'd had more trouble with during my training, but I liked to think I was getting pretty good. 'I'm not busy, and I'd love to come with you.'

Nina seemed exceedingly pleased with my convincingly enthusiastic response, so we arranged to meet in an hour down the street. I was there before Nina, but she wasn't too late, and I didn't mind. I spent the time mentally preparing myself, determined to build a good relationship with this girl. Once she trusted me, I was hoping that Dimitri and Valentin could be persuaded to accept me, and from there, I could work on getting involved with the gang.

'Hey!' Nina greeted me excitedly when she arrived, and led the way towards the nearby shopping district. As we walked, she explained the mission brief. 'I need a perfect dress for this new club opening at the beach tonight. I need to look hot, because there are gonna be a lot of girls there — dancers, you know — and I need at least a little attention on me.'

I laughed as we entered the first store.

'I never usually get invited, but this isn't business, you know,' she raised an eyebrow at me, knowingly, as she flipped through items on a nearby rail. 'It's open to anyone.' Her eyes suddenly widened. 'Oh my God, you should totally come!'

'Oh, I don't know.' I pulled out a simple black mini dress. 'How about this one?'

Nina wrinkled her nose. 'That's not really me. It would look great on you though. Try it on.'

'I'm not coming,' I told her, pressing the dress against my body to see the fit, despite my words. Of course I wanted to go, but I didn't want to seem too keen. 'I don't even know anyone.'

'You know me, and D, and Val,' Nina pointed out. 'Oh, and Doro, too. You know him, right? Besides, you belong there more than I do. Your dad was one of them.'

I chose to ignore most of what she said, mostly because she spoke so fast and I had to choose what to actually respond to. 'How come you're invited tonight? I mean, if you don't feel like you belong.'

Nina picked up a miniscule red dress. I shook my head, and she placed it back on the rail with a sigh. 'Oh, I've just known them for ages.' She waved a dismissive hand, continuing to search the rail. 'What about this?' She held up an ice-blue mini dress. It had way too many sequins and not enough fabric for me, but she looked like she'd already fallen in love with it, so I simply smiled and nodded.

'Let's try these on.' Nina pulled me towards the dressing rooms, and I followed, still holding the black dress.

I'd barely zipped the dress when Nina's face appeared around the curtain of my dressing room. I jumped, and shot her a glare. 'You're lucky I was dressed!'

She laughed. 'Let me see you.'

I stepped out, and admired myself in the full length mirror. The dress was skin-tight, though the jersey material stopped it from feeling constricting. The hemline brushed my knees, and the long lace sleeves made it look way more expensive than it was. I liked the way it looked, imagining how I would style my long dark hair, and what shoes to wear with it.

'You look amazing!' Nina enthused.

I turned my attention to her. She looked beautiful, and the dress looked much better on her than it had on the hanger. It was short, tight, and showed a lot of cleavage, yet she somehow carried it off without looking too tacky.

'So do you,' I replied, honestly.

'You have to come tonight. Please?' Nina begged, giving me her best puppy dog eyes.

I paused for effect. 'Do you think anyone would mind?'

'No, of course not. I told you, it's an open event. Is that a yes?'

'Maybe.'

Nina clapped excitedly, then turned back to the mirror. 'Do you think Val will like this dress?'

I smirked. 'Are you two a couple?'

'I guess so,' Nina replied, running her hands over the sequins adorning her hips. 'But you know what men are like.'

I nodded, as if I did know, though really I didn't have much experience in the way of dating. Prior to my undercover training, I had been living with a fellow officer named Ty, who I'd been with for years. Our relationship had always been pretty simple, since neither of us was the type to play games or mess around. It was almost two years since we had separated, but it still hurt a little to think about it all. I pushed the thoughts away, as I always did—I'd made my choice, and now I was here, and I needed to concentrate.

'I'm gonna buy it,' Nina decided. 'Are you going to buy yours?'

I checked my reflection once more, then nodded. 'Yeah.'

'And wear it tonight?'

'I'll have to see if I can get the night off work...' I warned.

Nina grinned.

We changed back into our own clothes and paid for our dresses before stopping for a coffee on the way home. Over our drinks, Nina explained that the club opening tonight was a recent purchase of Mikhail Ivanov, the gang boss. She reassured me that it was totally fine for me to be there, obviously assuming that I'd be worried about running into Mikhail, when really it was the best news I'd heard since arriving in the City.

I knew that my anticipation at meeting Mikhail was entirely the wrong reaction to have when faced with the possibility of a run in with the leader of the most feared crime syndicate in the City, but I was not the clueless civilian that Nina thought me to be. Mikhail was the target. Doro had been undercover, gaining knowledge, observing, learning, but we hadn't used any of the evidence to convict any of the gang members yet.

While there were other criminal syndicates operating out of the City, Mikhail's operations accounted for about 80% of the organised crime in the area. In other words, Mikhail was directly responsible for almost all of the violence, drugs and murder in the City, and for many miles surrounding it. The number of fatalities that had been attributed to his operations, whether that be direct gang violence or overdoses as a result of his product, was almost unfathomable. Yet even more unbelievable was that he had yet to be incarcerated, not counting the few low-level charges he'd faced as a teen. .

He was clever; he rarely got his hands dirty, at least, not where he could be observed. So, where Doro had been unable to facilitate any concrete evidence, I'd been sent in to approach this in a different way. If we could take down Mikhail, and then use all of the other evidence we had obtained to convict his most trusted members, then it was a safe bet that many of the other associates would flee the City, and the gang would be no more. And that was the ultimate end goal.

***

That evening, I was ready by eight thirty, fidgeting with anticipation. Leigh had agreed to cover my shift at the bar, and Nina had arranged that Dimitri would stop by my apartment and take me to the club. Theoretically, his company was to make sure I didn't get lost looking for the venue, but really, I was sure that Nina wanted to avoid my chickening out. Not that that was an option for me.

In efforts to dispel my anxious excitement, I'd focused my mind on the mundane task of getting ready. I'd curled my hair and spent significantly more time on my makeup than I ever usually did, but I was antsy, and even after a beer, I still couldn't seem to relax.

After what felt like an eternity spent pacing the limited length of my lounge, Dimitri finally knocked at the door, I answered almost immediately. He blinked at me, clearly surprised by the speed of my appearance. I looked right back at him, taking in his black jeans, boots, and a long-sleeved navy tee. He looked good, especially when he moved, and I could see the muscles in his shoulders under the thin fabric of his shirt.

'Ready to go?' his deep voice interrupted my dangerous line of thought.

I took a breath, telling myself to relax, and conjured a smile. 'Sure. Let's go.'

Outside, there was a cab waiting for us, which Dimitri paid for. We rode in silence, and when we got out of the car twenty minutes later, I was surprised to see that we were in a parking lot almost right on the beachfront. The moonlight glistened on the ocean, and the sound of the gentle waves did more to relax me than the alcohol had been able to. I loved the sea.

My hands trailed over the metal railings separating the car park from the sand, reminding me of sitting on them as a child, eating ice cream, avoiding swooping seagulls. 'It's beautiful here,' I said out loud.

Dimitri appeared in my peripheral vision, giving a vague 'Hmm' by way of response. He let me have a few more seconds, before walking away. I followed, as we crossed the car park and emerged onto a street of dated beachfront stores, which were closed at this time of night. We turned left into an alleyway, and through to a more industrial-looking area. I saw the club immediately, identified by a bright sign telling me the name of the place — *The Angel Rooms*. Music poured out of the building's open doors and, as we headed inside, my eyes adjusted quickly to the dim lighting.

The first thing I noticed about the place was the surprising number of naked women, even for a strip club. There were a number of podiums dotted around the large room, upon which they danced. Women in bikinis were carrying trays of drinks, or sitting with groups of men on some of the many leather sofas situated around the club. Despite the early hour, it was busy, and I was glad that I had Dimitri to clear a path as we made our way to the circular bar in the centre of the room.

'What are you drinking?' Dimitri asked me over the music.

'Desperados, thanks,' I replied, and he relayed my order to a nearby barmaid. In comparison to most other women in this place, she looked fairly respectable, where in reality she was barely clothed herself. My long sleeved, knee-length dress had looked sexy in the dressing rooms that afternoon, but now I felt more like a nun.

The barwoman brought over our drinks, and Dimitri didn't pay. He handed me a bottle, and pointed to the other end of the bar. Turning, I saw Valentin and Nina, and made a beeline for them.

'Hey, you're here!' Nina exclaimed as we approached, a wide smile splitting over her face. She pulled me into a familiar hug, and the sequins on her dress scratched my skin through the fabric of my own. 'It's pretty great in here, right?'

'Yeah,' I replied, pushing the wedge of lime into the bottle and taking a long sip of my beer. I'd been to many a questionable club in the past, but this was something else, for a reason I couldn't quite put my finger on. Maybe I was uncomfortable because I knew I wasn't here to have fun, I was here to work.

The four of us made our way to a small seating area in one corner of the room, made up of a small square table and some leather couches. Nina pulled me down next to her, and Val sat on her other side, while Dimitri took a seat opposite us. A few feet to my left, there was a podium upon which a girl in a bikini was displaying some impressive pole dancing moves. I had taken some pole fitness classes when I was a student, and I was enchanted by the fluidity of her movements, so much so that I almost didn't spot Doro on the other side of the podium. He waved, and I returned the gesture, signalling for him to come over.

'What are you doing here?' he asked when he reached our table.

'Nina invited me,' I told him.

He nodded, and held my eye contact for a second. I nodded in return, confirming that I was okay, and only then did he turn to greet the others.

'Dimitri,' Doro said, after pleasantries had been exchanged. 'Mikhail wants to see you.'

Wordlessly, Dimitri stood, and followed Doro away into the crowd, leaving me alone with Val and Nina. It wouldn't have been so bad, had they not started making out almost immediately. Sick of third wheeling, I decided to go in search of the bathroom, and took the opportunity to scope out the rest of the place and what was going on in here. Mostly, the clientele seemed to be middle aged men, interspersed with pretty young women.

The bathrooms were at the back of the club, and, surprisingly, there was no queue. As I checked my hair in the mirror, I witnessed a couple of the dancers snorting white powder from the surface of the plastic sinks. Exiting the bathroom, I decided to head back through the crowd to the bar, but was halted in my progress by a hand catching my arm.

Turning, I was surprised to see a vaguely familiar face. He was maybe my age, with olive skin and caramel hair. 'Do I know you?' I asked over the music.

'You're that girl from Dimitri's building, right?' he grinned, and the expression coupled with his words revealed the realisation. He'd been the second man standing outside of my building, who had grabbed my purse while his friend left bruises on my wrist.

'Don't touch me again, OK?' I yelled over the music, stepping away.

He held his hands up in surrender, then extended one for me to shake. 'I'm Fabio.'

I hesitated, but I shook his hand. I needed to make friends with these people, not enemies. 'Mari.'

He used my hand to pull me gently towards him before letting go. He spoke into my ear, his voice surprisingly smooth and pleasant. 'Look, I'm sorry about the other night. Tony shouldn't have got physical with you. We just really needed to talk to Dimitri.'

'Forget it.' What else could I say?

'So how do you like the club?' he asked, resting a hand on my waist. 'Are you here with Dimitri?'

'It's alright,' I responded somewhat coolly. 'And yeah.'

Fabio pulled back slightly to meet my gaze; his eyebrows raised. 'You guys dating?'

I couldn't help but laugh out loud, surprised by his assumption. 'No. Why?'

Fabio shrugged. His cheeky smile was infectious. 'If you're not dating D, you wanna dance with me?'

I smiled but shook my head. 'Sorry. I'd better get back to my friends.'

'Who are you with?'

'Nina and Valentin,' I replied, realising that I had no last names for either of them.

Apparently, I didn't need them, since Fabio's face lit up in recognition. 'Oh, I haven't seen Nina in forever. I'll come say hello. Lead the way.'

I obliged, taking his hand and leading him back to the couches where I had left Nina and Val, though when we got there, they were nowhere to be seen.

'They probably went outside,' I guessed.

'I'll wait.' Fabio used our joined hands to tug me down onto one of the sofas. 'So, how do you know Nina?'

I tried to subtly shuffle away from him a little, since he'd pulled me down practically on top of him. 'Oh, she comes into the bar where I work a lot — do you know *Arrows* up town?' Fabio nodded, and I continued, 'How do you know her?'

Fabio gave me a rueful smile. 'We went to school together. She was a couple years below me. We used to date.'

'Oh, really?' I wondered immediately if Fabio knew anything more about Nina's situation. 'I thought she dropped out of high school?'

'Yeah, she had some issues back then. We all did.' His expression sobered momentarily, then he forced a smile and changed the subject before I could ask any further questions. 'I haven't been to *Arrows* for so long, I guess I'll have to come see you, keep you company when you're working.'

I smiled, because I didn't know what to say.

Fabio leaned closer, and his arm stretched out over the back of the couch behind me. His lips brushed the skin beneath my earlobe as he spoke. 'I think we should pass the time with some shots. You drink vodka, babe?'

I held back the grimace that automatically came with the use of that pet name, and replied, 'I don't think you could keep up with me.'

Pulling back, Fabio laughed, his caramel eyes sparkling. He waved over a nearby girl in a bright pink bikini set, and she returned minutes later with a bottle of unopened vodka and a couple of large shot glasses. Fabio poured the liquid, and we clinked glasses before taking the first shot. The alcohol burned my throat in a familiar way, and I had to squeeze my eyes shut in order to swallow. Several shots in, it became a lot easier, and Fabio needed a time out.

'Damn, girl. You got a talent for vodka shots,' he laughed.

I laughed in return. I couldn't help it; Fabio was fun, and I was buzzed. We knocked back another couple and were getting a little giggly when Valentin returned with two men, both of whom looked familiar to me. I recognized one as Tony, the guy who had been with Fabio last week and bruised my arm outside my building. He was in his late forties, with greying hair, sallow cheeks and a long aquiline nose. The man next to him was slightly older, though a lot better looking, with fair hair and piercing blue eyes, wearing an expensive-looking shirt.

'Oh, hey,' Fabio said, looking up at his peers. He gave a one way introduction, gesturing towards me. 'This is Mari.'

'I know who you are,' Tony said, looking me up and down with an ugly look in his eyes. 'You're lucky Dimitri was there the other night.'

My stomach turned. 'So are you.' I was angry about the other night, how he had threatened me, and I wasn't about to take it again now. All four men smirked, apparently finding me amusing. Fabio's arm found its way around my shoulders, and I didn't shake him off.

'Relax,' Tony rolled his eyes in response. 'Dimitri warned us to stay away from you, and you're not worth the effort.'

I felt Fabio tense next to me, but he said nothing, and I decided to keep my mouth shut this time, too. That was difficult, given the automatic need I felt to defend myself, but instead I poured myself some more vodka in an attempt to calm myself a little.

The man next to Tony leaned forward to ask me, 'You like the club, Mari?' His voice lilting with an unfamiliar accent, his icy gaze demanding my attention. And suddenly it clicked. This was Mikhail. Of course I'd seen photographs of him before but meeting him in the flesh, was shockingly different. He had scars on his face that hadn't been visible in the photographs, yet there was something strong and commanding about him. I felt intimidated, yet awed. Charismatic confidence rolled off him, but the danger behind the façade was clear.

'Yeah, it's great,' I told him, swallowing my sudden nerves in favour for what I hoped was a confident smile.

Tony smirked at my response, and leered over at me. 'How much to get you up on one of those poles?' he asked, his tongue darting out over his thin, chapped lips.

I fixed him with a glare, reluctant to snap back at him again now that I knew I was in the company of Mikhail.

A weight next to me made the couch sink, and I saw Dimitri sitting down. As Fabio was already sat on my other side, Dimitri had to squeeze himself in beside me, but he didn't seem to mind. He looked at me, and his gaze shifted to Fabio's arm over my shoulders, but he didn't say anything.

'We were just asking Mari here what it would cost to get her up on the stage,' Tony told Dimitri.

'What did I tell you about her?' Dimitri's steely tone sent shivers down my spine, and not in a good way.

Tony rolled his eyes again. 'I won't touch her.'

I glanced up at Dimitri's face again. Despite the fact

that I already knew of Dimitri's high-ranking position within the gang, observing him effortlessly exert power over Tony chilled me. To be so highly respected by these other men must mean that he had done some scary things in his life and of course I knew the details better than most. The carefully blank expression he always wore was likely a shield to the terrible things he had seen and done.

But he had stopped Tony hurting me, and he'd looked out for me ever since, in his cold and slightly patronising way. He hadn't been inappropriate or particularly aggressive towards me, and his friendship with Nina and Val was quite endearing; although he didn't join in with their joviality, he clearly cared for them. He was hard to read, and it was frustrating, especially when I was usually a good judge of character.

I was so absorbed in my thoughts, that Fabio's whisper made me jump. 'You wanna go dance?'

I shook my head, mutely.

'Come on…' Fabio continued to speak into my neck, and his hand was back on my thigh, with more pressure this time. 'We can't talk here anymore.'

I understood then that Fabio was trying to subtly get me away from these men, either because they wanted to talk business some more, or because of the obvious tension lingering in the air. Maybe both. However, I was reluctant to be alone with Fabio; I wasn't sure how to continue rebutting his advances without causing offence. It had, of course, occurred to me that I could use his interest in me and his alcohol consumption to ask him some delicate questions, but I wasn't sure how much I could lead him on without it going too far. I also didn't know if my acting skills were up to par for this. Still, I didn't seem to have much choice, so I nodded and stood up.

I felt Dimitri's eyes on me as Fabio and I moved

towards the dance floor. I was surprised to feel glad that he was there, just in case anything went down with Fabio — I mean, sure, Fabio seemed like a nice enough guy, but I'd learned to never be too careful.

There was a small crowd on the dance floor, consisting mostly of scantily dressed young women and rapidly ageing men, who looked even older in comparison to the girls. There was something distinctly disturbing about the whole scene, but I suppressed my uneasiness as Fabio led me to the centre of the crowd. He placed his hands on my waist, and we began to dance. I was glad of the vodka I'd gulped earlier, as it helped me relax into the scene.

'So you work for these guys?' I asked, taking my chance.

'Yeah,' Fabio confirmed, running his lips from my earlobe to my chin and back again. 'But I'm no Dimitri.'

'Oh?' I wrapped my arms around Fabio's neck, and he pulled me closer. 'Why's that?'

'You know, I just don't do what he does.'

I knew what Fabio was referring to; Dimitri had been described in my training as Mikhail's right-hand man, who primarily worked as a hired killer. It was somewhat relieving to hear that the man whose arms were currently wrapped around me apparently did not commit murder, but I still wanted to find out more.

I turned my head as Fabio moved his lips up to my face, speaking into his ear. 'Do they ask you to do that?'

'Sometimes.'

'And you just say no? It's that simple?'

'It's never simple,' Fabio said, his breath warm on my jawbone. 'If they ask me, I just pay someone else to do it. Some of the kids — you know, the ones who wanna be in — will do anything for fifty.'

He was referring to the numerous teenage boys who

had grown up around this and wanted to be a part of it. They idolised the gang and the money and respect it would gain them, and would do anything to get in. I'd been briefed about them, and warned not to interfere — my boss knew that I wanted to help them, but that wasn't why I was here. I didn't know how much more I could press Fabio without raising suspicion, so I decided to change the subject for a little while.

'Do you go to places like this a lot?'

He pulled back to look at me, with an amused smile on his face. 'Obviously. It's basically part of the job. Don't you?'

'Not really.'

'You know, Tony is a creepy guy, but he had a point,' Fabio brushed a hand up my side, 'About you being hotter than all the other girls in this place.'

I forced a laugh. 'I don't think that's exactly what he said.'

Fabio smiled into the crook of my neck, and I resisted the urge to push him away; I needed as many contacts here as possible, but I couldn't let him carry on like that, either. Gently, I disentangled myself from Fabio.

'I have to pee,' I told him.

He looked disappointed. 'Oh. Okay. I'll be at the bar.'

I gave him a smile and dashed off to the ladies' room. This time, there was a queue, but it gave me more reason not to return to Fabio right away, so I didn't mind. As I stood in line, Nina emerged from one of the cubicles. I watched her wash her hands and fix her lip gloss before she spotted me.

'Hey!' she squealed, running the short distance over to me in her skyscraper heels. 'Where did you go?'

'Where did *you* go?' I responded. 'I went back to the couches and you weren't there.'

'Oh, sorry. Went for a smoke and ran into some

people. Are you okay?'

'Yeah, I was dancing,' I pulled a face.

Nina whacked my arm. 'You! Who with?'

'Fabio.'

Nina's expression fell, and she faltered for a second before regaining her composure. 'I didn't realise you knew him.'

'I don't really. He told me you knew each other. Sorry if that bothers you — I won't dance with him again,' I assured her. Fabio had told me they'd been an item while at school, but I hadn't considered that she'd be upset, and I needed my relationship with Nina more than I needed Fabio.

Nina waved a dismissive hand. 'Oh, honey, don't worry. It was years ago.' She smiled, but her eyes gave her away. I was pretty certain then that Fabio had been her baby's father, just by the sad expression lingering in her gaze.

Nina waited with me while I queued, telling me about Valentin's reaction to her dress (he liked it) and gossiping about some of the girls who were working here. I still didn't know the exact nature of Nina's role within the gang, but I was quickly learning that she knew everything about everyone.

When I'd relieved my bladder, we walked back to the corner seating area again, where Dimitri and Val were waiting for us. The other men had left, now, and that made me feel more comfortable. The bottle of vodka Fabio had ordered still sat on the table, though there was significantly less liquid in it than when I had left.

Nina curled herself around Valentin on one of the chairs, while I sat beside Dimitri on the couch, this time leaving as much space between us as possible, just to be polite.

'Where's Fabio?' he asked me, leaning in close so that

Val and Nina wouldn't overhear. Not that they were paying attention to anything besides each other.

'I left him on the dance floor,' I replied. 'I think he's expecting me to go back, but I'd rather stay here. Is that really mean?'

One corner of Dimitri's mouth tugged upwards. This time, the expression lingered, the first sign of any emotion I'd seen from him, and it changed his whole face. 'I'll get you a drink.'

'Just water,' I told him, sternly. 'Seriously.'

'Sure.'

When he returned with our drinks, I downed half my bottle of water right away. I was hot, and the alcohol had made me feel dehydrated. Plus, I still felt buzzed, and any more drinks would have pushed me over the edge. The four of us chatted for a while, and I actually felt myself relaxing a little in their company. At the nearby podium, I witnessed Doro slipping notes into a dancer's G-string, and threatening another guy that tried to pull down said underwear. I knew that he had been undercover for a long time, and he was damn good at his job, but it was still a little unnerving to see him looking so… authentic.

It was a little after two when Nina and Valentin finally took our advice that they should get a room and headed home. Taking our cue from them, Dimitri and I also decided that it was time to get out of there, and he offered to share a taxi again.

Following Dimitri through the crowd towards the door, I was surprised when a hand grabbed my wrist. I yelped as I was pulled sharply backwards. I thought it might be Fabio, catching me for another dance, but instead, I came face to face with Tony.

Chapter Four

Tony gripped my wrist tightly, his fingers digging into the bruises that already adorned my skin, and I winced.

'Hello again.' His voice was a growl.

I tried to pull my arm away, but he twisted his grip harshly, and I gasped at the shooting pain. 'Ow! What the hell? Let me go!'

'If you think you can keep disrespecting me, Mari, then you are wrong,' Tony snarled, his hot breath hitting my face.

'Let me go,' I repeated, with as much venom in my voice as I could muster.

Tony ignored me, pulling me so that I was pressed against him, his free arm snaking around my waist to hold me in place. He smelled like sweat, alcohol and stale cigarette smoke. 'Dimitri isn't here to save you this time, princess. He just left.'

I fought to get free, but his hold was iron. He made a low, appreciative noise in his throat as his free hand ran over my body. Panic started to rise in my chest as I struggled in his arms, knowing that yelling would do no good in this noisy, crowded place. Besides, a creepy guy forcing himself on a woman probably wasn't an unusual sight here. If Dimitri had left the club, I was sure he'd notice me missing and I hoped that he would return looking for me soon. I just needed to keep Tony busy until that time.

'Buy me a drink,' I said. 'And let go of my butt. Then I'll dance with you.'

Tony's sinister grin sent shivers down my spine, and I knew that a dance wasn't what he was after, but he dragged me over to the bar by my wrist and ordered us a couple of vodkas. I'd hoped that he'd let go of my arm, even for a second, but he held on like his life depended on it, no doubt guessing my plan for escape. The barmaid set down two glasses of clear liquid in front of us. Tony downed his and ordered another, which he also knocked back in seconds. No wonder he was so drunk. I held my glass in my free hand, but didn't take a single sip. I needed my wits about me right now.

Tony turned to me, and his hand took hold of my throat, though he applied no pressure. 'Come with me.'

'Where?' I asked.

He didn't answer, just pulled me away from the bar towards a section of the club that was separated from the main room by red velvet curtains. That was never a good sign. Through the curtains, I found myself in an area with several private dance tables, where some men were receiving lap dances, and some were receiving considerably more. To the left, there were some small booths, all with curtains for privacy. It was towards one of these booths that Tony directed me now. Inside, he pushed me face-first against the wall, my cheek pressing against the cool painted surface. He released my wrist, but I still couldn't get free, since his entire body weight pressed against my back.

'Let me go,' I said, my voice calm and stern.

Tony simply chuckled, and pressed his crotch against my butt, so I could feel exactly how excited this little power play made him. The panic in my chest increased in pressure, and I took a deep breath to calm myself. Tony's hand found the zip on the side of my dress, and slowly tugged it down, all the way to my hip, revealing the skin underneath. His fingers crept inside the fabric of the dress, splaying over my stomach. I cringed.

Tony took a step away, and his strong arms spun me around. 'Take it off,' he commanded, his voice gruff and thick.

I nodded, feigning compliance, and finally, he let go

of me, stepping back to watch the show. I didn't waste the opportunity. The short glass of vodka I still held in my hand became a weapon, as I lurched forward and slammed it into the side of Tony's face. Shards sunk into his flesh, and he cried out wordlessly, as the first drops of blood escaped from his skin. He stumbled back a couple of steps, and while he processed what had just happened, I hitched up my skirt enough to land a front kick that resulted in a stiletto to the stomach. Winded, he sank into the leather booth, and I ran for it.

I made it outside, looking desperately around for Dimitri. I spotted him talking to someone across the road. As I ran towards him, he looked up, and confusion crossed his features. I must have looked a state, frantic and flushed with adrenaline.

'What the hell happened?' he asked immediately when I reached him.

'Tony tried to force me to...' I began, completely out of breath, and a little panicked. It had taken me a lot longer to get away than I would have liked.

'I'll kill him,' Dimitri growled, interrupting me. His gaze caught the unzipped fastening of my dress, and anger blazed in his eyes. 'I will *kill* him.'

At that moment, Tony burst out of the club doorway. One side of his face was covered with blood, and I realised that I must have hit him harder than I thought; must have been the adrenaline. He saw us at the same time that Dimitri saw him, and both men started towards each other.

Beside me, the man with whom Dimitri had been speaking gave a low whistle. 'You did that to his face? I'm impressed.'

That voice sent chills of recognition over my skin — Mikhail. I looked up at him, hurrying to zip my dress with shaking fingers. Mikhail seemed pretty relaxed about the whole situation. I guessed he was used to it, given his career choice.

When I looked back towards the club, I saw that a fight was well underway. Tony was sprawled on the ground, Dimitri on top of him, landing punch after punch to Tony's already damaged face. If he didn't stop, he would kill him. My blood chilled, as I realised that was the norm for Dimitri. Except this time, he wasn't doing it for money, he was doing it because of me.

'Dimitri!' I yelled, hurrying towards him. 'Dimitri stop!'

He didn't stop.

I tried to grab his arm, but I couldn't catch it, and he didn't even notice my attempts. 'Stop! You're gonna kill him!'

Finally, Dimitri looked up at me. 'That was the point.' He had a scary, wild look in his eyes. I took an automatic step back. He saw my movement, and it seemed to knock him back to reality. His eyes changed, and he stood up, stepping away from Tony's motionless body.

Mikhail strolled over, still looking entirely unaffected by what had happened. Bending down, he checked Tony for a pulse, and I felt sick. What if he was dead? Luckily, Mikhail nodded, signalling that he had found a pulse. He waved to a couple of men who'd been watching the fight unfold and instructed them to bring a car around, take Tony home, and 'take care of this mess'. Whatever that meant.

'Mikhail,' Dimitri said, and the man in charge turned to look at us. 'We're good?'

'We're good,' Mikhail confirmed. 'Take your girl home. Come see me tomorrow. We'll continue our earlier discussion.'

Dimitri nodded, taking my left hand and leading me away. The physical contact caught me off guard, but I didn't dare pull my hand from his. I noticed that he held his other hand cradled to his chest; it was slick with Tony's blood, and probably needed medical attention. We walked together back to the parking lot where the cab had dropped us off earlier that night, and where another one was waiting. Dimitri must have called ahead. He held the door open for me and climbed in after me, telling the driver the address of our building in a quiet voice. It was strange to me how he could act so differently from minute to minute.

'They aren't gonna call an ambulance?' I asked, quietly, as the cab pulled away.

'No,' Dimitri replied. 'Hospitals ask questions.'

I swallowed. It was like being in a movie, except this was real-life. The crunch of the glass as I'd hit it against Tony's head replayed in my mind. The image of his bloodied face and his unmoving body flashed in front of my eyes every time I blinked. Maybe I wasn't as prepared for this as I'd thought.

Dimitri looked over at me, and it was like he knew what I was thinking. He took my other hand, and I winced. We both looked down at it to see that the glass had cut me, too, and small shards glistened on the skin of my palm as we drove past streetlights. There wasn't much blood, but it was enough to make me feel sick all over again. Gently, Dimitri cradled my hand in his own bloody pair the whole way home. At our building, Dimitri paid the driver and we went inside together. When I paused at my door, Dimitri simply shook his head, and led me upstairs to his place.

I steeled myself before stepping over the threshold, but I don't know what I was expecting to see, other than a perfectly normal apartment. Inside, it had the same layout as my flat, and was decorated with the same wooden floors and magnolia walls. The furniture was minimalist, and I noticed a distinct lack of personal items. The whole place felt very cold and uninviting, much like Dimitri himself. Except now, his expression was softer than usual as he sat me down on the black leather couch, switching on the table lamp next to me.

He disappeared into the bathroom, returning minutes later with a first aid box and a towel. He had taken the time to rinse his own hand and throw a bandage around it, though he seemed a lot more bothered by my relatively small injuries than by his own more serious ones. Sitting next to me on the couch, he laid out the towel over his legs, and set the box onto the coffee table. It was significantly larger than any home first aid kit I'd seen before.

I pushed the cuff of my dress up to the elbow, while Dimitri rolled up his own sleeves. He took a pair of tweezers from the box and began to remove the shards of glass, dropping them into the towel on his lap. He held my hand so gently, despite his own wounded knuckles, and worked quickly but precisely. It barely hurt, though that could be due to the alcohol or adrenaline, rather than Dimitri's delicate work.

'You've done this before,' I guessed.

Dimitri nodded. 'How did this happen?'

'I smashed a glass on Tony's face.'

Dimitri's hand stilled and he met my gaze. 'Seriously?'

I shrugged. 'I kicked him, too. I think I pulled a muscle in my leg. But at least I didn't rip my dress.'

A short, harsh laugh escaped Dimitri's lips, startling me. He shook his head and muttered something underneath his breath.

'I can take care of myself,' I said, more to reassure myself than him.

Dimitri began picking glass out of my palm again. 'I

assumed you'd gone to the bathroom, or something. I should have come and found you. I'm sorry.'

His apology surprised me, and I felt my guard start to dissolve. 'It's okay,' I told him. 'He didn't hurt me.'

Dimitri looked at me, sceptical, knowing that I couldn't actually be that naïve. 'He was going to.'

'But he didn't.'

In silence, Dimitri finished pulling the glass from my hand and set the tweezers down. He pulled a bottle of clear liquid from the first aid box and dabbed some onto a cotton wool pad, before applying it to my hand. This time, it didn't matter how gentle he was, it hurt. A lot. I gritted my teeth and shut my eyes. Finally, he placed a large square plaster over my hand, which covered all of the tiny cuts.

'Thank you,' I said, meeting Dimitri's gaze.

'Don't mention it,' he replied sombrely.

He gathered up the towel and the first aid box and carried it through to the kitchen, for cleaning, I assumed. Returning a few minutes later, he approached me slowly, taking a seat on the coffee table opposite, rather than the couch.

'Are you okay?' he asked.

'Yeah,' I replied. 'I'll be fine tomorrow.'

'What about right now?'

I took a deep breath. I had assumed that the carefully blank expression he usually wore was how his face always looked, but I'd been wrong; this was Dimitri's real face. So startlingly different, and so much younger, softer. I looked away. 'I just need to go to bed.'

Downstairs, I let myself into my own apartment with shaky hands, the after-effects of the adrenaline. In the bathroom, I stripped down, throwing my clothes onto the floor without a care, and stepped into the shower. I was careful not to get the bandage on my hand too wet, but I just really needed to feel clean. Standing in the hot water relaxed me and calmed me down. By the time I was done, the last of the adrenaline had faded, and I was exhausted. I didn't have trouble sleeping.

Chapter Five

The weekend passed quietly and slowly. I called my supervisor, Taylor, and updated him on the people I'd met, including Mikhail, though I left out the details of my run in with Tony. He seemed pleased with my progress, even though I personally felt like I hadn't yet achieved anything worthy of praise. After our quick phone call, I deposited my police phone back in its hidden compartment and reached for my other cell phone, the one that I carried day to day. I decided to send a tentative text message to Nina. I simply asked how she was, and almost immediately, my phone began to ring.

'Hello?'

'Hey, I got your text,' Nina said, her voice as bright as ever. 'I'm just walking home, so thought it'd be easier to call you. What's up?'

Her forwardness surprised me, but I felt triumphant that she was clearly already growing comfortable with me. 'Just felt like a chat. How are you?'

'I'm good, thanks. How are you?' Before I could answer, Nina continued, 'I heard about what happened with Tony on Friday night.'

'Uh. How?' I asked, wondering how far the gossip had spread already; it was only Monday.

'Dimitri told me,' Nina said. I could hear the noise of traffic in the background as she spoke and guessed that she was still walking. 'Have you seen him since it happened?'

'No,' I replied, lounging back on my couch. 'Why?'

'He's mad at Tony for going anywhere near you,' Nina told me. 'He specifically told Tony to stay away from you, and Tony directly disobeyed. People just don't do that to Dimitri, you know? Not without consequences.'

I bit my lip. I was really starting to understand that.

'He did beat Tony pretty bad,' I replied, pretending to be blasé about it all, like I'd seen it a million times before. Which, of course, I had, but not for the reasons Nina would likely assume, where she'd witnessed men fight each other at clubs and bars over women and drugs; I'd been the one in uniform called out in the middle of the night to break it up.

'Yeah, that's what I meant by consequences!' Nina laughed. 'Tony must have really been pissed at you to risk going against Dimitri. What the hell did you do to him?'

'To Tony? Nothing!' I protested. 'I hit him a few weeks ago, but only in self-defence.'

'Well, he's a guy. They hate being beaten by a girl.'

'Clearly,' I replied with an eye roll. It was my personal opinion that men like that were usually pretty insecure in their masculinity. I decided to change the subject, 'Did you have a good time on Friday?'

'Yeah, sure. I'm glad you came, even if it didn't end so well for you,' Nina apologised. 'We should hang out sometime soon, I'll let you know, okay?'

'Sure,' I replied with a smile in my voice. 'Talk to you soon.'

***

A few days passed, during which I went to work at the bar, and spent a lot of my free time in the gym dispersing my anxious energy. On Friday afternoon, I was half way through a vigorous clean of my kitchen when my phone chimed with the promised message from Nina.

Drinks tonight at Arrows, then party at a friend's place. You in?

I didn't hesitate, replying that of course I would come

along. I didn't even bother to enquire who said friend might be; it didn't matter, I just needed excuses to familiarise myself with Nina and her friends. I picked a slightly dressier outfit for work that evening, taking into consideration the party afterwards, and deciding on skinny black jeans, boots, and a sheer indigo blouse. It was suitable for both work and socialising, sexy without being too revealing. As I glanced over my reflection in my bedroom, I remembered that this was Ty's favourite of all my shirts. My stomach clenched at the memory of his smile, but I pushed it aside. Heading out into the cool evening air helped clear my head. The bar was busy, and since it was a Friday, Leigh was also working, which always helped pass the time more quickly.

Val, Dimitri, and Nina arrived a little after eleven, heading to their usual booth in the corner after greeting me and ordering their usual drinks. Leigh shot me a pointed look, and I knew I couldn't avoid her questions, so I bit the bullet.

'Dimitri lives in my building,' I told her. 'They come in here a lot. Nina doesn't seem so bad, you know. They all seem nice.'

Leigh raised one sharply pencilled eyebrow. 'Really? You're hanging out with them?'

I shrugged, wiping down the bar to avoid eye contact.

'You need to watch your back around those people,' Leigh warned, her voice low.

I resisted the urge to roll my eyes. 'Yeah, I will. Don't worry,' I placated her.

At closing time, Nina and the guys waited for me to lock up. As we left the bar, Leigh gave me another warning to 'be careful' and shot a glare in Nina's direction before stalking off into the night. Nina barely even noticed, simply shrugging it off, which I admired.

We followed Val and Dimitri in the direction of the

beach but turned off before we reached the seafront. Nina chatted easily to me as we walked, and it didn't take long before we approached a high rise building and let ourselves in through the propped-open front door.

'Fabio's place is much nicer than any of ours,' Nina told me as we trotted up the concrete stairs to the top floor.

A wisp of anxiety crept into my mind. I had abandoned Fabio on the dance floor last weekend, never going back to find him despite the promise that I would. I felt a little bad about it, and worried how he would behave towards me now.

'Does he know I'm coming?' I asked.

Nina waved a dismissive hand. 'It's fine, he said we could invite anyone we wanted.'

I took that as a firm *no*. We reached the top floor, and I saw that there was only one door on the landing, meaning that Fabio's flat must be a penthouse style, taking up the whole floor. Again, the door was open, and music flooded out into the stairwell. Once inside, I saw immediately that Nina had been correct; it was significantly nicer than my place. It was large, with an open plan design and a sleek finish. Black and white furnishings and sharp lines gave it a show-home feeling, and I couldn't imagine Fabio living here — it seemed so cold and pristine, and out of place with his bubbly personality.

'How does he afford this?' I asked Nina, having to speak up over the music, but keeping my voice quiet enough so that no one would overhear my invasive question.

'His job pays pretty well,' Nina replied dryly, giving me a sideways look. 'And Fabio likes the finer things in life.'

The main room was pretty crowded, and Nina took my

hand in order to pull me through an elaborate archway to the kitchen. She seemed to know not only the layout of the place, but also the organisation of the kitchen cabinets, and I guessed that she had been here before but decided not to ask; I didn't want to probe too much and risk upsetting her.

The kitchen was also decorated solely in black and white, quite futuristic in style. An array of bottles and punch bowls covered a glass table in the centre of the room, and we helped ourselves. While Nina had immediately made herself a vodka and coke, I decided to start with a beer instead. Appearing beside me, Dimitri also grabbed a beer, popping the cap on the side of the counter.

'How are you?' Dimitri asked, speaking his first words to me since the incident with Tony last weekend.

'I'm good,' I replied, taking a sip of my drink. 'You?'

'Fine.' Dimitri took a long drink over the silence that fell between us. His eyes were so dark in the overhead lighting that they almost looked black, especially against the perfect marble of his skin. His gaze fixed on mine, for two seconds, then he turned and disappeared into the crowd in the next room.

I sighed. I knew that he was my best shot and direct contact to Mikhail, given his high standing in the gang, but I was still struggling to read him, and I was starting to think that getting close with Nina and Val would be a much easier way in. Deciding to focus on that, I went in search of the couple, spotting them in the large open plan living room, leaning against the far wall. I joined them, paying close attention as they pointed out various people around the room, giving me brief descriptions of who each person was, followed by at least one piece of gossip from Nina. How she knew all these secrets about everyone, I wasn't sure. Almost an hour passed this way, but I was far from bored — I was eagerly soaking up every little bit of information Nina offered me, even if most of it was just rumours.

I was on my third drink when Nina and Val headed outside for a cigarette, leaving me to entertain myself. Sinking onto a nearby sofa, I surveyed the room. As I scanned the crowd, I saw several familiar faces whom I recognised from various mugshots I'd been shown during training. Unsure of my next move, I thought back to said training, trying to formulate a way to get more involved with the gang without being too obvious about it. It was during this contemplation that Fabio finally spotted me; he'd been working the room since we arrived, but hadn't looked my way until now. It seemed to me that he was trying to avoid Nina, although he'd been keen to see Nina that night at the club. Then it occurred to me that maybe it was Valentin he didn't want to see. I made a mental note to find out the whole story there.

'Hey!' he exclaimed when he saw me, a wide grin instantly spreading over his face as he weaved through the crowd towards me. Crashing down onto the couch next to me, I immediately smelled alcohol on him, but couldn't help but return his smile. 'Mari! I didn't know you were gonna be here!'

'I came with Nina,' I told him. 'I hope that's okay.'

'Sure!' he leaned in closer and spoke into my ear. 'It's good to see you again.'

'Yeah, you too. Sorry I left the club without saying goodbye the other night, I just…'

Fabio interrupted me. 'Hey, don't worry about it,' he drawled in his thick City accent. 'I heard what happened with Tony. You okay?'

'Yeah,' I looked down. 'Dimitri took care of it.'

'Heard that too.'

Meeting his gaze again, I frowned. 'Who told you?' I

was curious to know who was talking about this, and what their opinion was. Had I messed up by getting in between two of Mikhail's men?

'Mikhail,' Fabio replied with a shrug.

I was taken aback. That hadn't been what I'd expected at all. 'Really?'

Fabio smirked at my reaction. 'Relax. He was impressed with your self-defence skills — you smashed a glass over Tony's head! That's pretty bad ass.'

'It was self-preservation,' I corrected him, and he laughed.

'Seriously, don't worry about it. Mikhail was just curious about who you were, since none of us had ever seen you before. Dimitri sorted it, though. No sweat.'

I didn't know what he meant by that, but before I could ask, Fabio pulled me to my feet and towards the centre of the room, which was filled with bodies swaying in time to the heavy beat of the music.

'Enough talking about Mikhail and Tony,' Fabio laughed over the music. 'You owe me a dance!'

From a nearby table which had been set up like a bar, Fabio grabbed a bottle of top shelf whiskey. He took a long gulp before passing it to me. I obliged, the liquid burning my throat in a familiar way, and took another long drink before returning the bottle to Fabio. We each drank a little more, before he passed it away to another nearby party guest, and used his newly free hands to pull me closer. The music was fast, a thumping bassline reverberating through my body, and almost too loud now that we had moved closer to the large speakers, but the alcohol buzzing through my system transformed all of that into a bearable blur. The warmth of Fabio's large hands on my waist barely felt real as it travelled through my abdomen.

I don't know how long we danced for. All around,

neon yellow and green lights danced across the walls from some kind of light machine, the location of which I couldn't quite detect. In the relative darkness, Fabio moved closer. Our bodies were touching from head to toe, my cheek rubbing his as we moved with the crowd. When his soft lips touched my earlobe, I didn't turn away as I should have. I was lost in the music, for once forgetting my purpose in the City, and enjoying being held in a way that I desperately missed.

Fabio's mouth moved along my jawbone, until his lips met mine. He kissed me softly, then harder. And I let him. For about ten seconds — which was ten seconds too long. I pulled away, giving him an apologetic smile.

'I think I need some air,' I told him over the music.

He nodded. 'Want me to come with?'

'That's okay,' I replied. 'You stay — it's your party!'

He gave me an uncertain smile, and I took the opportunity to hightail it towards the door. In the stairwell, there were a few people dotted about, but it was a lot quieter, and a lot cooler. I sat down at the top of the concrete steps, dropping my head into my hands. What was I thinking? I shouldn't have let that happen. I'd had one too many drinks and let myself get carried away by the music and the touch of Fabio's hands. I guessed that spending so much time alone was starting to take its toll on me.

Chapter Six

I sat on the cold steps, mentally chastising myself for my stupidity. Everything suddenly felt very overwhelming. I don't know how long I stayed there, with my head in my hands, before I heard the familiar voices of Nina and Valentin echoing up the stairwell. Moments later, they appeared on the staircase in front of me, heading back up to the party from what I assumed was another smoke break. Nina was stumbling all over the place, obviously wasted. When I looked over to Valentin, he didn't look in much better shape, either. They were both in hysterics for no apparent reason, and when they spotted me, they only got worse.

Valentin bent down and scooped me up, tossing me over his shoulder as if I weighed the same as a bag of sugar.

'Oh my god,' I screamed. 'Put me down right now!'

Nina cackled with glee as she followed Valentin (and me, against my will) back into Fabio's apartment. It just kept getting busier and busier, despite the fact that my phone told me it was almost three a.m. by that point. Good thing I didn't have a job that required me to get up early in the morning.

My break in the stairwell had sobered me up significantly, and with my butt in the air, I felt entirely undignified as Val carried me through to the kitchen, which was surprisingly empty. Finally, Val put me down, sitting me atop one of the only clear counters. Every other surface was littered with glasses, cans, cups, and bottles. Nina poured herself a drink, and handed one to me, too. The plastic cup she gave me had several lipstick prints around the rim; I guessed they were out of clean ones. I set it down next to me with no intention of taking a sip. I'd had enough to drink.

As Valentin began to regale me with a story about a pigeon that they had just seen fly straight into a lamp post, Dimitri appeared in the room, followed by a couple of other men. I assumed that he had been discussing business with them, judging by their serious manner. Now, however, they set about getting drinks for themselves. Once he had a tumbler of straight vodka in his hand, Dimitri approached me, standing directly in front of me and making eye contact so intense that I looked away within seconds.

'I saw you and Fabio,' he murmured in a low tone.

I felt my cheeks heat up. I wanted to snap that it was none of his business, but his voice wasn't accusatory, and I didn't want to push him away. Instead, I decided to reply honestly. 'Don't worry, I stopped him and went outside to sober up.'

'I saw that, too.'

I made myself meet his gaze again. His molten chocolate eyes burned into mine. 'I shouldn't have let that happen. I'm not interested in him. Don't tell Nina, please,' I begged, remembering her reaction when I told her I'd danced with Fabio at the club.

'You don't have to explain yourself to me. I won't say a word.' Dimitri looked down as he took a long drink from his glass. Apparently he had found a clean one. I picked up my own drink, inspecting the lipstick on it; bright pink, not a colour that I could carry off, even if I'd wanted to. My wardrobe consisted entirely of dark colours, and my limited makeup collection followed suit.

'Here,' Dimitri held his glass towards me, noticing the marks on mine.

I took a small, polite sip. The vodka burned me in a different way than the whiskey had. I cradled the glass in my hands, my legs dangling off the side of the counter. Dimitri leaned back against the counter next to me, crossing his arms over his chest. I noticed that Val and Nina had disappeared, as had the two other men; we were alone.

'I've not been to a house party like this since I was a student,' I said, conversationally. Between the Tony fiasco and my kissing Fabio, I clearly wasn't in favour with Dimitri — he probably thought I was some kind of drama queen — so I was hoping that having a more respectful, normal conversation with him might help my cause.

'You went to university?' Dimitri looked at me, apparently interested. From my seat atop the surface, our faces were at the same level for once, and genuine interest sparked in his eyes. I was pleased to have caught his attention, since he usually seemed indifferent to most things.

'Yeah. I cleaned offices in the morning and did waitressing and bar work at night, to support myself while I studied,' I continued, the first bit of truth about myself I'd told anyone in a long time. Not only was it serving to gain Dimitri's trust, but it felt good to be real for a second. 'But I was still always broke.'

'What did you study?'

'Law.' I couldn't tell him that I'd joined the police right after graduation, once I'd realised that an office environment was never going to satisfy my need to make a difference. They'd accepted my application, and I'd worked my way up the chain. I was a quick climber, due to my absolute commitment to the cause, and the undercover unit had recognised me after a particularly successful honey trap job.

Dimitri raised an eyebrow. 'Damn. You're clever.'

I gave a short laugh. 'Why are you so surprised? Don't I look clever?'

He gave me a look. 'You wanted to be a lawyer?' he

guessed.

'Yeah,' I admitted. 'But then I realised that's not what I'm meant to do with my life.'

Dimitri twisted his stance against the counter so that his hip was propped on it instead, and he was facing me. 'So, what are you meant to do?'

I looked at his face. He was so intense and beautiful. And the vodka had obviously knocked my alcohol level right back up again. Dimitri never seemed to speak more than a few words at a time, and while I was glad that I'd managed to engage him in an actual conversation, his sudden interest was unnerving. I didn't want to mess up. I took a breath, focussing on keeping my tone and body language casual.

'I don't know yet.' I passed the glass that I still held back to Dimitri, and asked, 'What about you?'

He took a drink, looked away, shrugged. 'I'm not meant for anything, other than this.'

I blinked, taken off-guard by his response, and his earnest tone. 'What do you mean?'

Dimitri shrugged again. 'Look at what I do for a living. You think anyone is *meant* for that?'

'I don't know,' I replied, thoughtfully.

Dimitri turned and stared at me. When he spoke again, his voice was low and hard. 'You know what I do, right? For Mikhail?' He didn't break eye contact, and he didn't blink. 'I kill people for money.'

I was jarred by this admission, and my mind scrambled for something to say. I had known this, of course, way before I even met Dimitri. But I hadn't expected him to come out and say it like that, straight to my face, the cold, dead tone of his voice cutting through me like a knife.

'Don't look at me like that. You already knew,' Dimitri said, before I could respond.

'Yeah,' I agreed, working to keep my face neutral, despite the fact that it had apparently already given me away. 'But, I mean, is that because of you, or your situation?'

During my time working for the police, most of my time was spent on putting criminals like Dimitri behind bars, however I was not without my share of empathy. I'd always believed that the justice system failed many people who were forced into their criminal lifestyles, which is one of the main reasons I'd wanted to be a lawyer in the first place — to help. Even though my career path had changed, it didn't mean that my beliefs had. I knew that I should be careful to keep myself detached from Dimitri and the other gang members, but at that moment, I felt guilty about my false pretences for the first time. Dimitri had just admitted his guilt to me, and as soon as I had concrete proof, I would use his disclosure against him.

As we looked at one another, Dimitri's face changed almost imperceptibly, twisting into an expression that I could only describe as conflicted, though that didn't capture it exactly. 'You don't know what I've done, Mari.'

He was wrong; I did know the things he had done — murder, torture, violence. I'd seen him in action, I'd seen the killer look in his eyes, and he was by far the most intimidating person I'd ever dealt with in my life. I had no trouble picturing him carrying out horrific crimes. Except, right now, the man standing before me, without the careful blank shield on his face, just didn't seem capable of those things.

I didn't realise either of us had moved, but Dimitri was so close to me now, I could feel his breath on my face. I saw him swallow a gulp of air, and the rise and fall of his chest as he breathed. 'You wanna get out of here?'

'Yes.' I hopped down off the counter. When I wobbled slightly, Dimitri placed a hand on my hip to steady me.

On our way through the crowd towards the door, I spotted Nina and Val making out on a couch. I also spotted Fabio, with a drink in his hand, watching them with a strange, unfamiliar expression on his face.

Dimitri and I walked home in silence. I was going over the conversation we'd just had in my head, and I assumed that he was doing the same thing. I tried to think of the conversation as a police officer. Finally, I had got some real information out of someone, and a confession of guilt, no less. Of course, it was hardly useful in terms of conviction; I needed hard evidence, I needed to build a case, against more people than just this one man. But it was a start.

As we reached our building, my phone told me that it was 4.37 a.m. Definitely time for bed. But when we got to my apartment door, I found myself asking Dimitri if he wanted to come in. I don't know why. I hadn't meant to say it. To my surprise, he accepted the offer.

'So, give me the grand tour,' Dimitri said when we were inside.

I gave him a look. 'It's the same as yours.'

'Not true. For example, I don't have that pile of old magazines on my coffee table. Or that T-shirt on the floor over there.'

Embarrassed, I hurried to pick up the stray shirt; I'd thrown it off on my way to the shower earlier, and forgotten all about it. 'I'm definitely not giving you a tour if you keep pointing out things that need tidying!'

He smirked, and held up his hands, signalling that he'd behave.

I stared at him, at the light-hearted expression on his face, which I had never seen before. Who was this man? Because it wasn't the Dimitri I'd met those few weeks ago.

Humouring him, I gestured to the small room in which we currently stood. 'This is the lounge.' I pointed to the open door behind Dimitri. 'That's the kitchen.' I strolled to the other end of the room, and pointed to first one door, then the other. 'Bathroom, bedroom. That's it. The whole tour, over in one minute.'

Dimitri glanced around the lounge, then headed into the bedroom, so casually it was as if he owned the place. Although, I didn't doubt that Dimitri owned whatever room he walked into. I stood still for a moment, staring at the bedroom doorway as he disappeared through it. I didn't think I should follow him, but I also didn't know what else to do. My mind worked a million miles an hour—what the hell was happening right now?

Cautiously, I approached the bedroom and peered into the dim room, surprised to see Dimitri lying on his back on my bed. His eyes were shut, and his T-shirt had lifted a little to expose the hard marble skin of his stomach beneath. I tried not to stare.

'Your bed is comfier than mine,' he told me in a quiet voice, keeping his eyes shut.

I blinked. It had been only a week since I'd seen this man almost kill Tony, and it had been barely an hour since he'd admitted to me that he murdered people for a living. During my training for this job, I'd been warned to keep my guard up; the trick was to seem like you were trustworthy, without actually letting anyone in. These were dangerous men, I knew that. Ever since I'd first seen him, I'd been nervous around him, constantly aware that I was interacting with an exceptionally violent man.

But in that moment, I just didn't get that same feeling. And I wasn't sure if it was real, or the alcohol I'd consumed, or some kind of Stockholm Syndrome thing, but I was starting to feel a connection with him.

I could practically hear my boss yelling at me — or was it my own common sense? Either way, I ignored it. Kicking off my boots and switching the light off, I lay down on the bed next to Dimitri, on top of the duvet, leaving enough space in between us so that it didn't feel too intimate. I fell asleep listening to him breath.

Chapter Seven

'Mari! Are you home?'

Someone was shouting. And someone was hammering something. I squeezed my eyes shut, hoping that the noise would go away. It didn't. When I felt someone stir next to me, it knocked me out of my sleepy daze, and I sat up quickly. Looking over to my left, I saw Dimitri, still fully clothed, lying on top of the duvet next to me. For a single moment, I was confused, but then I remembered.

More banging startled me from my thoughts, and I realised it was someone at the door. 'Mari!' A male voice yelled.

Next to me, Dimitri propped himself up on his elbows. His hair was ruffled from sleep, and his eyes hadn't fully opened yet. He looked almost innocent, until he frowned. 'Is that Val?' the sleepy husk of his voice sent goose bumps over my arms.

I leapt off the bed, mostly because Valentin was still banging on the door and it sounded pretty urgent, but also to get away from dealing with the fact that Dimitri was in my bedroom.

Hurrying to the door, I pulled it open to see that it was indeed Val. He looked awful, wearing the same clothes as he had been in last night. I was still in my clothes too, but I had been asleep, while it was clear that Valentin had not.

'Christ, you took your damn time!' he snapped. I'd never seen him in any other mood than cheerful, so I knew something was wrong.

'What's going on?' I asked, squinting against the bright light of the stairwell.

'I don't know where anyone is! I've lost Nina, D isn't at his place — what the hell is going on?'

'Okay, just calm down,' I said gently. 'Dimitri's here.'

Val frowned, and opened his mouth to say something, but no words came. He seemed to stammer for a few seconds, before settling for, 'What?'

As if to prove my point, Dimitri appeared behind me, tugging his haphazard hair into place. 'What are you doing here, Val?' he asked.

'You know it's almost three in the afternoon, right?' Val asked us, though he clearly already knew that we had no idea. I had never slept in that long before, not even when ill, though it did explain why I felt so groggy.

'Val.' Dimitri seemed impatient. 'What's going on?'

'I don't know where Nina is,' Val explained, the worry in his eyes evident. 'I went to the bathroom last night, and when I went back to find her, she was gone. Someone said they saw her leave. She was totally wasted, and you know what she can be like. I still can't find her — it's been like ten hours. I tried her place, my place, tried calling her a million times. No sign.' He was looking more and more despairing. 'I'm really worried about her, D. This isn't like her.'

Dimitri rubbed a hand over his face, thinking, and let out a long sigh. 'Okay. She probably just passed out somewhere. I'll come help you look. If we work systematically from here to Fabio's, we'll find her.'

'Don't you think I've tried that?' Val snapped.

'Three pairs of eyes are better than one,' I pointed out softly. 'I'll come too. Just give me one second.'

I changed last night's blouse for a sweater and slipped on my Nikes, while Dimitri fastened boots that I hadn't even noticed him remove last night. He must have done it after I'd fallen asleep, and the knowledge that he had consciously chosen to stay with me last night made my stomach knot. As for me, the fact that I'd been comfortable enough to fall asleep in a room with a man who killed people for a living was an entirely separate problem.

Val waited for us impatiently, then the three of us hurried out onto the busy street. I called Nina, to make sure that it wasn't just Valentin that she was avoiding, but got no answer. I was worried too; Dimitri was right, she probably had just fallen over and passed out somewhere, but that wasn't safe, especially not in this neighbourhood, and especially not in this temperature.

We combed the streets, checking every alleyway, and continuing to call her cell phone with no luck. We made it all the way back to Fabio's apartment with no sign of Nina.

'I'll run up and ask Fab,' Val said. 'You two check around the building. I looked already, but I might have missed her.'

We did as we were told, but she was nowhere to be seen.

'Do you think she's okay?' I asked Dimitri in a quiet voice as we made our way back to the front of Fabio's building to wait for Valentin.

He didn't look at me. 'I don't know. Sometimes Nina does stupid things.'

'What does that mean?'

Dimitri didn't answer my question, and seconds later Val emerged from the building.

'Fabio hasn't seen her since last night,' he told us, a frantic edge sharpening his voice.

'Why don't we try going to Nina's again? She might have got home by herself by now,' I suggested, clutching at straws.

Val sighed, hopelessly, but nodded agreement. We headed in that direction, the tension obvious between us as we became more and more worried. Silence fell as we hurried along the sidewalk, and when Valentin's cell phone suddenly beeped, it made me jump. He scrambled to retrieve the buzzing phone from his pocket.

When he looked at the screen, his face immediately relaxed. 'It's Nina,' he breathed, before raising the cell to his ear with a shaking hand. When he heard her voice, he let out a long sigh of relief, but as the seconds passed, he seemed to get angry and a heavy frown darkened his usually cheerful face. He hung up without saying a single word to her.

'She's okay?' I asked, anxious to know what she had said to Val.

'She's fine,' he almost spat. Avoiding my gaze, he looked right over to Dimitri to explain. 'She got called for a job last night. Only just got the time to look at her damn phone.'

Dimitri nodded, dropping his gaze to the ground. I looked to both men for an answer, but neither gave me one. Taking my hand, Dimitri tugged me gently away, as Valentin took off in the opposite direction, again without a word.

When he was out of earshot, I turned to Dimitri. 'What the hell just happened?'

He dropped my hand, and I had to hurry to keep up with his long strides. A sigh escaped his lips. 'I can't tell you this stuff, Mari.'

I raised an incredulous eyebrow. 'Nina is my friend. I was worried about her, too, you know. I helped look for her, and you can't even tell me why?'

Dimitri glanced over at me, but remained silent until we reached our building. At my door, he didn't ask before following me inside. He stood in the middle of the lounge, an irritated expression drawing his features together. Since he hadn't taken a seat, I didn't either, choosing instead to stand opposite him, arms folded over my chest to show my determination.

Dimitri didn't wait for me to ask again before jumping into an explanation. 'Sometimes Nina gets a call from Mikhail, and she has to go to the beach, to do a job for him. She doesn't have a choice, and she isn't supposed to tell anyone. Mikhail wants to keep it on the down low, and Nina doesn't exactly want everyone to know either.' His words were hurried, as if he was trying to get it all out before he changed his mind. 'There's a particular guy who visits from Europe every few months, he stays with Mikhail at the beach, and he... well... He doesn't want any of the girls at the club, he asks specifically for Nina. I guess he flew in late last night and requested her.'

I felt my eyes widen. 'She's a prostitute?'

Dimitri frowned and shook his head. 'Not really. It's only this one guy.'

I was having trouble processing this. I hadn't expected it at all. 'But I didn't think she worked in your... business.'

'She doesn't really. But if Mikhail wants you to do something, you do it.'

That reminded me... 'Fabio told me that Mikhail was asking about me.'

Something flashed in Dimitri's eyes. 'He was. But you don't need to worry.'

I looked down. 'Yeah, Fabio also told me that you *sorted it out*, whatever that means.'

'It means that Mikhail won't ask about you anymore.'

'What was he even asking?'

Dimitri ran a hand through his hair and turned to the window, shifting uncomfortably. 'He just wanted to know who you were. He was impressed by the damage you did to Tony. That's all.'

I narrowed my eyes; I didn't believe him, but I didn't want to press him anymore. He'd already told me a lot of stuff that he wasn't supposed to talk about.

I joined Dimitri at the window. The view wasn't great, but it was a busy street, and people watching was a way to pass the time on a dull afternoon. We stood there for a moment, both staring down at the sidewalk, until Dimitri made a move towards the door. He thanked me for helping look for Nina, said a quick goodbye — then he was gone. I remained where I was for a few minutes, staring at the door that Dimitri had just closed behind him.

During my training, I'd been warned about the dangers of forming real relationships with people while I was undercover. At the time, I'd brushed the advice off, believing that I knew what I was doing, and I would be able to stay completely focused. But now, I was starting to understand the warning, though the real danger was the difficulty distinguishing fake relationships with real ones. I needed to stay focused. That meant no more sleepovers with hired killers. I had to get the information, and get out, before I was in too deep.

Chapter Eight

Tuesday night, I arrived at the bar for my shift, to find an unfamiliar young man behind the bar. Beside him, Jono — the owner of the bar, who rarely came down from his office, was showing him how to work the till. I approached curiously, rounding the bar and stashing my purse on top of the rarely opened wine fridge.

'Mari, this is Tad,' Jono introduced. 'He's going to be taking over Leigh's shifts from now on. As Tuesday is usually a quiet night, I thought it would be a good opportunity for you to train him up a little.'

'Leigh quit?' I asked, incredulous.

'Yeah, on Sunday. Luckily, a friend recommended Tad, and he was able to start right away.' Jono beamed, and slapped a hand on Tad's back as if they were old pals. 'He's got bar experience, so he should pick it up pretty quick.'

With that, Jono headed back upstairs to the safe retreat of his office. I doubted that he really had so much work to do that he couldn't spare the time to come downstairs once in a while, but I never questioned what he did up there. I preferred him out of the way. Next to me, Tad was smiling nervously. He looked very young, with surfer blonde hair, blue eyes, and dimples. Contrastingly, tattoo sleeves covered both of his arms and peeped out from underneath the round neck of his black T-shirt. I wondered just how much of his skin was adorned with the intricate ink designs.

'So, you have bar experience?' I asked.

'Yeah, loads. Been doing it since I was eighteen.' His low voice didn't suit his boyish exterior.

I raised an eyebrow. 'How old are you now?'

'Twenty-one,' Tad beamed proudly.

I resisted the urge to roll my eyes — I'd been right, he

was young. 'Okay. Well, I guess Jono showed you how to use the till, and where everything is kept. It's not a hard job, no one really asks for very complicated drinks in here. You'll do fine.'

As we worked, Tad told me that he was two months away from finishing his degree in psychology, that he lived with three untidy girls and hated it, and that he couldn't wait to move down south next year. He seemed nice enough — surprisingly green, considering that he had apparently grown up in the City, and he was easy to work with, so I was content with Jono's choice of hiring. Despite this, I couldn't stop thinking about Leigh, and wondering if she had quit because of my budding friendship with Nina, Dimitri, and Valentin. It seemed petty, but Leigh had had such a strong reaction to Nina last time she'd seen her, it wasn't entirely improbable.

Nina herself arrived at the bar a little after eleven. When she walked through the door, I waved, but she ignored me, turning away instead to give the man behind her a kiss. I balked when I saw that it wasn't Valentin. This man was older — maybe in his mid-fifties, with dark hair and wearing an expensive looking suit. As the pair of them made their way over to the bar, it was clear that Nina had already been drinking for a while.

'Two vodkas,' the man ordered.

'Sure.' I poured the drinks, trying to make eye contact with Nina as I did so, but she expertly avoided my gaze. The man paid me for the drinks, and took Nina over to the booth furthest away from the bar, where they sat too close together. I didn't need to be told that this was the man who liked to *request* Nina when he visited the City. Even without this knowledge, he still would have made my skin crawl.

'You okay?' Tad asked me.

I blinked. I guess I'd been staring at Nina and her date.

'Yeah, yeah. I'm fine. I'm gonna take a five minute break, you'll be okay?'

'Sure, no problem.'

I smiled my thanks and grabbed my purse from underneath the bar on my way outside. Luckily, I had Dimitri's number saved in my phone; Nina had given it to me the night of the club opening, when Dimitri had agreed to go with me to the Beach, in case I needed to rearrange the time or anything.

He picked up right away. 'Hello?'

'Hey, Dimitri. It's Mari.'

'Is everything okay?'

'I'm fine,' I told him. 'Just… I'm at work, and Nina is here with that guy. You know, *that guy*.'

'I know who you mean.' Dimitri's tone had lowered significantly. 'So what's the problem?'

I frowned. 'He's so creepy. Watching them is making me uncomfortable.'

'So don't watch them.'

I hung up on him. Angrily, I kicked at a discarded beer can on the sidewalk in front of me. I knew I couldn't do anything to help Nina out of this situation, and I hated how useless that made me feel. I don't know what I'd been thinking to call Dimitri, I knew he couldn't help either, but it made me so mad that he didn't even seem to care. He was just used to it.

Back inside the bar, I avoided Tad's questions about my sudden mood change and concentrated on doing my job. Tad took all the orders from Nina's table, and, as lousy as it had been, I took Dimitri's advice and tried my hardest not to look in her direction, though I couldn't help but check every now and then to ensure that she was okay.

The evening dragged, and I was getting more and more frustrated by how useless I felt. Finally it was nearing closing time, and Nina's booth was the only one still occupied. Tad and I were chatting aimlessly about countries we wanted to visit, when the door opened, revealing Dimitri. Relief washed over me.

Choosing the barstool directly opposite me, Dimitri gave me a small smile that I couldn't help but return. I slid a vodka towards him, telling him that it was on the house.

'Are we allowed to do that?' Tad asked me quietly a few minutes later, as I restocked the soda fridge.

I shook my head. 'I wouldn't make a habit of it. This is a one off.'

'Who is that guy?'

'He's a regular,' I replied dismissively.

When it was time to lock up, I showed Tad how to cash out the register and the location of the safe and the keys before he left. Nina had to be supported to the door by her date, due to her level of intoxication. When the two of them stumbled out onto the street, Dimitri rolled his eyes, and hurried to steady them.

'Dimitri!' the man exclaimed upon seeing him. 'I didn't see you. What are you doing here?'

'Hello, Olivier. Just came for a drink,' Dimitri replied, still holding onto Nina in case she fell again, which was looking pretty likely.

I finished locking the door and approached the three of them slowly. Nina finally acknowledged me — I guessed she was now too drunk to keep up the pretence of not recognising me.

'Mari,' she drew out my name horribly, and reached out for me.

Seeing this, the man — Olivier — pulled Nina away from both me and Dimitri, who was forced to let go of her. 'I've got this from here,' Olivier said, pulling Nina towards a nearby taxi.

'She's barely conscious,' Dimitri pointed out. 'Let me take her home.'

'I said I've got this.' Olivier's simple words sounded dangerous, and I felt a chill go through me.

Dimitri, however, didn't seem fazed as he took hold of Nina's arm. 'I'll take her home, and you should go to the beach. Mikhail opened a new club recently, have you been yet?'

'What the hell is your problem?' Olivier snapped.

'Look, I'm just trying to help,' Dimitri said in a low but friendly voice, as if confiding a secret. 'I know Nina — she'll be throwing up and passing out very soon. I'm sure you'd rather be enjoying the new club than dealing with this.'

Olivier seemed to think about this for a moment, before releasing his hold on Nina, pushing her away from him, suddenly disgusted. Dimitri caught her, and Nina barely seemed to notice what was going on.

'Fine,' Olivier snapped. 'But you tell her that I won't be paying for her time tonight. She needs to learn to handle her alcohol.'

With those final bitter words, Olivier jumped into the waiting taxi and took off in the direction of the Beach. I let out a breath that I hadn't even realised I'd been holding. If Dimitri hadn't turned up, I don't know what I would have done. Seeing Nina in this state with that man made me feel physically sick, and again, I worried that I was starting to care too much about these people. Only thing was, I didn't know how to stop caring.

Nina's flat wasn't far from the bar, but it took a long time to walk her home. Dimitri supported most of her weight, and I kept her balanced on her other side. When we finally reached her building, I found her keys from her clutch and we helped her inside. Her apartment was a small and messy studio, smelling strongly of cigarette smoke, poorly masked by perfume. Dimitri placed her down on her bed then left me to take off her shoes and tuck her in. I managed to find a clean glass in the tiny kitchen and filled it with water before placing it next to the bed; I knew what hell it was to wake up hungover and dehydrated.

I was reluctant to leave her, but before long, Valentin showed up.

'She's in bed,' Dimitri told Val, handing him Nina's key. 'She's okay, just wasted.'

'Thanks,' Val replied. He sounded out of breath, and I guessed he'd ran over here. His devotion made my heart ache.

Dimitri and I left, closing the door behind us and starting down the stairs.

'You called him?' I asked.

'Yeah.'

Dimitri and I walked home together without speaking, as was quickly becoming our custom. I knew that I was supposed to be gaining his trust, which was probably a little hard to do without talking to one another, but I also knew that Dimitri valued his silence, and I didn't want to pressure him into conversation.

Only when we reached my front door did I finally dare to speak. 'Thank you for coming to the bar. I don't know what I would have done if you hadn't been there.' I tried to ignore the sick feeling in the pit of my stomach as I thought about what Nina would have gone through tonight if Dimitri hadn't been there to rescue her.

'Mari.' The harsh tone of Dimitri's voice commanded my attention, and a closed off expression hardened his face. 'I don't want you to keep getting involved with this stuff,' he told me.

I blinked. 'What?'

'I just don't think it's a good idea.'

'Nina is my friend,' I argued, taken off guard by this line of conversation.

'She has a very different life than you,' Dimitri said, keeping his voice carefully blank. 'We all do. And it's dangerous for... people like you.'

'People like me?' I repeated, incredulously.

'You might have been born into it, but you weren't raised in it. You don't understand it.'

I frowned. 'Where is this coming from? Do you have some kind of problem with me?'

Dimitri ran his hand over his short, dark hair, frustrated. 'No. Look, you remind me of someone, okay? Someone who got hurt because of their association with me. And after what happened with Tony, and now having met both Mikhail and Olivier, you should stay away. These are very dangerous men, Mari.'

I looked up at him. 'Well, so are you, by your definition. But I'm not scared of you.' At least, I wasn't anymore.

Dimitri's eyes flashed. 'Maybe you should be.'

I didn't know what to say. I'd thought my getting involved with the members of the gang would make me part of their lives, but there was a fine line between being accepted and pushing them away with one step too far. As far as Dimitri was concerned, there was no reason that would explain my wanting to keep integrating myself with their lives.

While my mind struggled to find a response to Dimitri's warning, he raised a hand to my face, and ever so lightly brushed a thumb over my cheekbone. His touch left a warm trail over my skin, contrasting against the cold disappointment I felt in my chest.

'I appreciate your concern, but you can't tell me what to do,' I said, after a long pause. 'Nina is my friend, and I'm worried about her. Do you expect me to just cut off all contact with her? And Val? And you?'

'No,' Dimitri replied, dropping his hand to his side. Irritation hardened the line of his mouth. 'Nina cares about you, too. I just don't think you should come to the Beach anymore, or Fabio's parties.'

My own frustration deepened. 'I don't think that's up to you. I can handle myself.'

'I'm just trying to look out for you.'

'Why?' I snapped. I knew that I was being defensive in response to feeling rejected, but I couldn't stop the annoyance in my voice. I'd never met anyone who turned from hot to cold as quickly and frequently as Dimitri; one minute he was sleeping over at my place, the next he was telling me to keep away.

A muscle in Dimitri's jaw twitched, and I knew he was holding back his response. He held my gaze intensely for a moment, before simply turning and walking away. I stood wordlessly in my doorway watching his legs disappear up the stairs in front of me. What the hell had just happened?

Chapter Nine

The next day, I vented my frustrations with an intense workout at the gym, and a vigorous cleaning of the flat before heading in to work. I worked alone, and it was surprisingly quiet for a Wednesday evening. It was just after eleven when Nina appeared. She was alone, and gave me a tentative smile as she made her way over to the bar. I noticed that she was wearing jeans and a hoodie, her hair messy and her face bare of makeup; I had never seen her look like that before. She was still pretty of course, but she looked a lot younger, and very vulnerable.

'You okay?' I asked, sliding a vodka and coke towards her to make up for my inadequate words.

Nina took a seat on a barstool, giving me a half-hearted shrug. 'I guess… Val and I had a fight this morning,' she confided, clasping her hands around the glass in front of her as if to anchor her down.

'About Olivier?' I guessed.

She nodded. 'Yeah. Val hates that I have to do this whenever Olivier comes into town. And I totally get it, but I don't have a choice.'

'Surely Val understands that?' I asked, trying to sound sympathetic when all I really felt was angry.

'He does,' Nina said, taking a small sip of her drink. 'That makes it even harder for him. He knows it's not my choice, so he won't leave me, but he can't stay with me knowing that I have to sleep with another man. Neither of us know how to deal with this problem.'

My heart ached for her. I leaned forward on the bar, reaching a hand out to touch Nina's arm gently. 'It must be hard.'

'I just don't know what to do.' Nina sighed miserably, sinking further down onto the stool, and further into herself.

'Nina…' I took a deep breath. 'Have you ever thought of going to the police? There's witness protection, and you could…' I trailed off when I saw Nina's horrified expression.

'Are you insane?' she exclaimed, her eyes darting around the bar to make sure no one had overheard. 'They'd *kill* me. Witness protection is a joke. No one who has turned on Mikhail has stayed alive long enough to even *attempt* a new life.'

I couldn't help but take her criticisms a little personally, although she was at least partly right. We couldn't help everyone, no matter how hard we tried. But I could damn well help Nina. She didn't deserve this, and I swore to myself then that I would do whatever I could for her.

'Okay, maybe you're right,' I backtracked quickly. 'I'm sorry. I just wish there was something I could do to help.'

Nina gave me a sad smile that didn't reach her eyes. 'I wish there was, too.'

I was relieved that my mention of police protection hadn't raised her suspicions, but my relief was short lived; I just felt so useless. 'Well, I can be here for you. Honestly, whatever you need.'

Nina's eyes glistened. 'Thanks, Mari. I don't know what I'd do without you.'

I smiled in what I hoped was a reassuring way. A middle-aged man approached the bar and ordered another round of drinks for his table. When he had paid and taken the tray of glasses over to his friends, I turned back to Nina. She had finished her drink, so I poured her another.

She smiled. 'Thanks. How much?'

I shook my head. 'I'll add it onto Dimitri's tab.'

Her smile deepened, her teeth finally showing through. 'Val told me how you and Dimitri got me home last night. I don't remember, but I really appreciate it.'

'Don't mention it,' I replied. 'I couldn't have done it without Dimitri, so it's him you should be thanking.'

She gave me a look that I couldn't decipher, and I was reminded of Dimitri's similar expression last night. I still didn't know what to do about that — I had been under the impression that I was earning Dimitri's trust, but after our conversation, I'd realised that he still saw me as an outsider.

When Nina's phone beeped, she reached for it out of her purse and sighed heavily when she read the message. 'It's Val,' she explained, a sad line settling over her mouth.

I propped a hip against the glass washer. 'You okay?'

Nina pulled a face, tucking her phone away without replying to Val's message. 'I dunno. I mean, I love Val. But this is so hard for him, it's not fair. And sometimes I think it would be better if we weren't together — I went straight from one serious relationship into another, and I've never really been on my own.'

I was surprised by her admission, but jumped on the chance to gain some more information. 'You mean Fabio?'

'Yeah,' Nina replied. 'That was so intense, and I was so young. We started dating in high school.'

I raised my eyebrows questioningly, and that was all it took for her to finally explain the full story. Well, that and the fact that she'd now had a few drinks.

'Fab was my first boyfriend, and I got pregnant,' Nina began. 'I dropped out of school. He told me that he would get a proper job, and support me and the baby. But when I had him — my baby, Mikhail forced me to give him up for adoption.' Nina sighed, and my heart ached for her, as she continued, 'Fab had been working for Mikhail since he was fourteen, so what Mikhail said was pretty much the law. We had no choice.'

'Why would he do that? Make you give up the baby?'

Nina shrugged. 'Because he can, because he has this control over all of us. And Fabio would never tell you this, but Mikhail practically raised him, he's like a father to him. Guess Mikhail thought a baby would distract Fabio from his work, or something. I don't know.'

'And you and Fabio broke up?' I asked, my voice gentle.

'Not right away.' Nina's voice was unbearably sad. 'He really did love me, and I had no one else, so I moved in with him in this tiny little flat he shared with a couple other guys. That was before he made enough money to move out on his own. It was the worst year of my life. Fabio and those guys were high every day, and the place was always trashed and dirty with needles and shit all over the floor... There were always random people coming in and out, and it's a good thing I never kept my baby, because that was no place for a child.'

I let out a long breath, waiting to hear the rest. I'd had no idea that Nina had been through so much, and at such a young age.

'I met Valentin and Dimitri at a party at the Beach,' Nina continued, finishing off her drink. 'Val was so sweet. He helped me get a job, and gave me enough money for the first few months' rent on my own place — the one I'm still in now. He helped me get away from a horrible situation, and I couldn't help but fall in love with him. Obviously leaving Fabio was hard, and he was hurt, but I'd already fallen for Val.' As she spoke, the sadness in her face was erased by a small smile that played on her lips. 'He saved me.'

I returned her smile. 'Give me ten minutes to close up, and I'll walk you home, okay?'

Nina nodded, and watched as I set about the closing

duties, despite it being ten minutes before time. When I was done, we headed out onto the dark street, and towards Nina's flat. Before we reached it, I took her hand and turned off in another direction.

Nina looked at me confusedly. 'Where are we going?'

'I'm taking you to Val's,' I told her, wrapping my arm around her. She didn't object.

After leaving Nina with Valentin, I headed back across town to my own place. My walk home led me past Fabio's street, and I found myself fixating on Nina's story. I couldn't imagine how hard it must have been for her to give up her baby and live in that awful situation while she was so young, but nothing she'd said led me to believe that Fabio himself was really a bad guy. Even after all that had happened between them, she hadn't said a bad word against him.

When I got into bed what seemed like hours later, I lay there in the dark and thought about everything I'd found out, and about the very real possibility that Dimitri would never let me into his life the way I needed him to. I felt inexplicably sad.

***

The following evening, I was at work again, trying desperately to think of a way to reconcile with Dimitri. I needed to get him to trust me, but after his warning about the dangers of hanging around with him, I knew that any normal girl would back off. If I was too persistent, I would raise suspicion. The intensity of the undercover life was worse than I could have ever imagined, but I knew I needed to keep focussed and press forward. Somehow.

The night was fairly busy, and I was thankful for the distraction. Midway through my shift, Val and Nina entered, closely followed by Dimitri. My heartbeat quickened when I saw him, and he met my gaze for only a second before looking away.

Nina and Val hopped onto barstools opposite me, but Dimitri remained standing. When I looked at him questioningly, he gestured to the door, indicating the desire to speak to me alone. I frowned, uncertain of what he could possibly want, given how we had ended our last conversation, but followed him out of the bar and onto the street.

'I can't stay out here long,' I warned, peering through the glass of the door to keep an eye on the customers. Everyone had drinks, aside from Nina and Val, but I would still get in trouble if Jono saw the bar unattended. Not that there was a particularly high chance of that happening, since he seemed to be constantly occupied in his office upstairs — doing what, I had no clue. Although, I was pretty sure he also lived up there, so for all I knew, he could just be watching TV while I ran his bar for him.

Dimitri crossed his arms over his chest, keeping his expression carefully blank, as usual. He didn't meet my eyes when he spoke, choosing instead to study the pavement on which we stood. 'Look, I'm sorry about what I said the other day — it obviously came across wrong. I didn't mean to offend you.'

I blinked. I hadn't expected that. 'Oh. Uh, don't worry about it.' I stumbled over my words, fighting the urge to make a sarcastic comment in favour of getting back into Dimitri's good books. I knew that I needed him for information, but I simply couldn't figure out how best to get him to open up. Nina trusted me, and after a few drinks, she'd tell me pretty much anything I needed to know. And with Fabio, I knew a few flirtatious comments would get him on my side. But Dimitri was just so hard to read, and that made me nervous.

Dimitri let out a sigh. 'What are you doing tomorrow night?'

'Working,' I replied. 'But I can get Tad to cover for me. Why?'

Dimitri hesitated. 'I want to take you somewhere.'

I frowned. 'Where?'

Dimitri shook his head. He wasn't going to tell me. 'Will you come, or not?'

'Uh... Okay.' It went against all my instincts to walk into an unknown situation, but I was intrigued, and couldn't really afford to pass up the opportunity to spend time with him.

'Good. I'll see you tomorrow night, at nine.' With that, Dimitri turned on his heel and disappeared into the night, leaving me entirely confused.

Back inside, I hurried to the bar, glad that no one was waiting to be served. I poured Nina and Val their usual drinks, and added them to Dimitri's tab.

'Thanks,' Nina smiled. 'Where's D?'

'He left,' I replied. 'He said he wants to take me somewhere tomorrow.'

Nina frowned. 'Take you where?'

I shrugged. 'Your guess is as good as mine.'

Nina glanced at Val, and he mirrored her clueless expression.

'So, if you don't know where you're going,' Nina mused, sipping her drink, 'then how do you know what to wear?'

I grabbed a nearby dishcloth and flicked it at her. 'That's hardly the biggest concern I have right now.'

She grinned, avoiding the cloth expertly. 'Sorry. He really didn't say anything to us, though, so I can't help you.' She turned to Val. 'I'm gonna smoke, you want to come out with me?'

'Yeah, be there in a second,' Valentin replied, giving Nina a sweet kiss on her forehead before she skipped towards the door. When she was safely outside, Val turned his attention back to me. 'Mari, I want to thank you.'

I blinked. 'For what?'

'Bringing Nina to my place last night.' Val's gaze dropped to his almost empty glass. 'I don't know what I'd do without her. We had a fight, and I was really starting to think that was it for us. Thanks for talking her round.'

I leaned forward on the bar. 'I didn't talk her round, she talked herself round. She was telling me how you met, and how much she loves you, and I think she realised that she wouldn't know what to do without you, either.'

Val lifted his gaze to mine again, and the tenderness in his eyes surprised me. 'Well, thank you for being there. You're a good friend to Nina, and to me, as well.' He reached over the bar and gave my hand a quick squeeze, before finishing his drink and heading outside.

Chapter Ten

When Dimitri knocked on my door the following night, I leapt to answer. Tad had happily agreed to cover my shift, and I'd spent the afternoon mentally preparing myself for whatever this evening might involve. Although I had dismissed her remark, Nina had been right about not knowing what to wear. Given that I doubted Dimitri was taking me any place particularly nice, I had gone for the safe option of jeans, boots, a grey tee and my favourite leather jacket. Luckily, I seemed to have chosen correctly, as I saw that Dimitri was wearing a pretty similar outfit. I also couldn't help but notice that he looked good in it.

'Hey,' he greeted me as I locked the door behind me. 'You ready to go?'

'You gonna tell me where we're going?'

'Nope.'

I felt tense, as I always did when I wasn't aware of all the information about a situation. I still had no idea where I stood with Dimitri, or why he no longer seemed to be his stoic, rude self. There seemed to be two very distinct sides of his personality, though I had a suspicion that one was the defensive shield he portrayed to the world, and the other was the real Dimitri, that he didn't reveal to anyone. Why he would reveal it to me, though, was a mystery. Maybe I was better at my job than I'd thought, and he was starting to trust me. But maybe not.

Outside, I pulled my jacket tighter around me against the cold night air. Following Dimitri to the underground station, we took the train east, changed once, and emerged almost half an hour later.

'Okay, seriously, where the hell are we going?' I demanded, my patience wearing thin as we walked down an unfamiliar street in a part of the City I didn't know well. Dimitri had been quiet during our journey, and now he ignored my question, increasing my level of anxiety. I followed him for another few blocks until, suddenly, I figured out where we were going.

We turned a corner, and the cemetery gates loomed before us. 'What are we doing here?' I asked, my voice quiet.

Dimitri weaved his way through the headstones, towards the newer plots at the back of the land. He stopped in front of a small stone plaque that lay in the long grass, marking a fairly recent cremation.

'Here.' Dimitri pointed, and I read the name on the plaque in the glow of a nearby lamp.

Max Peters, 1960–2019, Gone but Not Forgotten
Oh.

I stepped back instinctively. 'Dimitri, what the hell? I don't want to be here.'

He turned to look at me, his face cast with deep shadows in the dim lighting. 'I figured you'd never seen this.'

'Don't you think there was probably a reason for that?' I was starting to panic. I wasn't a good enough actress for this. I couldn't care less that Max was dead. In fact, it was a good thing for the public of the City. I didn't know how to play this.

Dimitri regarded me coolly with his imperceptible dark gaze. 'Are you upset?'

'No,' I replied, honestly. 'I told you — I barely knew him. I don't know what you expect me to say right now.'

'I don't expect you to say anything,' Dimitri replied, stepping towards me. 'I just wanted to show you what happens to people who get involved with this life. He was your father, and he's dead.'

'So what?' I snapped, uneasiness swirling in my stomach.

'I'm trying to make you realise how dangerous this is for you!' Dimitri raised his voice, exasperated.

'I can take of myself,' I defended, for what felt like the millionth time.

'Not anymore,' Dimitri replied, the harshness of his tone slicing through the cold night air. His icy gaze met mine. 'Mikhail seems to think that a child of Max's should be involved with the *family business*. Remember how he was asking about you? He wanted information, to see how he could use you. At first, he wanted you for the clubs, thinking that he could make a lot of money from a pretty face like yours, but I pointed out that Max — even being the pig that he was — probably wouldn't want his daughter being whored out to strangers.'

I recoiled. I hadn't expected any of this, and I was caught completely off guard.

Dimitri continued, 'Seeing how you handled yourself against Tony that night at the club, how you smashed a glass over his head... It was impressive — none of us knew you had that in you. And he had a different idea about how you could work for him.'

'Doing what?' I asked, carefully keeping my voice controlled.

'Mostly drugs, like Fabio,' Dimitri replied. 'It's nothing compared to what I do, but it's still not something that I want you involved in.'

'What are you saying? Why would Mikhail want me?' I asked, feeling completely blindsided by this information, and struggling to figure out how my *character* would react to this. 'I mean, look at me!' I gestured down to my small frame. 'I'm hardly intimidating.'

'I think that's the point. People who owe us money, they see us coming and run a mile. They see you, they let you into their homes. Then you beat the money out of them, just like any other *employee*. You see? This is why you have to stay the hell away from Mikhail, and from the Beach. I can't keep holding him off.'

'Have you known about this the whole time?' I asked, incredulous. 'That Mikhail wants me to work for him?'

'I won't let it happen.'

'But you knew that's what he wanted. Why didn't you tell me? Don't you think I needed to know?'

'I tried to warn you to stay away,' Dimitri told me, his expression carefully guarded. 'I didn't want to scare you.'

'So dragging me out to the cemetery at night and telling me all about it, that's not supposed to scare me?' I exclaimed. I hated being unprepared, and being caught off guard, and I was beyond pissed that I hadn't been aware of Mikhail's plans for me. It felt like information I should have known. I hated that Dimitri had control of the situation.

Dimitri cursed, kicked angrily at the grass in front of him. Seeing him lose his composure startled me. 'No! I thought that seeing your father's grave might remind you how dangerous this all is. It's not a game, Mari, its life and death. If you work for Mikhail, you will die, sooner or later.' Dimitri sighed, his momentary anger seeming to fade away, replaced by a sad kind of resignation. 'We all will.'

His words chilled me, and there was a silent pause. When I spoke, my tone was as cold as the tension between us. 'Dimitri listen to me. I don't need your protection, okay? I'm not your responsibility. I can protect myself.'

Dimitri frowned. 'It's not like you'd have a choice, you know, if Mikhail decided he really wanted you.' He sounded as though he was explaining something simple to a child, and was sick of trying to get the message to sink in. 'Val, and Nina, and me — none of us have a choice. I need you to stay away from the club, away from Mikhail.'

I sighed, choosing not to reply to that request. I couldn't help but think that this was an opportunity; although my working directly under Mikhail hadn't been the plan, it would allow me to get into the middle of the action, see first-hand all the things that I needed to see, rather than relying on information from other people. It hadn't been the intention of my undercover persona, but I couldn't let this chance pass me by without at least considering it.

Only, I couldn't exactly turn around and tell Dimitri that. Especially not after he had gone to such lengths to keep me out of it. I just needed Mikhail to decide he wanted me to work for him, once and for all, but it would have to look accidental on my part. I needed to call Doro; he was the only person who would be able to help me with this. But only after I got the permission of my superiors to make a slight change of plan... It wouldn't be easy, but I knew I had to convince them.

Dimitri let out a long, ragged breath, drawing back to the current moment. He held his hand out to me, and I took it. I shouldn't have. He'd gone from barely tolerating me to actually seeming to care about my well-being in a matter of days. My brain screamed at me to keep my guard up, but my body disobeyed.

Gently, Dimitri led me to a row of memorial plaques further along in the cemetery, and stopped in front of a slightly older looking stone, before letting go of my hand. I read the engraving.

Isabel Marlow, 1991-2018, Beloved Daughter, Sister, and Friend, Tragically Taken Too Soon, Forever in Our Hearts

I looked up at Dimitri.

He didn't meet my eyes. 'My girlfriend.'

My heart seemed to stop.

'She had nothing to do with the business. She didn't even really know what I did, I always lied to her about it,' Dimitri continued, staring ahead into the darkness. 'I wish I'd told her. Maybe then she wouldn't have come looking for me at the Beach that night... She got so pissed when she found me in a club, she stormed right over and demanded that I come home with her, right that second. Except I couldn't. We were in negotiations with a rival group.'

I sucked in a breath. My mind raced. Was he actually confiding in me?

'I left with her, because what else could I do?' Dimitri shook his head, looking at the ground. 'The guys I was with, they saw it as disrespectful, and they followed us out of the club. I didn't even notice them — I was too busy arguing with her. They shot at us. I don't know if they were aiming for me, or her, or just trying to scare us... but they hit her. She died right there, in my arms, in an alleyway.'

'Oh my God, Dimitri...' I breathed. I'd had no idea.

'I killed them both, the guys who shot her. It was easy.' Dimitri's voice was empty. 'But it didn't help. She is the only person I have ever loved, and I'm the reason she's dead.'

I wanted to tell him that he was wrong, that he couldn't have known that would happen, but I finally understood what he was trying to tell me; the truth was that anyone involved with him was in danger. And the ache that settled in my chest made me painfully aware that I, too, was approaching imminent danger with impressive speed.

***

On the way back to our part of town, we decided to get a drink, so less than an hour later, we turned up at *Arrow's Bar*. It was pretty quiet, save for a bored-looking Tad behind the bar. When he saw us, however, a warm smile spread over his face.

'Hey Mari,' he said when we reached the bar. 'What are you doing here on your night off?'

'Drinking,' I replied. 'Can I have a vodka lemonade?'

Tad nodded, and looked over to Dimitri, who ordered a vodka on the rocks. As he got our drinks, Tad chatted away about how quiet the night had been, and how he much preferred it when we worked together. I agreed; the shifts went much faster when there was someone to talk to.

Sliding our glasses across the bar, Tad winked at me. 'On the house.'

I felt a smile lift my mouth, despite the sadness that I felt surrounding me. 'You're not supposed to do that, remember?'

'You do,' he shrugged. 'I'm just following by example.'

I pulled a face, and Tad laughed, but then I glanced over at Dimitri and my smile faded instantly. His blank shield was firmly in place, but the emptiness in his eyes was real. We chose a booth in the corner of the large room, and sat opposite each other, sipping our drinks in silence, both lost in our thoughts. I was still reeling from everything I'd just found out about Dimitri's past, and Mikhail's interest in me. I still wanted to call Doro to see if I could get myself fully involved with Mikhail and the organisation; being on the outside gathering information in this way wasn't enough. I craved the action, and I wanted to bring down Mikhail first-hand. But I was very aware of just how angry Dimitri would be if I did end up working for Mikhail. And given everything Dimitri had just told me about his life and the awful tragedy he felt responsible for, I wasn't sure he'd ever forgive me.

Dimitri finished his drink within minutes, and waved to Tad for another. Only after Dimitri had downed that second shot of vodka did he break the silence, to ask, 'You okay?'

I looked up at him, surprised that he was checking on me, when he was the one who had a real reason to be upset. 'Yeah, I'm fine. I just… Are you?'

'I don't want you to feel bad for me.'

I hesitated. 'You can't blame yourself.' I don't know why I wanted to console him.

He looked me dead in the eye. 'Of course I can. It's completely my fault.' He sighed, dropped his gaze. 'You remind me of her, you know.'

'How?'

Dimitri shrugged. 'I'm not exactly sure yet.'

I didn't know what to say. I picked up our empty glasses. 'Another?'

Dimitri nodded, and I wasted no time getting up from the table and heading to the bar. I took the time to mentally shake myself. I was letting myself get too emotional, too close. I needed to focus.

'Another round?' Tad asked, when I put the glasses down on the bar. I nodded, and he poured the drinks. 'You know it's only fifteen minutes until closing, right?'

I blinked. Was it almost 1am already? 'Uh, yeah. No worries. Last order, I promise.'

Tad lowered his voice to say, 'That guy's in here a lot. I didn't realise you were friends.'

I glanced over my shoulder at Dimitri, who was staring down at the table in silence. 'We're not.'

'Whatever that means…' Tad handed me the drinks, and I returned to Dimitri.

'Thanks,' Dimitri took the glass from me as I slid back

onto the bench opposite him. 'You know that guy likes you right?'

'What?'

'The bartender.'

I almost choked on my drink. 'Tad? Are you joking? He's a kid.'

Dimitri's eyebrows rose in sudden amusement. 'You didn't notice? He was trying to flirt with you earlier.'

'He was not!' I exclaimed, and Dimitri laughed. The deep sound rumbled in his chest before it met his lips, resulting in a brilliant smile. His mouth was wide, and his lips were a little fuller than most men's, hiding straight white teeth, which created a startling contrast next to the dark stubble that dusted over his jaw. His eyes changed, too, when he laughed; they shone and swirled, like molten chocolate, framed by his thick, dark lashes.

I blinked. Had I been staring? I wasn't sure. Dimitri was staring right back at me, though, and I blushed, breaking our eye contact and finishing my drink very quickly. Dimitri followed suit, and we stood up to leave.

We walked back in silence, which we both apparently preferred to small talk, and said goodbye at my door.

The second I got inside, I phoned Doro.

Chapter Eleven

As we had discussed on the phone, Doro arrived at the bar the following night while I was at work. Better to have this kind of conversation face to face. He turned up late, right before closing, meaning that he was the only customer, and we were alone.

'What's up?' he asked, sliding onto a barstool fairly gracefully, considering his substantial size.

I leaned over the bar towards him. 'Mikhail wants me to work for him. And I think I should do it.'

'What?'

'Dimitri told me that Mikhail wants me to work for him,' I explained, ignoring Doro's incredulous expression. 'I know it's not why I'm here, exactly, but it's an opportunity that's just fallen into my lap. I really think I should take it.'

Doro hesitated, considering, then surprised me by saying, 'That's not a bad idea.'

'Great!' I'd expected him to argue with me. 'So my only issue is that I don't think I'll get supervisory permission. I'm supposed to focus on the peripheries, not work directly for Mikhail. It was never considered that I would have that opportunity, given his usual approach to us womenfolk.'

I couldn't help the disdain in my voice. Men like Mikhail saw women as having precisely one use — sex. Working for Mikhail directly was never the plan for me; he only hired women to work in his clubs, and a dancer would likely not have access to any particularly useful information. I was a little proud of myself, in a weird way, that he actually saw me as more useful than that. Not that a dealer was an especially high-ranking position in the gang. But, still, it was more than my superiors had anticipated, and I knew I'd be able to get more information than if I stuck to the original plan.

'I agree. They won't give you clearance — you know they won't,' Doro said, again surprising me by agreeing without persuasion. 'You'll see stuff that I don't see. He uses me purely for muscle, intimidation. He'd use you for more *vocal* jobs. You'll get more information that way than you ever could just by befriending a couple of hired guns and a part time prostitute.'

I flinched inwardly at his choice of words, but nodded. 'That's what I thought. But I don't know if it's a good idea to go in without asking Taylor. I'll get in serious trouble.'

Doro shrugged. 'Just tell them I gave you permission.'

I gave him a look. 'I don't think that will go down too well. You aren't my boss.'

His eyebrows drew together, distinctly unimpressed. 'I've been here for years. I know everything that goes on in this world, I've seen it first hand, and that gives me far more right to give you instructions than some over-qualified prick in a suit.'

'You know Taylor is more than that,' I argued, a little prickle of anger working its way up my spine.

Doro rolled his eyes. 'Oh, yeah? If he's so good at his job, then why am I still here? They keep telling me they're "building a case" but with everything I've seen and reported, the case should be closed, and Mikhail should be rotting in a cell. So tell me again how great Taylor is.'

I frowned. 'They can't base a whole case on your testimony, you know. You're only one person. That's why I'm here. Corroboration, and the parts of the business that you don't see.'

'Right, and that's why you need to get involved with Mikhail directly. Pussyfooting around the outskirts of the gang won't get you anywhere. But if you ask for permission and you get denied, then you're screwed.' Doro shrugged again. 'I say, just get in there. Once you're in, and you start getting real, useful information, then they won't pull you out.'

'They might,' I responded, uncertainly.

Doro looked at me. 'Then don't tell them. Trust me, your time is better spent in Mikhail's inner circle. Now, how do you plan on getting in?'

I sighed, propping my elbows on the bar. I guessed that I'd just have to take Doro's advice, and go ahead with my plan without Taylor's permission. It felt wrong, but I also knew that Doro had a point — he was the one with first-hand experience, I had to believe that he knew best.

'Well,' I began. 'Mikhail has already expressed an interest in me working for him, especially after seeing the way I beat up Tony. Only problem is that Dimitri has convinced Mikhail against it. But I think that if Mikhail sees me in action again, he'll insist on getting me involved in the business.' I bit my lip, pausing to get my thoughts in order before continuing. 'Okay, so obviously Dimitri has to think I'm being coerced into it, because I can hardly just go down to the Beach and volunteer my services.'

'So, what's your plan?' Doro asked.

I pulled a face. 'I need to get myself into a situation where I need to defend myself, and where Mikhail can see me do it, since he was so impressed last time.'

Doro nodded. 'I've got it. Tony's been baying for your blood since you kicked his ass. He'll be at the *Angel Rooms* this weekend. You could get your little gang together for a night out, and just happen to run into him there.'

'No,' I shook my head. 'I want it to really look like I had no choice, not like I put myself in the situation. Tony needs to come to me.'

He thought for a moment. 'Okay, I'll get Mikhail, Tony, and some other guys to come here. There's no CCTV, Mikhail knows Jono... I'll think of a reason to be nearby, then suggest a drink.'

I hesitated. Actually, there was CCTV at *Arrows*; I guessed that Jono kept it quiet to avoid losing patrons. I briefly considered the legalities around that, then remembered that I wasn't here to work on data protection laws.

'While I'm working?' I asked, unsure if it was a good idea to start something while behind the bar. If I lost my job, I'd lose a lot of my contact time with the gang members who frequented the bar as clients.

'No, your next night off. Just make sure you're in here drinking, so we cross paths. Tony won't start anything in an open, public place like this, so you'll have to antagonise him a little.'

I smirked. 'I don't think that'll be a problem. My next night off is Sunday. I'll suggest to Nina that we come for a drink.'

Doro nodded, and stood to leave. 'Then it's a date. See you Sunday. Prepare yourself for the big time.' The grin he gave me had a dangerous edge.

***

My side of the plan worked perfectly; on Sunday night, Nina and I were chatting amicably in the bar. We were a few drinks in, and while I was aware that I shouldn't drink too much in order to keep my wits about me, I also needed a little extra courage. I did my best to join in with the conversation, but the butterflies in my stomach made it a little hard to act normal. Not that I needed to; Nina was holding most of the conversation by herself.

I was on edge, waiting expectantly for Doro and Tony to walk through the door at any moment. It wasn't nerves, exactly, just anticipation. I had planned my moves as much as I could, but everything depended on Tony's behaviour tonight, so all I could do was wait and see. I hated that.

It was almost 11 by the time Doro arrived at the bar, and I'd been beginning to lose hope of him showing up at all. He headed to the bar, closely followed by Tony, Mikhail, Fabio, Dimitri and two other men who I did not know by name. My heartbeat quickened, and I felt the fiery jolt of adrenaline hit my veins. I licked my lips; it was time to put this plan into action.

Dimitri noticed me immediately, and visibly tensed, a dark look settling in his eyes. He knew my shifts by now, and had clearly not expected me to be here tonight.

At that moment, Doro spotted me, too, and called over. 'Look who it is!' He picked up his freshly made drink and strolled towards us. From behind the bar, Tad shot me an anxious glance, which I had to ignore; I knew he was worried about me in this situation, but I couldn't spare the time to placate him. Besides, I knew I'd be fine. Well, probably.

After a quick greeting, Doro joined the other men at a large table on the other side of the room.

'You OK?' I murmured across the table to Nina, who was staring at her hands.

She nodded, but didn't look up.

Glancing to my left at the table of gang members, I saw that Dimitri, Tony and Fabio all had their eyes fixed on me. Tony licked his lips, pointedly, and smirked. His face was almost entirely healed by now, except for the faint shadow underneath his left eye. I didn't know if that was from Dimitri's assault, or a more recent fight, and I didn't care. Next to him, Fabio raised his glass to me, and

I returned the gesture with a smile, before turning my attention back to Nina.

'Want to go for a cigarette?' I asked her. She looked so nervous, and I was trying to give her an excuse to get out of here.

She nodded, of course, and practically sprinted to the door. I hurried after her, and watched as she lit a cigarette. She offered me one, but I shook my head.

'I don't know what they're doing here,' she fretted between puffs. 'They never drink here.'

'Is it Fabio you're worried about? Or Mikhail?' I asked, hugging my arms around myself against the cold night air.

'Both,' Nina replied. 'Aren't you worried, too? Tony is here! You should leave.'

'No. I'm not gonna let them chase me out of my own bar,' I argued. 'Shouldn't I show them that they don't bother me?'

'I guess…' Nina looked entirely unconvinced. 'Would you mind if I headed home?'

Sympathy tugged at my heart; she had been through so much because of these men. 'No, of course not. You go. I'll just sit at the bar for a while, show them I'm not scared, and then head home myself, okay?'

'Okay,' Nina agreed. She stamped out her cigarette under her heel, then pulled me into a hug. 'Be careful. If they even look at you wrong, get out of there. Something about them being here just feels wrong.'

'Sure,' I agreed. *If only she knew…*

Back inside, I did as I'd said and hopped up onto a barstool. Tad slid a fresh drink over to me.

'Who are those guys?' he asked, clearly uneasy.

'They're friends of Dimitri's,' I replied. 'They work together.'

'Okay…'

'Chill out,' I told him. 'It's less than an hour until closing.'

Tad gave me a small smile and nodded, changing the subject and asking me about my plans for the coming week. We chatted easily for a little while, and I felt myself relaxing a little. At least until Fabio approached the bar to order another round of drinks. Tad jotted down their order, and offered to bring the drinks to the table.

Fabio declined. 'No, I'll wait. Mari can help me carry them.' His eyes were on me as he spoke, and this did not go unnoticed by Tad, although he said nothing.

Fabio took a seat next to me, leaning close to whisper, 'You look beautiful tonight.'

I didn't have to force a smile. 'Thanks. I haven't seen you here before.'

His trademark cheeky grin flashed across his face. 'Well, I did promise I'd come in to see you sometime.'

'I'm not even working tonight,' I pointed out.

'But you're still here,' he replied. 'Bit sad, really, that you come into work on your days off.'

I pulled a face at him. 'I was having drinks with Nina.'

Fabio's light-hearted expression faltered. 'Did she leave?'

'Yeah, she was tired.' My lie was obvious.

Fabio nodded, paused for a second before raising another smile. 'Why don't you join us, instead of sitting over here by yourself?'

'I'm not by myself.' I gestured to Tad, who was filling tumblers with vodka and ice.

Fabio's gaze flicked over Tad, and he smirked. 'Okay, but you know I'm a lot more fun.' He was flirting with me.

I raised my eyebrows. 'Oh, really?'

He laughed, and hopped down from his bar stool. He twisted my stool so that my body faced him, and he positioned himself between my thighs. Our faces were mere centimetres apart. 'I'm sure I can convince you,' Fabio murmured, holding my gaze, his own eyes smouldering. 'I can show you just how much fun I am.'

Even though I had no real interest in Fabio, I had to admit that my pulse had spiked. He was good at this. Besides, flirting with Fabio was as good a way as any to incite Tony's anger.

I leaned forward so that Fabio had a better view down my shirt, and our lips were almost touching. 'And how are you gonna do that?'

Fabio swallowed, and reached a hand up to my shoulder, brushing over my collarbone and up to my chin, where he cupped my face gently. 'I can think of a few ways,' he whispered huskily.

He closed the miniscule space between us, and I prepared an excuse to avoid the kiss, but our lips had barely brushed when he was pulled roughly away to reveal Tony. My flirting with Fabio had worked, and now it was time to kick this plan into action.

Chapter Twelve

Tony sneered at me, holding the back of Fabio's jacket in his fist, with which he had ripped Fabio away from me. Fabio cursed, and yanked himself out of Tony's grip.

'What the hell, man?' Fabio spat.

Tony ignored him, instead pinning his narrowed gaze on me. 'Mari,' he growled, a dirty smirk on his face. 'You refuse to dance for me, even when I offer to pay you, yet you give yourself up to this little boy for free?'

'Maybe it's *because* he didn't try to pay me,' I retorted, my heart thumping and my adrenaline roaring. This was my moment. I had to piss him off until he got physical with me, so that I could fight him off right under Mikhail's nose. 'Or maybe,' I continued, boldly, 'it's because he isn't a creepy old man. You're old enough to be my father, right?'

A sinister smile spread over Tony's thin lips. 'Ah yes. I knew your father. He was a good man.'

I shrugged, taking a sip of my drink in an effort to appear casual. 'If he spent any time at all with a lowlife like you, I doubt that. In fact, I can't imagine anyone wanting to spend time with you. I guess that's why you have to pay people.'

Before I knew what was happening, Tony's hand was on my throat. 'You stupid bitch,' he snarled in my face. 'I'm going to…'

I interrupted him, brazenly meeting his angry gaze. 'Going to what? Hit me?' I was daring him with my tone.

'Hey!' Fabio's face appeared in my peripheral vision. I'd forgotten he was even there. 'Tony, back the hell off, man.'

Again, Tony ignored him. 'Mari, I'm going to do so much worse than hit you. You won't walk after I'm finished with you.' His hand moved from my throat to my hair; he knotted his fingers in my dark curls and pulled me to my feet. I pressed my lips together against a yelp of pain as he yanked me to the door by my hair. Fabio followed us, voicing his protests, but made no effort to actually help me. I didn't need his help, and I understood the rankings within the gang; Fabio was essentially helpless in this situation, as he had been the first time Tony had got his hands on me.

Over my shoulder, I saw Dimitri raise to his feet, his eyes darker than I had ever seen them. I lost sight of him as Tony dragged me out of the door and onto the street.

That's when I took my first swing at him, aiming my fist at his jaw, and making solid contact. He grunted and took a step back. Now, I couldn't help but cry out in pain as I felt my hair being pulled from my scalp.

I stepped back, but Tony followed me, slapping my face hard but open handed. He was obviously trying to shut me up, rather than really hurt me, or he would have used a fist. His mistake. I swung back, and my own fist buried into his gut, and he grunted again. Tony grabbed my throat with a lightning-fast movement, squeezing. I gasped for a breath, and began to panic when I couldn't draw one in.

Thinking fast, I raised my knee with all the strength I had to meet with his groin. He howled in pain, the noise more satisfying than I could ever have imagined. He stumbled backwards, losing his grip on my throat but grabbing my arm on his way down. I fell on top of him, bracing my knees either side of his stomach on the cold cement ground. Tony's hands flew to my throat again, but this time I was prepared; I used both of my hands to grab fistfuls of his thinning hair, taking all my strength into lifting his head off the ground, then slamming it back down into the concrete as hard as I could. Twice.

While I didn't have the sheer strength to do any lasting

damage, the hard crack was satisfying, and Tony's grip on me loosened enough that I could pull away. Deftly, I leapt backwards and onto my feet, just as Dimitri flew out of the bar and onto the sidewalk.

He looked ready to fly into action, but halted when he saw Tony flat on the floor cradling his balls with one hand, and his head with the other. Dimitri turned to me, his eyes wide and wild. He knew what was going to happen when Mikhail saw this.

Seconds later, Tad rushed onto the scene, looking absolutely terrified, closely followed by Mikhail, Doro, and the other men. They all took in the scene before them with surprise. After a moment of silence, Mikhail laughed. It was not a pleasant sound.

'Well, shit,' he chuckled. 'Tony just keeps getting beat by this girl.'

'Oh my God...' Tad murmured. He looked at me, horrified. 'I called the police.'

Oh, no. I took a step towards Tad, but I was too slow. Doro grabbed Tad by the front of his T-shirt and shoved him against the wall. 'Don't you know who we are, kid?' Doro spat. 'The only thing the police are gonna find is your bloodied corpse!'

'No, stop!' I yelled.

Doro ignored me, landing a hard blow to Tad's young, innocent face. I cried out in dismay, rushing forward to grab Doro's arm before he could swing again.

'Get the hell off me!' he bellowed. His face twisted in rage, and he didn't look like the man I knew. Despite my heart threatening to burst out of my chest, I held on insistently with both hands.

'Stop,' I told him, my voice steady. 'Tad has nothing to do with this. Leave him be.'

Angrily, Doro pulled his arm out of my grasp, and hit Tad again, before letting him go and turning on me. Doro grabbed my chin between his thumb and forefinger, getting in my face. 'Don't do that again.'

I felt my eyes widen, taken by surprise. I nodded, because I had no other choice, and Doro let me go. When he stepped out of my line of vision, I saw everyone staring at me. Tony had stood up, finally, and was shooting a murderous glare in my direction. As my gaze shifted to Dimitri, I saw that he also looked like he wanted to kill me. I'd never seen him look so angry, not even when he beat the crap out of Tony the other week. I had to look away.

Doro gave me one last filthy look before simply walking away. I didn't care if he was mad at me, there was no way I was going to let him hurt Tad.

When my gaze landed on Mikhail, his expression was the most terrifying; he wasn't angry, he looked impressed. My plan had worked, but for some reason, it didn't make me feel good.

Mikhail turned to the remaining men. 'The police are coming. Let's go.'

The men scattered, all heading in their own direction. Fabio avoided my gaze as he left. Dimitri strode off like he couldn't wait to get out of there, without even another glance in my direction. Mikhail watched them all go, before turning back to me.

His voice was low. 'I expect Dimitri has told you of my interest in you, yes? Come to the Beach tomorrow. *The Angel Rooms*, at midday. If you don't show, I will simply come to visit you instead, and it will be a significantly less pleasant conversation.' He nodded his head towards Tad, who was a bloody heap on the floor. 'Take care of your friend.'

With that, Mikhail turned away. When he was out of sight, I rushed to Tad, who, thankfully, was conscious. I helped him up and took him back inside. Luckily, there were no other customers, so I locked the door behind us and walked Tad to the men's bathroom. Dragging a chair in from the bar, I sat him down and grabbed the first aid kit from behind the bar.

I knelt down in front of him. 'Tad?'

'Mari,' he replied. His nose and lip were bleeding, and discolouration was forming already around his nose and over his left cheekbone. But he was conscious, and after a careful inspection, didn't seem to have any serious injuries. I cleaned up his face despite his protests, and grabbed some painkillers from my purse.

I was disposing of the bloody tissues when I heard a knock at the door. I half expected it to be Tony coming back to finish me off, but it was just a pair of police officers. I opened the door and explained that there had been a bar fight, but it had broken up and everyone had gone home. I apologised for wasting their time, and they simply nodded and went on their way.

Tad emerged from the men's bathroom, looking a little more stable, and I felt a wave of pity as I took in his appearance once more.

'I'm so sorry, Tad.' I hadn't even considered him when I'd made my plan. I should have known that he'd try to protect me in some way.

'It's not your fault,' he tried to reassure me.

'It is though,' I sighed. 'I'll call you a taxi.'

Ten minutes later, the car arrived, and I bundled Tad into it. Only when I was back inside going about the closing duties did it really hit me. My throat burned, and the back of my head throbbed angrily. I guessed the adrenaline and my concern for Tad had distracted me until now. I reached up to the back of my head where Tony had pulled the hair from, and whimpered involuntarily when I felt a patch of bare scalp, maybe two inches across, jagged in shape.

Tears sprung to my eyes. I knew I was being ridiculous. Losing a bit of hair and some faint neck bruising was actually a lot less of an injury than I'd expected to get tonight, but I couldn't help my vanity. When I took my hand away, I saw little spots of blood on my fingers.

Still, my plan had worked. I would go and see Mikhail tomorrow, and start working for him directly. But my triumph was dulled by Tad's injuries, Dimitri's anger, and the fact that Doro's acting was just a little too convincing.

Chapter Thirteen

That night, I barely slept. At 7 a.m. I gave up trying and went for a run instead. Usually that made me feel better, but not today. I took a shower and got myself ready for my meeting with Mikhail. My first instinct was to dress up nicely, but then it occurred to me that this man did not deserve my effort. The only thing I made sure to do was style my hair in a half-ponytail in order to cover the hairless patch at the back of my head.

I took the underground to the Beach, just about remembering how to get to the *Angel Rooms*. The door was closed, but unlocked when I pushed it. I'd never been in a club during the day before, and it felt a little strange. It barely resembled the place I remembered; the room seemed a lot bigger, the ceilings a lot higher, and the décor even more minimal, by which I mean there were scrapes on the walls and tiles missing from the floor. It had only just opened, but I guessed that a high-quality finish wasn't necessary to attract business in this industry.

My footsteps echoed as I walked towards the bar. Behind it stood a man who was taking inventory of the alcohol. I didn't recognise him, but he must have been expecting me, because he greeted me curtly and led me through to the private dance area. There was a door that I hadn't noticed last time I'd been there, although I guess I had been a little distracted. It was through this door that I found Mikhail's office. It was a large room, decorated with wooden flooring, leather chairs and dark chestnut furniture, clearly designed to intimidate. Behind the formidable desk sat Mikhail, tapping something onto a laptop in front of him.

He looked up when I entered, waving for the barman to leave and flashing me a smile. It was not a warm expression. 'Mari, come in. Sit.'

I did as I was told, lowering myself cautiously into one of the two chairs in front of the desk. Waiting patiently while Mikhail finished typing on his laptop, I took in the room around me, wondering exactly how many awful crimes had been planned within these four walls.

'Okay.' Mikhail shut his laptop and folded his hands on top of it. 'Let's get to business.'

I met his gaze. 'Let's.'

He smirked. 'I like you, Mari. You're not scared of us.'

'No,' I agreed, although he did make me a little nervous.

'I assume that is because your father was one of us?' Mikhail guessed.

I simply shrugged, allowing him to interpret that as he pleased.

'You know I want you to work for me,' Mikhail continued.

'Yes. Dimitri told me.' My heartbeat was quicker than I would have liked, but my voice was steady and confident.

Mikhail rested his chin on his hands, and tightened his lips, displeased. 'Yes. I knew he would. He warned me away from you, convinced me that you wouldn't be useful. Dimitri is my best employee, so I allowed him to influence my decision. But I keep seeing you, and I know he is wrong. You would be very useful to me.'

'I don't think I would,' I argued, in efforts to look unwilling. 'I have no experience in this kind of thing.'

'You are beautiful,' Mikhail surprised me by saying. 'You're strong. You can clearly defend yourself. People will like you, you're approachable, which — you may have noticed — is something that a lot of my men lack.'

I raised an eyebrow. 'You could say that.'

Mikhail smirked again, and I got a little thrill at the idea that I impressed him. 'Yes, I definitely like you.' He sat back in his seat. 'Work for me.'

I leaned forward in my own chair. 'No.'

His smile widened, showing straight white teeth. For some reason, it surprised me that he had all of his teeth. I guessed, since he had so many men working for him, that he didn't need to put himself in the kind of situations where teeth might be lost. Although I also knew that he'd worked damn hard to get to where he was today, in charge of the whole gang. Maybe he just had a really good dentist.

'What can I offer you to change your mind?' Mikhail paused, then guessed, 'Money?'

'No.'

Mikhail sighed, and held my gaze for an intense few seconds. 'Okay, how about this. If you work for me, I *won't* break every bone in Nina's body.'

His threat didn't rattle me; I'd been expecting it. 'You wouldn't do that. You need Nina, for when Olivier comes into town.'

Mikhail's eyebrows rose marginally, and I liked that I had surprised him. 'How do you know of Olivier?'

I simply shrugged, choosing again to be evasive.

'Hmm.' Mikhail didn't look too pleased. 'Well, I could always send him your way instead. I'm sure he wouldn't mind a trade.'

Maintaining eye contact, I kept my mouth shut. Sometimes silence showed more confidence than a smart ass comeback.

Mikhail continued to speak. 'I guess if that isn't enough incentive, then I could always go back to the bar and finish off that bartender kid. Tad, isn't it? You seemed to care about him. I could have my men at your apartment every hour of every day — you live below

Dimitri, correct? Or, hey, I could do it the old fashioned way, and just torture you until you agree to work for me.' A sinister grin flashed over his face.

I sat back in my seat, careful to keep my expression blank. The admittance that he knew who Tad was, and that he knew where I lived, did not surprise me; Mikhail wasn't a man who went into things without doing his homework first. The fact that he only threatened Nina and Tad was reassuring, though, as it meant he hadn't managed to find anything further into my past. Not that there was anything to find, besides a bank account and student loans in my fake name, plus a couple of police cautions from my fictitious youth, if someone was looking really hard. It was all set up to look realistic, but Marianna Harris did not exist, and there was nothing else to find.

Still, I knew that I had to at least act distressed by Mikhail's threats, so I fidgeted in my seat and took a deep breath. 'What kind of work would you want me to do?' I asked, as if he had persuaded me.

Mikhail's triumphant expression made me want to pick up his laptop and slam it into his smug face. 'Easy jobs. Drugs. Mainly deliveries and payment collections, since I know you can take care of yourself, and my product. Negotiations, if you are smart enough. Work in the clubs if you are not.'

I hesitated, before nodding slowly. 'Alright.'

'I want to be clear about a few things.' Mikhail's voice had remained calm and almost jovial through our entire conversation, until now. His tone deepened considerably, and I finally understood why he was the boss, because I wouldn't dare say no to this voice. 'You don't talk about your work for me with *anyone*. You don't alert the police. If you do, I will know, and I will kill you.'

My stomach fluttered, and this was the first time I'd

felt a flicker of real fear since beginning my undercover role. I knew that it wouldn't be the last, now that I'd agreed to work for Mikhail. Swallowing my nerves, I nodded.

Mikhail continued. 'Also, if I ask you to do something — whatever it might be — you do it. Or the same consequences apply. Do you understand?'

'Yes.' My voice was strong.

Mikhail nodded, clearly satisfied, and opened his mouth to say something, but before he could get the words out, he was interrupted by a frantic knocking on the door. Irritated, Mikhail barked, 'what?!' and the barman entered the room. He looked a little panicked, and my attention immediately focused on whatever he was going to say.

'Mikhail, I'm sorry, there's been… It's Tony. We need instruction,' the barman stammered.

Mikhail rose to his feet. 'What's happened?'

The barman glanced at me, questioning whether I could be trusted, and Mikhail waved him on. Clearly my verbal contact was in effect already.

'Tony is dead.'

Now I, too, shot to my feet, though I wasn't sure why. 'What?' I demanded, without meaning to.

Mikhail sighed, slowly rounding his desk to stand beside me. He was barely within reaching distance, but he still felt too close for comfort. 'Where is the body?' he sounded neither angry nor surprised by this news. I, on the other hand, felt sick.

'In his flat,' the barman replied. 'Some of the guys went over there this morning. Door was unlocked, Tony was inside. Shot.'

'In the head?' Mikhail asked, as if he already knew the answer.

The barman nodded gravely.

Mikhail cursed and sighed. 'Okay. Take a van and take care of the body.'

The barman hesitated. 'But… It's Tony.'

'I know! I said take care of the damn body!' Mikhail snapped.

With a frantic nod, the man scurried out of the room, the door slamming behind him.

I stood there, frozen to the spot, unsure of how to deal with the information that Tony was dead. Of course, I knew exactly who had killed him — Dimitri had sworn that he'd kill Tony if he touched me again, and after last night, I should have expected it. Mikhail knew that Dimitri was responsible, too, which was why he'd asked about the location of the bullet wound; Dimitri always shot his victims in the head, executioner style.

Mikhail tossed a notepad at me, snapping me out of my daze. 'Write down your number and get out of here,' he barked.

I grabbed a pen from the desk and did as he'd asked.

'This is your fault,' Mikhail said, and my eyes shot up to meet his. 'You know that, don't you?'

I nodded, turning and exiting the office with my tail quite clearly between my legs.

***

I practically ran back to my building and hurtled up the stairs two at a time, rushing straight past my apartment and up to Dimitri's. Hammering on his door, it took him only seconds to answer. He was dressed in a way I'd never seen before, in nothing but a pair of grey tracksuit bottoms. I had been ready to lay into him, but now all I could seem to do was take in the sight of his body. His torso was hard and toned, covered in intricate black ink in an array of patterns and images. Over his pectoral muscles was a display of black roses, the crawling vines of which reached up and over his shoulders. Below the joining of his ribs, there was a skull. Many others crept over his arms and ribs, and I could safely assume that his back would also be pretty covered, too. Sculpted, cut muscles lay just beneath the skin over his stomach, running down into the waistband of his tracksuit pants, and it was all I could do to keep my eyes from lingering.

'What do you want?' The harsh and cold tone of Dimitri's voice brought me back to the present, and I swallowed, hard, as I remembered exactly why I was there.

'I know what you did,' I told him, in an equally cool voice. 'To Tony.'

Dimitri's eyebrows rose, and he seemed surprised that I had already found out. 'How?'

I shook my head. I'd been clinging to the vague hope that it hadn't been him who had shot Tony, but he hadn't even tried to deny it. He didn't even care — murdering a man was just a normal start to the day for Dimitri. This was not the man who'd fallen asleep beside me, and told me about the pain of losing his girlfriend. This was the man who worked for Mikhail, who had a police file as thick as the bible, who did unspeakable things without hesitation.

I decided not the stick around for any more of the conversation, not that there was anything left to say anyway. I turned on my heel, and heard Dimitri's front door slam shut before I even reached the first step down to my floor. Clearly, he wanted just as little to do with me as I did with him at that moment.

Chapter Fourteen

A week passed by, during which time I heard nothing from Dimitri, Val, or even Nina. I guessed that she'd heard about what happened with Tony, and she had probably decided to keep her distance from me. I didn't blame her, really. I didn't hear from Doro, either, although I decided that was probably a good thing, since I wouldn't know what to say to him. I'd clearly pissed him off, and I was starting to become uncertain about where Doro finished and Steve — the police officer I'd known before — started.

I knew I should have called Taylor to update him on the situation, but I didn't want to get into trouble, and I really didn't want to risk getting pulled out of the job for disobeying orders. Doro had been right about that at least — Taylor wouldn't like me going against his carefully thought out plan. But even if I didn't disclose my working for Mikhail, I should still have told Taylor about Dimitri killing Tony. That was first degree murder, and I'd had Dimitri's guilt confirmed by both Mikhail and Dimitri himself. Yet, even though I felt sick every time I thought about Dimitri ever since the realisation about who he really was had finally hit me, I couldn't bring myself to turn him into my boss just yet.

So, I didn't call Taylor. It went against all my training, and all my natural instincts (I'd always hated breaking the rules), but I knew that I was on my own now, and I had to show that my decision to work for Mikhail had been the right one. It was all about keeping my head down and getting the evidence I needed to bring the gang down, once and for all.

The only person I spoke to all week was Tad, when we worked together on Friday night. His face had started to heal, but the damage was still obvious, and my guilt weighed heavy on my chest. He hadn't been himself for the whole shift, which was entirely my fault, of course.

It was the next day, Saturday, when I received my first text from Mikhail. I was almost relieved — being so isolated from all the action and all the people I'd met so far had been making me feel a little crazy.

Meet Fabio, East Street Station, 8pm

That was it. That was all the text said. Of course, I was meant to work at the bar that night, but I had a feeling that excuse wouldn't mean anything to Mikhail, so I sent a message to Tad explaining that I couldn't make my shift. He sent back a short, blunt text saying that he'd cover for me. His clear distrust of me was painful, but there was nothing I could do about it now; I had to focus.

All day, I was full of nervous energy, and when it was finally time to leave, I practically ran out of the door. It was a ten-minute train journey to the station where I was supposed to meet Fabio, and sure enough, he was there waiting when I stepped off the train.

When he spotted me, Fabio's face broke into an automatic smile, and I felt instantly better. Spending so much time on my own had allowed too much space for me to doubt myself, and for loneliness to set in, so the familiarity of Fabio's cheerful expression helped push that away. The last time I'd seen him he'd basically abandoned me to Tony's mercy, so I really should have been pissed at him, but I knew that Tony outranked him. Besides, his lack of interference had actually served to facilitate my plan.

As I approached him, Fabio burst into laughter. 'Did you dress like a ninja on purpose?'

I frowned, glancing down at my all-black ensemble, and shoved his arm. 'Shut up.'

He may have had a point, though. I guess I'd been trying too hard to look inconspicuous and it might have actually backfired a little. But my black leggings, boots and sweater were comfortable, at least, and I could run in them if I needed to. I'd also made sure to tie my hair back, both for practicality and to hide the bald patch.

Fabio raised his hands in surrender. 'Sorry. For future reference, you can wear whatever you like. In fact, the more normal, the better.'

We ascended the stairs to the pavement, and I followed him as he headed south, towards the downtown district. This was a predominantly middle-class area, known for its expensive shops and restaurants, so I rarely had a reason to come here.

'What are we doing?' I asked as we walked.

Fabio shrugged. 'Simple collection. Just watch and learn, okay? You'll usually do this on your own, unless it's a particularly nasty client.'

As we continued on our way, the streets became wider, brighter and tidier. The difference between this area and the district I lived in astounded me. People talked a lot about equality, but we were nowhere near achieving it, that was clear.

'I'm sorry about Sunday night,' Fabio said, breaking our silence.

I didn't look at him. 'Don't mention it.'

'You heard about Tony?'

'Yep.'

Fabio exhaled harshly. 'I'm sorry. I should have done something. I should have stopped him.'

'Forget about it,' I told him, my voice coming out a little harder than I'd anticipated. Every time I thought about Tony, my stomach hurt. I mean, of course, he'd had it coming, but I hated that Dimitri had been the one to kill him. I'd really believed that Dimitri was a good guy in a bad situation, but the fact that he'd done that of his own accord showed me that I'd been mistaken. The truth hurt, for reasons that I didn't understand, and didn't like to think about too much.

Fabio didn't seem to want to let it drop. 'I was going to come by the bar this week, but I've been really busy, I'm sorry.'

'Seriously, shut up,' I snapped. 'I really don't want to talk about this.'

He looked a little hurt by my tone, but at least he stayed quiet this time. A few minutes later, he pointed to a modern apartment building in front of us, with balconies up the side and well-watered plants either side of the marble-pillared entrance. When we reached the door, Fabio pressed a button, and a woman's voice greeted us over the intercom.

'It's Fab,' Fabio said.

'Oh, shit,' the woman cursed. 'Uh... Okay. Come up.' She buzzed us in.

The foyer was decorated with marble floors and more matching pillars. Stairs with a gold banister curled up to our left, but there was also an elevator, towards which we headed now. When we reached the eighth floor, we alighted, and I followed Fabio to the nearest door, where he knocked loudly.

Almost immediately, the door was pulled open and a very young woman — a girl, really — appeared, with long bleached hair and 0% body fat. She ushered us inside, where I found myself in a brightly lit and expensively decorated sitting room.

'Hey, Bethy. How are you?' Fabio asked, flashing his best flirtatious smile.

The girl blushed. 'Uh, I'm okay.'

'Well, good, but you owe us five hundred,' Fabio replied. His voice was light and friendly, and I liked that he wasn't trying to intimidate her any more than necessary, especially considering that she was so young and obviously in over her head.

'I don't think I have it.' She turned to look at me, her big blue eyes pleading, clearly hoping that I'd be more sympathetic to her cause.

I kept my mouth shut, since I was just there to observe, and Fabio stepped forward, commanding her attention once more.

'Sweetheart,' he drawled, 'you better get it for me right now, or I'm gonna have to tell mummy and daddy just how much trouble you're in.'

'Oh, God,' Bethy almost sobbed. 'Okay, hang on. Please don't tell my parents.'

We sat down on an immaculate white couch while she made a frantic phone call, and waited for barely five minutes until someone else knocked at the door. Bethy ran to answer it, revealing a skinny guy with slick black hair and bad skin, probably in his mid-thirties. When he greeted her with a kiss, I grimaced, because she was at least half his age. He snaked an arm around Bethy's waist, holding her tightly to him, and held out an envelope to Fabio.

Fabio stood, peering inside to quickly count the money. He nodded, obviously satisfied, and tucked it away inside his jacket. 'Good girl, Bethy. Don't make me come back here again, okay?'

Bethy nodded, wordlessly, her cheeks flaming. The man tightened his grip on her, and glared at Fabio, who simply grinned cheerfully. I followed Fabio out of the door, and just like that, my first job for Mikhail was complete. This was starting to get very real.

Chapter Fifteen

As we left the apartment, I tried to process the surreal scene I'd just witnessed, feeling more than a little uneasy about leaving that young girl with that creepy man. Fabio, on the other hand, seemed to be in a significantly better mood, apparently forgiving me my harsh words earlier. As we left the building, he slung his arm around my shoulders and pulled me closer to him.

'So, how was your first time?' he asked with a wink.

'Surprisingly simple,' I replied, honestly.

Fabio laughed. 'I thought you'd say that. You see what I mean about not needing your ninja suit?'

I swatted at his chest, but felt a smile raise to my lips, infected by his good mood. 'I will break out my ninja skills if you keep making fun of me. And you'll never see it coming.'

'You want to get a drink?' Fabio asked. 'We're in the fancy part of town, with a lot of money. Think of the possibilities…'

'Isn't that Mikhail's money?' I asked, as we continued to stroll down the sidewalk, looking to the rest of the world like a happy couple out for an evening walk.

'We both get our cut,' Fabio replied. 'And I want to spend mine on you.'

I rolled my eyes, but my smile deepened. His mood was catching, and my own elation at finally making progress after a week of standing still felt a lot like real happiness in that moment. 'Well, then, choose a bar.'

Minutes later, we were sat the bar of a fancy cocktail club, perusing the extravagant drinks menu.

'*How* much for a drink?' I whispered in disbelief.

'Don't worry baby, it's on me,' Fabio whispered back, and I laughed quietly.

We selected the most ridiculous cocktails on the list,

and it took the bartender nearly ten minutes to make the drinks. I was glad that at my bar, the most complicated thing I had to do was add soda to vodka. When our drinks were ready, however, they definitely looked impressive, and I couldn't help but snap a photo on my phone, despite usually judging other people who did such things.

The drinks tasted good, too, and three rounds later, we were laughing and joking as if we were best friends. The mixture of different spirits I had consumed was something I wasn't used to, and I was more buzzed than I should have been by that point, but I also felt like I'd had a tough week, and I decided it was okay to reward myself. I knew that Fabio wasn't the best person to be rewarding myself with, but he was apparently the only person who was speaking to me at the moment, so it's not like I had a whole bunch of options.

The night turned blurry as we hopped between bars, and it was nearly 2am when we stumbled out onto the pavement to finally head home. I barely felt the cold night air as we zig-zagged towards the nearest underground station.

'I really am sorry that I didn't call you this week,' Fabio said as we descended the stairs to the platform. 'You must have been having a hard time.'

'Yeah, I guess,' I replied. 'I just don't really have anyone I can talk to here.' I don't know why I said that.

Fabio's eyes shone with sympathy. He reached out to touch my arm. 'Mari, I'm always here if you need me. You know I like you — you must know that. You've been through a lot, and you're still here. You're the strongest woman I've ever met.'

'I wish that was true,' I whispered, gazing up at Fabio's hazel eyes.

He brushed a strand of hair away from my eyes, his hand sweeping down my neck and over my collar bone.

At that moment, a train hurtled into the station, and I was able to step away from Fabio under the pretence of boarding the carriage. It was pretty empty at that time of night, so we sat beside one another for the short journey.

'Fab, you know we're friends, right?' I said, feeling bad for leading him on a little, but knowing that I needed to clarify our relationship. Everything was complicated enough without having to deal with this, too.

A small smile raised his lips, but he knew what I was saying. 'Sure. Don't worry about it.'

'I had a fun night, though,' I placated him with a kind smile. 'I mean, considering it started with the collection of drug money from a teenager.'

Fabio laughed, and the awkwardness was dispelled. We chatted easily for the rest of the journey, and parted ways at the next stop, heading back to our own homes respectively. I felt a little bad; Fabio was a good guy, and he'd been nothing but nice, but if I succeeded here, he'd spend the rest of his young life behind bars. Which is what criminals deserved. Right?

***

The following morning, I woke up to someone knocking on my front door. Rubbing sleep from my eyes, I threw on a sweater and some pyjama shorts and shuffled out of my room to answer it. My head felt slightly hazy after the alcohol I'd consumed last night; my increasing inability to drink without consequences was the surest sign of aging. Or that my alcohol intake needed reviewing.

Pulling back the door, I was surprised to see Nina standing in the corridor. She wore a fitted grey tracksuit and a smile on her face. 'Hey,' she greeted me, brightly.

'Hey,' I replied, cautiously. 'What are you doing here? It's so early.'

She raised an eyebrow. 'It's not that early, hon. Did you have a late night?' she teased.

I rolled my eyes. 'No. Not in the way you're thinking, anyway.'

She laughed. 'Well that's boring.'

I gestured for her to come inside, and as I shut the door behind her, Nina looked around for the kitchen then made a beeline for the coffee. I followed her into the kitchen, apprehensive. She hadn't made contact since everything had happened last weekend, with Tony, and I wasn't sure where I stood with her. Obviously I had got what I wanted out of the situation, aside from the overlooked consequences, but as far as Nina knew, I'd experienced something horrible. And she hadn't bothered to even send me a text asking if I was okay. Now she was acting as if everything was normal between us.

'Nina,' I said, leaning a hip against the counter. 'Why are you here? Is everything okay?'

'Oh, yeah…' She looked a little guilty. 'I really just wanted to make sure you're okay. I heard about last weekend…'

'Oh, you mean how Tony tried to assault me, so Dimitri killed him, and now I'm stuck working for Mikhail?' I said, deadpan, letting my irritation take control despite my better judgement. 'Is that what you're referring to?'

Nina grimaced, and avoided my accusatory gaze in favour of putting the kettle on to boil. 'I'm sorry, I've been a bad friend. I really did mean to call and check on you, but honestly, I didn't know what to say. I mean, this is all my fault, you know?'

I blinked. I hadn't seen that coming. 'What are you talking about?'

She grabbed a couple of mugs from the draining board and set about making the coffee, keeping herself busy as she spoke. 'Well, if I hadn't invited you to the *Angel Rooms* opening party, you never would have met Mikhail or Tony. And if I hadn't left you last weekend, maybe I could've helped.' She shrugged. 'I just figured, it might be better for me to keep my distance from you, considering what's happened since you met me.'

I stared at her. 'Are you serious? You can't really think that any of this is your fault?'

Nina shrugged again, handing me a steaming mug, for which I was more grateful than she knew; my head was starting to throb now that I'd been standing upright for more than a few minutes.

'Nina, it's really not your fault,' I told her. 'I already knew Doro before I met you. My father worked for Mikhail his whole life. I work at a bar where a lot of the guys in the gang regularly come to drink. I'd already run into Tony, and I'm sure I would've met Mikhail at some point too, whether I had met you or not.'

Nina nodded slowly, clearly wanting to believe my words and absolve her guilt. 'I guess... I just feel so bad though. Especially about not calling you this week — I really am sorry. Are you okay?'

'I'm fine,' I reassured her.

And I meant it. Being back in contact with Fabio, and now Nina, had re-focussed me. I was here to do a job, and I was finally making real progress. Time to stop feeling sorry for myself and get my head back in the game.

'Really?' Nina seemed disbelieving.

'Really. I mean, it's not like Tony can bother me anymore, you know?' I said, dryly, taking a sip of my coffee.

Nina's expression turned rueful. 'Yeah. I think you should talk to Dimitri.'

'I already did,' I told her. 'I asked him if he was

responsible, and he confirmed that he was. There didn't seem to be much to talk about after that.'

'Yeah, he's pretty pissed at you,' Nina laughed, humourlessly. 'But he's pissed at me, too, if that helps.'

'At you? Why?' I propped a hip against the kitchen counter; my head was foggy, and I just needed a little support if I was going to keep standing.

'We, uh, had a fight.'

'What?' I exclaimed, surprised. I couldn't imagine that at all; they seemed to have such a close friendship that I couldn't picture them arguing about anything.

Nina sighed, and began to explain. 'He's mad about you working for Mikhail. He tried really hard to get Mikhail to forget about you, and he's mad that it didn't work. He's mad at Tony for even going near you, let alone hurting you. He's mad at himself for not stopping Tony, and for what he did to Tony after. Mostly, I think he feels useless because he couldn't stop any of this from happening. So, he's mad about all this stuff, but he's not actually angry at you.' Nina shrugged. 'When I pointed this out, he cursed me out, and we got into an argument. He's just being stubborn, and seems to be blaming you even though it's pretty obvious that none of this is your fault. Even Val can't make him see sense. So I think you should go talk to him — you'd be able to talk him around.'

'Yeah, right!' I scoffed. 'He barely looked at me the last time I saw him.'

Nina's lips curved in sympathy. 'You two were getting close, weren't you?'

I shrugged. There was no clear answer to that.

But Nina took my silence as confirmation. 'I thought so. He doesn't really make new friends — not since Isabel, you know.' Nina's face melted into a sympathetic expression. 'Val and I are the only people who really know him. But he likes you. I think that's why he's so mad, you know, because he wanted to keep you out of all this.'

The coffee had started to help my headache, but this conversation was just making it a whole lot worse again. 'I still don't think talking to him is a good idea.'

Nina looked at me with a strange expression in her eyes. 'Trust me.'

Chapter Sixteen

It was Wednesday when I received a call from Mikhail. He told me he needed me at the club that evening for a job. Luckily, Tad agreed to cover my shift at *Arrow's* again. I had been working alone at the bar for the past few days, and hadn't seen him for a while. Every time I thought about him, I felt a deep stab of guilt, and I wished there was a way I could make it up to him, but of course there wasn't. I also hadn't spoken to Dimitri yet, despite Nina's advice. A couple of times I'd thought about going up to his apartment, but I just had no idea what to say to him, and I'd chickened out both times.

At ten o'clock that evening, I took the train to the Beach. It was cold, especially in my short dress — Mikhail had told me to 'dress sexy' — and my thin jacket wasn't doing much to keep me warm. When I reached the *Angel Rooms*, it was still early and therefore quiet. The bouncer waved me inside, and I spotted Mikhail and Fabio at the bar in the centre of the room. Fabio saw me first, and shot me a bright smile.

'Mari,' Mikhail greeted me. 'Take off your jacket.'

I did as instructed, although I didn't appreciate the order, and Mikhail took it from me, stashing it behind the bar and giving me a once over.

'Good.' He clearly approved of my outfit choice.

I frowned at him, biting back my sarcastic response. I hopped up onto a barstool beside Fabio. 'So, what's going on?'

'We are meeting with the Thai organisation,' Mikhail said, referring to a neighbouring gang with whom Mikhail had a certain understanding. 'You don't need to worry about the business side of things, I will take care of that in my office. Nick and Alexander will be with me,' he gestured to two of his men, who were chatting to a waitress at the other end of the bar, 'While you and Fabio will stay out here with the rest of the Thai men. Make sure they have all the drinks they need, whichever girls they like the look of, coke if they want it, whatever they require to have a good night. You understand?'

I nodded. It sounded easy enough. 'Yeah.'

'Good. Fabio will brief you.' With that Mikhail headed to his office, Nick and Alexander following closely behind.

'They aren't here yet,' Fabio told me, entirely unnecessarily.

'Ok. Is there anything we need to do to prepare for their arrival?' I asked.

Fabio smirked. 'Good little hostess, aren't you?' He shook his head, clearly finding me very amusing. 'Nah, Mikhail told you to get here in advance in case you bailed, or needed to settle your nerves.'

I frowned. 'Oh. Glad to see he has such confidence in me.'

Fabio laughed. 'Well, you were here on time, and you seem totally chilled, so you're doing good so far.' He rounded the bar, and held up a bottle of vodka. 'We've got some time to kill — drink?'

'Why not?' It would help me relax.

Fabio lined up four shot glasses on the bar and filled them. 'Two for you, two for me.' He gestured to the glasses. Together, we took the shots, and within minutes, I felt better. I'd severely underestimated how much of a role alcohol played in this 'business' and how much I'd actually consume during my time undercover. I was becoming accustomed to the bitter burn of straight vodka, which was both beneficial and worrying.

As we waited, Fabio and I chatted easily over the bar, which he remained behind in order to keep the shots flowing. The dancers emerged from the back rooms of the club a little before eleven, at which point a steady stream of customers began rolling in, and the bartenders kicked Fabio out from behind the bar.

It was almost midnight before our guests arrived, but when they did, I suddenly became nervous. They were not as intimidating as Mikhail — I doubted anyone could be—but at least with Mikhail and his men, I was somewhat familiar with their operations; the Thai gang was relatively new in the large-scale organised crime game, and I had limited knowledge of their structure or the major players.

Five men approached us, including an obvious leader; he was maybe in his sixties, older than Mikhail, with a harsh, worn face. Mikhail must have been alerted to their arrival, as he appeared from his office to greet the men with formal handshakes. The Thai boss and one of his men followed Mikhail back to his office, leaving Fabio and I with the remaining three. They were all a lot younger — only in their twenties and thirties, and significantly less intimidating.

Fabio greeted them in a friendly but respectful way that I admired, then introduced me. The five of us ordered drinks before heading over to a vacant seating area near a side stage upon which a pretty young redhead was dancing. The three Thai men were preoccupied with her admittedly impressive moves, and they didn't seem interested in conversation, so Fabio and I sat quietly to one side. I sipped my drink (I'd switched to beer, to avoid intoxication) and wondered what I was supposed to do now. Should I try and make conversation, or leave them to enjoy the dancer's show?

As if sensing my uncertainty, Fabio leaned over to speak into my ear. 'They don't like us, so they won't chat. We just need to keep their drinks topped up, and keep the girls coming.'

He was correct. As the dancers rotated around the different podiums, the men seemed content. Most of the evening passed in a very similar manner. Fabio and I didn't speak, but I was comfortable enough just sitting with him, looking around the club. It really was interesting to see the range of different people here, from hired murderers knocking back shots, to boys who looked barely legal staring around at the half naked women with wide eyes. I was engrossed in my people watching, so at first I didn't notice Valentin sitting at the bar. But when I did, and our eyes met, I could read the disappointment on his face regardless of the distance between us.

I tried to smile at him, but he didn't immediately return the expression, which hurt a little. Seconds later, another familiar form appeared beside him. Dimitri. Following Val's gaze, Dimitri turned his head and his eyes found me. He blinked, then looked away, and I felt like I'd been punched in the stomach. I couldn't bear Dimitri being angry with me, although I had no right to care this much. I wanted to go over to him, but I was here to work, and I was happy to use that as an excuse.

Turning my back on the bar — and Dimitri — I met Fabio's inquisitive gaze, and gave him a reassuring smile. He shifted closer to me, the glow of drunkenness clear in his bright eyes. Trying to distract myself from Dimitri, and prevent Fabio from starting something I would have to stop, I stood up to offer the three men another refill from the fresh bottle of vodka we had just opened. While two simply accepted the alcohol and returned their attention to the dancer, the other man grabbed my wrist as I reached for his empty glass, and pulled me down on top of him. Vodka sloshed out of the bottle I held and soaked into the thin material of my dress.

Running his hand over my now wet stomach, the man murmured in my ear, 'We'll have to take this off to dry.'

I tried to stand up, but he had a firm grip on me, so I had no choice but to remain on his lap where he had positioned me. 'I'm fine,' I assured him. 'Can I get you another drink?'

In response, he grabbed the bottle from my hand and took a long slug before placing it back down on the table. His hands slid over my body, making my skin crawl. I longed to struggle away from him, but I knew I couldn't. Having this creep feel me up wasn't pleasant, but I was sure it would be preferential to Mikhail's anger if I fought him off.

'What was your name, again?' I asked, hoping to start a conversation.

'Ram,' he replied in his grumble of a voice.

'I'm Mari,' I told him with a smile, despite Fabio's earlier introductions. 'Are you sure I can't get you anything else from the bar?'

'No, you can stay right where you are.' Ram ran a hand through my hair, which I had styled in a half up-do in order to disguise the bald patch, which much to my dismay, had yet to regrow any hair. 'You have beautiful hair.'

My face was directly in line with Ram's, since I was sitting on him, and I gave him the brightest smile I could muster. 'Thank you.'

He stopped talking then, and focused his attention back to the blonde dancer who currently occupied the podium in front of us, although his hands remained on my body. I hoped he couldn't tell how tense I was. As Ram stroked a light hand up and down my bare thigh, I tried to remind myself why I was doing this.

When I felt a hand on my shoulder, I expected to see Fabio rescuing me from Ram's clutches. Instead, I turned to see Dimitri. He leaned into Ram and said something to him that I didn't catch. Ram nodded, and released his hold on me. Another display of Dimitri's influence.

Dimitri pulled me up by my arm, and dragged me away. I had no choice but to let him pull me along wordlessly as he led me towards the restrooms. Dimitri pushed open the men's bathroom door. There were a few guys in there, but when Dimitri barked at them to get out, they hurried to leave, and we were alone.

'What are you doing?' I asked, irritated by his caveman behaviour. 'I am working here. I can't just leave when I'm supposed to be...'

'Supposed to be what?' Dimitri exploded interrupting me. 'Letting them grope you?'

'Well, yes!' I exclaimed. 'You're the one who told me there are no choices when working for Mikhail. Whatever those men want, I have to give them.'

Dimitri yelled wordlessly in frustration, tugging hard on his hair. 'I can't believe you let yourself get into this position! I warned you! You should have listened to me, Mari.'

'What was I supposed to do?' I asked, taken aback by his aggression. 'It isn't like I volunteered my services.' Well, not exactly...

'You should have stayed away!' Dimitri finally looked at me, and his eyes were wild. 'Don't you get it? I can't protect you anymore.'

'You don't seem to understand that I don't need protecting,' I argued. 'I can handle this.'

'No, you can't!' Dimitri shouted, his angry words echoing around the empty bathroom. It took all of my strength not to shrink away from his rage. 'You have no idea what you're doing, or what you're in for. And there's nothing either of us can do about it now.'

I spread my arms in defeat. Nothing I could say would calm him or make this better. For me, this situation was a means to an end, but as far as Dimitri knew, this was my life now.

A silence fell between us, during which I stared at the dirty, tiled floor. I heard Dimitri move, and when I looked up, I found him standing less than two feet away from me. I hadn't been this close to him for what felt like a long time, and my heartbeat quickened in automatic response. It must have been the adrenaline; I knew an argument was coming.

Except, I was wrong. Dimitri stepped forward and enveloped me into his arms. For a second, I simply stood there, confused as always by his mood swings, but eventually I couldn't help but relax into his embrace. We'd never touched like this before, but it felt natural, and it felt so good to be held, especially by him. I didn't realise until that moment that I had missed him. And that was not okay.

'I can't watch you with those men,' Dimitri murmured into my hair.

'So don't look,' I repeated the advice he'd given me weeks earlier, in relation to Olivier and Nina.

Dimitri pulled back to look at me. He looked unimpressed. 'It's not that simple.'

I stepped back, breaking contact. 'Then leave. You know I have to do this, and I really should get back out there.'

Dimitri sighed, heavily, but nodded. I turned to leave, but he caught me arm, and when I looked back over my shoulder, his gaze held mine. 'Let me take you home. I'll wait until you're done.'

Chapter Seventeen

Returning to Fabio, I was greeted with the sight of a couple of naked women lying across the three men. There were hands everywhere, and it was entirely indecent, although I supposed it was a pretty normal sight here. I had to pretend like it wasn't making me want to vomit. At least it wasn't me on Ram's lap this time.

'You okay?' Fabio asked as I sat down beside him, averting my gaze from the display opposite us.

I nodded in response, and we didn't have to wait long after that before Mikhail and the other men joined us, clearly having finished their business discussion finally. The Thai boss gestured wordlessly to his men, and they stood instantly, brushing the poor girls aside like used napkins after a dinner party. Only when they were gone did I finally relax.

Mikhail took a seat opposite me, and leaned forward to speak over the music. 'How was she?' he asked Fabio.

'She was great,' Fabio replied, enthusiastically. 'They were pretty hands-on with her, but she didn't react.'

I frowned, irritated that they were discussing me like I wasn't even there, but kept my mouth shut. Fabio didn't tell Mikhail that I'd disappeared with Dimitri for twenty minutes, and I appreciated his discretion, so I didn't want to show him up by making a scene now. At least they were being complimentary about me. Well, kind of.

'Good,' Mikhail nodded, finally glancing in my direction. 'See, Mari, it's not that hard, is it?'

I just looked at him. I had no fake smiles left.

Mikhail stood, and waved a dismissive hand towards Fabio and me as he walked away. 'You can both go. I'll be in contact.'

Fabio turned to me. 'You want to get a celebratory drink?'

'Celebratory?' I asked, standing up and stretching. I felt wiped. My phone was in my jacket, which was still behind the bar, so I had no idea what time it was. I made a mental note to buy a watch before the next job.

'Yeah, you were a hit with those guys!' Fabio beamed like a proud parent.

'Oh, thanks, but Dimitri is waiting for me.' I glanced over to the bar, and sure enough, Dimitri was there, his eyes on me. I guessed Valentin had left, since Dimitri sat alone.

Fabio followed my gaze, and his face fell. 'Oh, sure, okay. I'll see you around, then.' He wrapped his arms around me in a too-intimate hug, his hands on my back pressing our bodies together. I suspected that Fabio was making a show for Dimitri's benefit, although I thought he should know better than that.

I pulled away, and gave him a stern look, to which he rolled his eyes and nodded, clearly understanding my silent chastisement.

'I'll see you soon,' I told him, with a smile to soften the mood.

He returned the expression. 'Sure, see you round.'

I made my way over to the bar, to Dimitri. I asked the nearby waitress for my jacket, which Mikhail had tucked beneath the bar, and was relieved to see that it hadn't been spilled on; that thing cost more than my monthly salary at *Arrow's*. Shrugging into the warm leather, I followed Dimitri out into the cold night, surprised to see that it was almost 4am when I checked my phone.

'What time does this place close?' I asked, curious. All the clubs back home kicked out at three, latest.

'Whenever people leave,' Dimitri replied.

Dimitri hailed a nearby cab. The journey was quiet. At my door, Dimitri paused.

I lingered in the doorway. He seemed to be waiting for

something. 'Do you… want to come in?'

He hesitated, then nodded, following me inside. I was exhausted, and needed to get out of my alcohol-sticky dress, so headed straight for the bathroom, shutting the door before Dimitri could speak. He obviously wanted to talk, or he wouldn't have come in, but I wasn't sure that I was in the mood to be yelled at.

Peeling off the dress, I changed into a clean camisole and pair of pyjama shorts from the cupboard. I wiped off my makeup, splashed my face with water, and dragged a brush through my knotted hair. Ready to sleep for twelve hours, I emerged from the bathroom to see Dimitri leaning against the nearby wall, waiting.

I hesitated. 'I'm really tired.' I was being avoidant, but after everything that had happened in the past few weeks, I was a little too emotionally drained to deal with whatever he wanted to say, and to be honest, I wasn't sure I wanted to know.

Dimitri looked at me for a moment. 'Okay.'

I gave him a small smile. 'Thanks.' Passing by him, I headed into the bedroom, hoping that he would let himself out, but I had barely walked through the doorway when I heard Dimitri suck in a deep breath from behind me. Turning, I saw him staring at me with a strange expression—sympathy, hurt, and… guilt? Understanding clicked, and I realised that now I'd brushed out my hair, the bald patch was plainly visible. My hands flew up to the back of my head, hurrying to bunch my hair into a ponytail and cover the ugly gap. But it was too late. He'd already seen the damage, and the look on his face was more than I could handle.

I turned my back on Dimitri in favour of crawling into my bed and pulling the duvet up to my chin. Minutes later, I was surprised to feel a weight on the bed next to me. I rolled over to see Dimitri lying down next to me. It was dark, but I could tell that he was still fully clothed and on top of the duvet, rather than under it. I guessed he was trying to be respectful, but it was cold, so I pulled up the cover, inviting him in. He hesitated for a second, but then he kicked off his boots and obliged. His body heat radiated instantly through the bed, although we weren't touching.

My body longed for sleep, and I tried to close my eyes, but my mind was too busy focusing on Dimitri's gentle breathing, and the smell of his skin on my pillows. Giving in, I opened my eyes, and saw his shining back at me in the dim room, lit only by the streetlight creeping in through the blind. He watched me, an indecipherable expression on his perfect face.

'Do you want me to leave?' he asked, softly.

'No,' I whispered in response. The way he was gazing at me made my chest hurt.

Dimitri sighed, rolling onto his back. 'Fabio would kick my ass if he knew I was here.'

Frowning, I pushed myself up onto my elbows. 'What?' the increased volume of my voice cracked through the darkness like a whip. I switched on the bedside lamp, so that I could see Dimitri's expression, though that didn't help. He was so hard to read.

'You and Fabio,' Dimitri said, his brows drawing together. 'I'm not blind. I see the way he looks at you.'

I frowned in return. 'There's nothing between me and Fabio.'

Dimitri raised one eyebrow sceptically, and I thought about the numerous times he'd seen Fabio kiss me, dance with me, flirt with me, and I could see why he might not believe me.

'I'm not going to pretend like Fabio isn't interested, or that we've never flirted, but honestly, nothing has really happened between us. I'm not interested in him,' I said. 'I mean, he's fun, but he's a friend.' It was important to me that Dimitri knew that.

Dimitri shifted next to me. His fingers brushed the underside of my chin, and I raised my face to meet his gaze. It was surreal to see him like this, in my lilac bed sheets, looking almost vulnerable. His shield was fading.

'I am so sorry that I didn't stop Tony that night.' Dimitri's voice was a husky whisper.

I blinked, staring into his molten eyes, almost black in the glow of the lamp. I hadn't expected to hear that, given our last conversation. After he'd killed Tony. The thought sent ice through my veins, but even though I knew what he'd done, I just couldn't reconcile that part of Dimitri with the man lying beside me now. It was like they were two different people, at least in my mind, if not in reality. I was in trouble.

'I saw you with Fabio, and I got so mad, and I turned away,' Dimitri continued, his voice low, regretful. 'I didn't even see Tony approach you, and next thing I know he's dragging you outside by your damn hair.' He exhaled sharply, and his hand fell from my face to rest on the sheets between us. 'I'm just so sorry, Mari.'

My breath hitched in my throat as I tried to understand the emotions behind his words. 'It's not your fault.' I hesitated. But then I said what I was thinking. 'You were so mad at me.'

Dimitri shook his head gently. 'I was mad, but not with you. I should have done something, saved you from this whole situation.'

'It isn't up to you to save me, Dimitri,' I told him softly.

His eyes locked with mine, and emotion sparked in his irises. My stomach fluttered at the heat in his gaze. Dimitri closed the space between us and pressed his lips against mine, gently. I was so used to kisses being demanding and aggressive, that this sweet and soft kiss took me entirely by surprise. My heart pounded, and I kissed him back, leaning in, deepening. This didn't feel real.

Dimitri's hand brushed my cheek, gently moving to the back of my neck, where it lightly rested. There was nothing commanding about this, and yet it was the most compelling contact I'd ever experienced. I knew Dimitri wouldn't push this, but my body was responding strongly to his touch, and all my common sense had been brushed aside by the feeling. Needing more, I moved to press my body against his, pushing my fingers through his thick, dark hair.

The kiss deepened. I raised my leg, draping it over Dimitri's hip and using it to pull him closer to me. I could feel every inch of his body through the thin fabric of my clothes, and it still wasn't enough. His hands stroked down my back, and I shivered in the best possible way, throwing my head back and allowing a small moan to escape my lips. It was as if that noise flicked a switch within Dimitri; he pulled my head back down to his, kissing me harder this time. I welcomed it. He tugged at the hem of my camisole, and I pulled back, raising my arms so that he could pull it over my head and toss it aside.

He rolled us over so that I was lying on my back and he hovered over me, kissing my mouth deeply, before moving his attention to my neck, and down over my breasts. I threw my head back, enjoying the sensations as he caressed and kissed my chest in just the right places. My fingers twisted in his hair, gently tugging, and he moaned.

His kisses travelled lower, over my stomach, and to the waistband of my shorts. Hooking his fingers over the elastic, he tugged them down, revealing my underwear. I wriggled, helping him remove the shorts, and was rewarded with the feeling of his hot breath against my most sensitive area, only the thin lace of my panties separating his soft mouth from me. Pushing them aside, he slipped a finger into me, and I cried out wordlessly. It had been so long, and this was so… different. He was different.

'Dimitri…' I whispered. I couldn't form any more words.

A growl rumbled in Dimitri's throat when I said his name, his dark hair tickling my belly as he leaned into my skin. He moved his finger inside me, and I arched my back, helping him hit the right spot. He started a rhythm, and my breathing began to quicken. When he stopped, I opened my eyes, confused momentarily until he tugged my panties down, and returned to his previous actions. This time, I was exposed, and his hot mouth found the bundle of nerves that he'd already set on edge. I yelped at the surprising pleasure. He sure as hell knew what he was doing. His tongue worked quickly, in rhythm with his hand, and I squeezed my eyes shut again, concentrating solely on the feeling he was creating.

'Oh, God…' I heard myself moan.

Dimitri groaned in response, his tongue moving faster across me, and my legs tensed, my hands fisting in the bed sheets, as the pleasure reached its height. I cried out, loudly, and he moaned, continuing to taste me until I was done, my muscles finally relaxing.

Before I could recover, Dimitri's face returned to my vision, and I felt him press against me. I don't know when he took his clothes off, and I didn't care. I wrapped my hand around him, and he inhaled sharply. He was perfect.

'Mari,' he begged, his lips parted and his eyes gleaming, fixed on mine.

I moved my hips upwards, and guided him into me. Dimitri inhaled sharply, and I gasped at the unfamiliar feeling of him inside me. He took it slow at first, but his breathing became heavier, and his movements faster. I dug my fingernails into his back, urging him to go harder. I'd never felt anything like this before, it was like our bodies just fitted so perfectly together. Dimitri rolled his hips, and the feeling intensified. He kissed me, urgently, our sweat covered bodies creating a powerful friction between us. Harder, faster... Dimitri moaned my name again, and again, as we both got closer to the edge, until finally, he tensed in culmination, and I followed. As he relaxed onto me, breathing heavily, I took in the familiar scent of him, and everything felt right. We stayed that way for a long time.

Chapter Eighteen

A week passed, during which time I completed three solo drug deliveries and one debt collection in the company of another one of Mikhail's employees — a burly man in his fifties named Jag. Everything went pretty smoothly, with the exception of the collection with Jag; the debtor was refusing to pay on the grounds that Mikhail's cocaine quality had significantly reduced in the last few months. Jag managed to elicit the monies owed, of course, and I tried to ask him about the quality issues afterwards, but he shrugged it off.

Besides that, Doro had been right — my direct involvement with gang activities was invaluable. Not only had I seen Jag beat someone almost to death, but I was also starting to get to know Mikhail's core dealers and customers — no doubt at least some of them would be willing to testify for the right sum, or the right level of protection.

Things with Dimitri were complicated, of course. We'd avoided each other for a few days after our first night together, but when he turned up at my door midweek, I couldn't say no to him spending the night. And again a couple of days later. I wasn't sure what was happening between us — it's not like we sat down to discuss it — but I couldn't seem to stop it, as much as I knew that it was a terrible idea. It just didn't *feel* terrible.

The end of the week finally rolled around, and it was a quiet Sunday night in the bar. Only when I finally locked up and stepped out into the night air did my night get interesting. Doro was waiting for me, dressed in his usual intimidating all-black gear, a cigarette between his thin lips.

My throat tightened; the last time I'd seen Doro, he'd hurt Tad and then threatened me, but I swallowed the nerves. 'If you wanted to talk, you could have come inside,' I said, dryly.

'I thought I'd walk you home instead,' Doro replied in his gruff tone, dropping his cigarette on the ground and treading on it as he fell into step beside me. 'Besides, the last time I was in that bar, things went very wrong.'

I rolled my eyes. 'Don't be dramatic. We got the outcome we wanted.'

'Tony is dead.' Doro's words, and his icy tone, sliced through me.

I shot him the coldest look I could manage as we walked. 'That was not my fault. It would have happened either way — the moment Tony touched me, he was a dead man. We both should've seen that coming.'

'If you weren't screwing Dimitri, it wouldn't have happened.'

I stopped in my tracks, gaping up at Doro in shock. I hadn't told anyone about the recent developments in my relationship with Dimitri. And I knew Dimitri wouldn't have said anything, either.

'Don't look at me like that,' Doro spat, nastily. 'Everyone knows. What the hell are you thinking?'

'Okay, are you really telling me that since you got here, you haven't slept with a single person? Really?' I fumed. 'Besides, there's nothing going on with Dimitri and me. He wasn't even speaking to me at the time that Tony died.'

'You're not supposed to get involved, and you know it,' Doro's voice was low, threatening. Clearly he didn't like me calling him out on his own sexual escapades.

I started walking again, in the direction of home. The quicker I got there, the quicker this conversation would be over. 'I'm not involved, I know what I'm doing.'

'You expect me to believe that?' Doro scoffed.

'I needed Dimitri to trust me, and I think it's going

pretty well so far,' I replied.

Doro gave a short, humourless laugh. 'You're in over your head, you've got no idea what you're doing. I should never have helped you get in with Mikhail. He'll be the end of you.'

I felt myself frown; I wasn't sure exactly when Doro had experienced this change of opinion regarding my apparent inability to do my job, but something felt off. This whole conversation had set me completely on edge, and I was relieved when we finally reached my building. I grabbed my keys, and hurried to get inside.

'Well, it was lovely to see you, and thanks for your vote of confidence.' I attempted to shut the door behind me, but Doro caught it before I could.

Leaning close, his voice dropped to a harsh growl. 'Just one more thing before I let you go. If you ever touch me again when I'm working, I will knock you out just like I would anyone else. You got that? And if you mess this up, I will not let you take me down with you. You are on your own.'

My eyes went wide. 'Don't you dare threaten me. And don't come see me again.' I shoved against the door, and this time, Doro stepped back, and the lock clicked into place.

Upstairs at my apartment, I was glad to see that Dimitri wasn't waiting for me tonight. I crawled into bed alone, completely unable to believe the things Doro had just said to me — he was supposed to be my ally, someone I could turn to if I got into trouble. Obviously, that was no longer the case. Ironically, while he had accused me of being too involved, I knew that he was the one in over his head. I could no longer see Steve — the person he really was — beneath the façade. Dread settled over me, because now I was truly alone, and if an experienced officer like Steve had sunk under the weight of his undercover persona, then what hope was there for me?

***

The next morning, I was woken early by a text from Mikhail commanding me to come to the *Angel Rooms* ASAP. I rolled my eyes. It wasn't even nine in the morning. But I still dragged myself from my bed, throwing on jeans, boots and a sweater before making my way down to the beach.

The club door was unlocked, as usual, and I made my way straight back to Mikhail's office.

Inside, I saw Mikhail sitting behind his formidable desk, typing on his phone. He glanced up when I entered the room, and gestured for me to take the seat opposite him. I obliged, and waited patiently while he finished up whatever he was doing. When he finally set down his phone and made eye contact, I forced myself to hold his gaze.

'Mari,' he rolled my name over his tongue, and I felt a little violated. 'You've done good work for me the past few weeks. I like you.'

I shifted in my seat; I knew he hadn't dragged me down here just to compliment me.

'It is time to test your loyalty.' Mikhail reached into a drawer in his desk and pulled out a handgun, setting in on the table surface and pushing it over towards me. I swallowed, and made no move to take the weapon, simply waiting for Mikhail to continue, which he did, almost gleefully. 'I've recently been informed of a rat in our midst, and I need you to take care of him.'

I raised my eyebrows. 'You mean kill him?'

Mikhail nodded. 'Of course. A simple test of your allegiance. An initiation... if you like.' He smirked. 'You

145

know, you're lucky. Historically, women would have to be intimate with all high-ranking members in order to be accepted into our business. So, you're getting a nice easy task.'

'Oh, yeah, thanks.' I rolled my eyes.

'The rat's name is Henry, a prospect from around here. He had potential, too, until the police got to him. He is unaware of our knowledge. Tonight, you will go to his home, and carry out your duty.'

My heart pounded, but I took a deep breath and thought about how I should react.

'He lives alone?' I asked.

'No.' Mikhail looked impressed by my question. 'He lives with several other prospects, and it's my understanding that their place is regularly used as a gambling room.'

I frowned. 'So you want me to shoot him in a room full of other people? How the hell am I supposed to do that without getting killed myself?'

Mikhail shrugged, a smile playing on his crooked mouth. He was enjoying this. 'You will have to figure that out yourself. Take the weapon. I will text you the address, and you will go there tonight.'

Sucking in a breath, I reached for the gun, the weight familiar in my hand, and stood to tuck into my waistband, pulling my sweater down to cover it.

'Is that everything?' I asked, stepping towards the door.

'That's it. Don't screw up, Mari,' Mikhail warned, his tone low. 'You remember I told you the consequences of failing to do something I have asked of you.'

He meant death, of course — how could I forget? I nodded, before making my exit. I felt the gun against my skin the whole way home.

Chapter Nineteen

That evening, I called Jono and told him I was sick so I couldn't make my shift at the bar. I dressed in black jeans, heavy duty boots, and a long-sleeved dark tee. I tucked the gun into my waistband and threw a jacket on to hide the bump under my shirt. Heading out a little after nine, I took the underground to the beach, and followed the map on my phone to the address that Mikhail had text me.

Taking a moment to survey the area, I guessed that there were at least 15 flats in the building, meaning somewhere around 30 people would hear a gunshot — not that I planned on firing one. Equally high buildings rose on either side of my target, adding to the number of witnesses. There was no way that this task could be carried out without the culprit getting caught, and there was no doubt in my mind that Mikhail knew that. But why set me up to get caught? Was it part of the test?

Not that it mattered. Of course I wasn't going to kill anyone.

That afternoon, after Mikhail had sent me the address, I'd called Taylor and told him to have a car at either end of the street, ready to take Henry into witness protection. Whether he was a rat or not, I didn't know, but after I told him I'd been sent to kill him, he'd surely do whatever it took to protect himself.

I took the stairs up to the fifth floor, and knocked on the door numbered 13. Only seconds later it was pulled open by a kid who was no older than fifteen. From inside the flat, I could hear music and several low voices, interspersed with laughter.

'You Henry?' I asked, praying that he wasn't.

'No,' he replied, much to my relief. 'Who the hell are you?'

I raised my eyebrows, impressed by his gall. I imagined that hanging out with gang members did wonders for a teenager's sense of self-importance. 'My name is Mari, I work for Mikhail. I gotta talk to Henry, so is it okay if I come in?'

The kid hesitated, looking me up and down, then nodded, stepping aside so that I could enter the flat. He shut the door, and led the way through a cramped hallway and into a small lounge room where a game of poker was mid-way through. I noticed substantial stacks of cash on the table, and several bottles of spirits, half-empty. As I entered the room, the five men crowded around the makeshift poker table turned their attention to me, and one particular gaze struck me with familiarity. Oh, no.

Dimitri held my gaze. His face remained carefully blank, but that meant nothing. I wondered again, had Mikhail known Dimitri would be here?

'Yo, who's this chick?' one of the younger men demanded.

The kid who'd let me in spoke up from behind me. 'Said she works for Mikhail. Wants to talk to Henry.' He turned to me, and pointed to a door behind Dimitri. 'Henry's in there, think he's still sleeping off last night.'

There were a few snickers from the men as I crossed the room towards presumably Henry's bedroom. It was a small apartment, and my arm brushed Dimitri's as I squeezed around the table. I felt him tense.

I didn't knock before opening the door. It was dark inside, but I could see someone was in the bed. He didn't move when I entered. I closed the door softly behind me and approached the bed, slowly. My hand reached for the gun in my waistband, my pulse quickening. He could wake up any second. As my eyes adjusted to the dim room, I could make out his face. There was a dark pool around his head.

Blood.

He was already dead.

The door clicked behind me, and I whirled on my heel, pulling the gun out and pointing it at the intruder. But even in the shadows, I knew who it was, leaning against the closed door with his arms folded across his chest.

'What did you do?' My voice was low.

'What I knew you couldn't.' He held up a gun, with a silencer attached.

I felt sick. I lowered the gun and turned to look at the bed. My heart ached. Henry looked barely eighteen. He was skinny, with bad skin and very fresh tattoos. His eyes were frozen open. I didn't have to look any more closely to know that he'd have a bullet wound in his temple.

'We need to go,' Dimitri said.

I turned to look at him. 'How could you do this? He was just a kid.'

'Committing murder for Mikhail is initiation. We've all done it,' Dimitri explained in a quiet voice, holding my gaze intensely. 'If you can't do it, you die.'

'So I'm supposed to be grateful to you?' I spat.

The hard black of his eyes bore into me, as he tucked his weapon away underneath his jacket. 'We need to go.'

Dimitri opened the window, and indicated for me to go first, but I couldn't move. Dimitri swore. He grabbed the gun from my shaking hand, and pushed me out onto the fire escape. My body acted without conscious decision. I half climbed half slid down the rusty metal stairs until my feet hit concrete. The cold wind hit my face and I realised that there were tears on my cheeks.

Dimitri grabbed my wrist, tugging me harshly around the corner of the building and into an alley. My stomach churned, and I just managed to turn away from him before vomiting.

Whether I pulled the trigger or not, Henry was dead

because of me.

I wiped my mouth with the back of my hand, and stood up straight. Dimitri was watching me. He opened his mouth to speak, but I cut him off. 'Not here.' I was very aware that there were police officers nearby.

We took the underground train home together in silence. I could barely stand the sight of Dimitri, but I couldn't seem to take my eyes off him. When we reached my flat, he followed me inside. He held out the handgun Mikhail had given me, but I didn't take it. After a moment, he set it down on the coffee table.

'You killed him.'

Dimitri stood with his arm folded, still looking at me with that blank shield expression. 'One of us had to.'

'No!' I exclaimed. 'No! I wasn't going to hurt him, damn it! I just…'

'Just what?' demanded Dimitri. 'What the hell were you going to do, then?'

I bit my tongue. I couldn't tell him the truth.

Dimitri let out a single, humourless laugh. 'You are a naive little girl.'

'Better than being a murderer.' The cold tone of my voice sliced through the room.

He stared at me for a long, painful minute. Then he spoke, his voice as empty as his expression. 'You tell Mikhail that you killed Henry. He'll trust you now.'

Chapter Twenty

I couldn't sleep, but I waited until a reasonable hour in the morning before I headed out to go tell Mikhail that I was now officially initiated. I emptied one bullet from the chamber of the gun, since I was sure Mikhail would check once I handed it back to him. Henry was dead, and there was nothing I could do about it, but I wasn't going to let his death be meaningless by getting caught out in a mistake now.

I had barely taken two steps down the stairs when a noise caught my attention. I stopped moving and listened. Indecipherable muffled shouting, clattering, banging… I suddenly realised that it was coming from Dimitri's place.

I turned and ran up the stairs. His front door was closed, but when I tried the handle, it opened. I shut it gently behind me, pulling the gun out and holding it out in front of me, like I was trained to do.

Dimitri's voice echoed through the apartment. 'Stop smashing things!' He sounded irritated more than anything else.

I edged towards the lounge doorway. Judging by what I could hear, I thought that there were at least two men in the apartment, besides Dimitri. Slowly, I peered around the doorframe and into the room. Sure enough, Dimitri was in the process of fighting off two men that I didn't recognize. I could see the bright red of blood dripping from his nose, and my stomach clenched. While he was engaged in a physical fight with one man, I saw the other pull a gun from his jeans, and point it at Dimitri.

I stepped into the room and yelled, 'Hey! Put the gun down.'

All attention was on me. I held my gun confidently in both hands, aiming it towards the armed man. He hesitated for a second, and then he shot at me, the bullet embedding into the plasterboard wall next to me. Adrenaline and hard-core police training fuelled my responsive shot, and I was a better aim than him. The bullet hit his knee. He was knocked spectacularly onto the floor, losing grip on his own weapon. It skidded across the floor and under the couch.

The man wailed in pain, and his accomplice turned to see what was going on. Dimitri took advantage of the distraction, and landed a heavy blow to the man's skull. The man stumbled to his knees, and Dimitri was on him in a second, landing punch after punch, until the intruder was no longer conscious. His friend moaned continuously, writhing on the floor, clutching at his leg as blood pooled on the floor.

Dimitri surveyed the damage to the two intruders before finally looking over at me. 'Where the hell did you learn how to do that?' he asked, sounding breathless.

I relaxed my arms, replacing the safety mechanism on the gun, and shrugged. 'Learn what? The guy shot at me first, Dimitri. It was pure luck that I hit him.' But of course, it wasn't. I'd aimed for the lower leg on purpose, so as to incapacitate him without too much permanent damage.

'Who are these guys?' I asked.

'They were at Henry's place last night playing poker,' Dimitri replied. 'I killed their friend and took all their money. Guess they weren't too pleased about that.' He shrugged, and it disturbed me how blasé he was about this. How often did this kind of thing happen to him? Actually, I probably didn't want to know the answer to that particular question.

The bleeding man groaned as he tried to crawl forward. I stepped forward, and pressed my heel into his injured leg. He wailed, his pain piercing through the room. His blood spattered over my boot and up the leg of my jeans, and I felt the warmth of it seeping through to my skin. When I pressed harder, he seemed to crumple beneath me, passing out either from the pain or the blood loss.

Dimitri looked distinctly impressed. 'Remind me never to piss you off.'

I hid the smug smile that wanted to rise. 'What do we do with them now?'

Dimitri shrugged. 'Kill them or let them go. What do you think?' He wasn't really asking.

I frowned. 'That's not even a choice.'

He raised an eyebrow. 'For you, maybe.'

'Dimitri. We can't kill them.'

He looked at me for a second, his face blank, then he sighed. 'Okay, okay. Go down to the beach, get a van, one without windows, and bring it back here.'

'Then what?' I asked.

'We'll drive them out of the City while they're unconscious and dump them somewhere.'

I considered this. My initial response would be to hand them over to the police, but of course that wasn't an option for Dimitri.

Dimitri rolled his eyes at my hesitation. 'Hell, Mari, what would you rather we do? Make them breakfast?'

I narrowed my eyes at him. 'Fine.' I pointed to the man I'd shot. 'Wrap his knee while I'm gone, he's losing blood.'

At the *Angel Rooms*, I found the front door unlocked although no one seemed to be in the bar. Luckily, when I knocked on the office door, Mikhail shouted from inside for me to enter.

He didn't look surprised to see me. 'Ah, Mari. How did it go last night?'

'Fine. Henry's dead.' I reported, carefully keeping my

voice steady, ignoring the sharp stab I felt in my stomach. I hadn't pulled the trigger, but I was the reason that kid was dead. I would never forgive myself.

'I know. Well done.'

I held the gun out to him, but he shook his head.

'Keep it,' he told me.

I hesitated, but then shrugged. 'Fine. Uh, there's something else. I need a van. With no windows.'

Mikhail startled me with a harsh, ugly laugh. 'Damn, you are like one of my boys already.' He pulled open a drawer in his desk and tossed me a set of keys. 'It's parked on the next street.'

'Thanks,' I replied, relieved that he hadn't asked any questions. I guessed that he was used to this kind of request from his employees.

When I got back to the apartment, the two men were already dead. The van was for moving the bodies. I threw the keys at Dimitri, and told him I never wanted to see him again. I should have known I wouldn't be able to stick to that.

Chapter Twenty-One

'Hello.' The familiarity of Taylor's voice washed over me like a comfort blanket. He was my boss, but he was also my mentor, and he was my only contact from my real life. His voice was like an anchor, which I very desperately needed.

'It's me,' I replied. It was late, and I was in bed, but I still couldn't sleep.

'Are you alright?' Taylor asked, sounding calm and controlled as always.

'Yes.' Lie.

'We didn't pick up any one last night at that address.'

'It didn't go down as planned.' Understatement.

'What happened?'

'Nothing.' Denial.

Taylor paused. 'Harper, what's wrong?'

I sighed, and sank back into my pillows. 'It's harder than I thought. Don't say you told me so.'

But of course, he wouldn't even consider saying that. Instead, he asked, 'Do you want out?'

'No,' I replied immediately. 'I'm in a good position. I'm seeing a lot, learning a lot. I'm getting closer with Dimitri and Nina, and Mikhail, too. They trust me.'

Then I bit my lip; I'd forgotten that I never actually got supervisory permission to start working directly for Mikhail. I knew that I should tell Taylor now, but I couldn't bring myself to do it — the risk that he'd pull me from the field was too great, especially now that I was starting to get real, useful information.

'How's Steve?' Taylor asked, surprising me with the use of Doro's real name. 'He hasn't made contact for a long while, and I'm starting to worry. Do I need to?'

I hesitated. I didn't want to tell on my fellow agent, but Doro had threatened me, and I knew he was in too deep. It was for his own good. 'Actually, yeah. I think there might be a problem there.'

'I had a feeling there might be,' Taylor replied, with a heavy sigh. 'I'll send someone to his place. Thank you, and good work.'

I didn't reply. I felt guilty.

'It was good to hear from you. Keep me updated,' Taylor said. 'And stay safe.'

I hung up, turned the phone off and replaced it in the hiding place. That hadn't helped at all. I wasn't sure that anything would.

***

Days passed, during which I heard nothing from Mikhail, and nothing from Dimitri. The weekend arrived, and I worked at the bar, again. Tad hadn't been in for a few weeks, although Jono reassured me that Tad hadn't quit, he was just taking some time out. I wasn't sure what Tad had told Jono about that night, and the way Jono looked at me didn't help; it was like he suspected me of something, but he didn't vocalise his thoughts, whatever they were.

The practicality of working alone meant some busy weekend shifts, because of course Jono still didn't deign to lend a hand behind the bar. But I didn't really mind working alone; being busy kept my mind occupied. I thought about calling Tad, but I guessed that he probably wanted time away from me just as much as he wanted time away from the bar, so I gave him space.

The Friday shift was hectic, and the Saturday shift was worse. Afterwards, I cleaned up quickly and began the walk home. My thoughts shifted to Dimitri, as they tended to do at night, when I was alone. Twisted feelings tangled in my stomach. I felt sick about him, horrified and repulsed by what he did, and yet I almost *missed* him. I was in too deep. Staying away from him was the only option.

My building came into view, and I hurried to get into the warmth. Jogging up the steps to my floor, I was fumbling in my purse for the keys, and didn't immediately notice the figure waiting outside my door. Only when he moved towards me did I realise who it was.

Doro.

He grabbed me and slapped a hand across my mouth before I could even think about making a sound. Snatching the keys from my hand, he unlocked the door and shoved me inside so forcefully that I lost my balance and stumbled forward onto my knees. Doro slammed the door shut behind him, before taking a menacing step towards me.

I hurried to my feet, adrenaline already pounding, backing away instinctively, but never taking my eyes from the man before me.

'What the hell do you think you're playing at?' he snarled. The inhuman anger in his eyes made him almost unrecognisable — this was not the man I knew.

'I don't know what you're talking about,' I replied, struggling to keep my voice steady.

'The hell you don't!' Doro bellowed, taking another step forward. 'An officer showed up at my place today, sent by Taylor. Apparently, they're under the impression that I've lost my way, forgotten why I'm here. I wonder where they got that idea.'

'Listen,' I began, but I was cut off when Doro lunged for me, grabbing me by the throat and hurling me back against the wall. He held me there, a tight grip around my neck. I could breathe, but barely.

'No, you listen, bitch!' His pupils were huge, and I

smelled whiskey on his breath. 'You *told* on me. Who the hell do you think you are? You think you can tell me how to do my job?'

'No,' I managed to croak.

The grip on my neck tightened, and I gasped for breath. I needed a gun, but my service weapon was safely tucked away in my bedroom, as was Mikhail's gun. There was no way I could get to them, even if I wasn't pinned to the wall. Frantically, I rolled my eyes to the side, searching desperately for some other kind of weapon within reaching distance.

'I've been here for years,' Doro continued, 'I've given my life to this job, and you waltz in here, get straight into Mikhail's favour, and decide that you're better at this than I am. But you forget—this is my *life*.'

I was starting to have real trouble breathing, gulping for air, my throat burning. Still trying to spot a suitable heavy object, I cursed myself for not being the type for ornaments or vases. There was nothing within my immediate reach.

Doro moved closer, and our entire bodies pressed together uncomfortably. 'This is my life,' he repeated, growling. 'I'm not afraid of doing the tough jobs. I'm not afraid to hurt people, especially when I need to teach someone a lesson...' I heard a metallic click, and as Doro raised his free hand, the gleam of a switch blade caught my eye.

Panic rose in my chest. He thought I'd betrayed him, and he was going to do what Mikhail would do to a traitor. If anything, this confirmed that I'd been right in reporting Doro to Taylor, because he clearly was in too deep, unable to tell the difference between his persona and his reality.

But being correct about Doro wasn't helpful in the moment. I needed to save myself, or I was going to pass out from lack of oxygen. Out of the corner of my eye, I noticed a dirty ashtray on the windowsill that had been there when I moved in. It wasn't particularly heavy, but it would be enough to get Doro off of me, if I hit him hard enough. Problem was, it was just out of reach.

Doro's knife was moving closer to my face by the second, in time with the increasingly sick smile on his face. A sudden heat burned my left cheek, and it took a few seconds to realise that Doro was actually cutting me. Even as the pain seared through my skin, I could still barely believe that this was really happening. My body was pinned, and my vocal cords were ineffective; the only sound I could make was a gargled whimper. There was nothing I could do but stand there as he sliced a thin, curved line from the outer corner of my eye all the way down to my chin.

When he finally pulled the blade away from my face to admire his work, the slick warmth of blood trickled down my face and neck. Tears of pain and frustration leaked from my eyes against my best efforts of control, and Doro's smile widened. He was really enjoying this.

Blood seeped into my mouth, and I impulsively spat it out, spraying it into Doro's face. Surprised, he took a step back, loosening his grip just a little, and I took the chance to lunge to my left. He hadn't expected my sudden movement, and my fingertips were able to brush the edge of the ashtray. Doro pulled me back towards him, but I managed to grip my makeshift weapon and swing it with all my strength into the side of his face.

It made a satisfying *thunk* upon impact, and Doro yelled, inadvertently releasing me from his clutches. He stood between me and my bedroom door, and thus my guns, so I ran for the kitchen instead. I pulled open the cutlery drawer, but before I could grab a knife, Doro was on me again. He yanked me back by my shoulders and tossed me aside. My hip slammed into the side of the counter, and I yelped. Frantically I grasped for something — anything — and found a discarded mug on the surface. Doro was quicker than me, though, and knocked the mug from my hand before I could do anything with it. It smashed on the floor, and he grabbed my arms so I couldn't reach for anything else. In our struggle, the plate rack tumbled to the ground with a deafening crash, smashing around my feet.

I tried for a kick, and made contact with Doro's upper thigh, but there was no strength behind my blow. Doro swung a fist, making sharp contact with my already injured cheek. I screamed, and my pained throat burned angrily against the strain of the noise.

Desperately trying to organise my thoughts into some kind of feasible plan, I used all my strength to throw my body into Doro's, pushing him back into the fridge. His head connected with the cold metal, and I was able to pull one wrist free of his grip. I landed a clumsy but adrenaline-fuelled punch to his face, his nose crunching satisfyingly, blood pouring.

He growled, and hit me again, this time in the stomach, winding me. Another blow landed on my face, and my vision momentarily blurred. I tried to swing again, but I was too slow, too dizzy. Doro's hand flew up, fisting in my hair, and he spun me, slamming my face into the door frame. Pain erupted; everything went black. If Doro hadn't still been holding onto me, I would have crumpled. I tried to suck in a breath, but my nose was blocked... I tasted blood, thick and heavy. I gasped for air through my mouth, but couldn't seem to find any. My ears rang. There was a crash, and some shouting, but everything was spinning and I couldn't hear properly, and then suddenly, no one was holding me up anymore. Dizziness overwhelmed me. I didn't even feel the impact of my body hitting the floor.

Chapter Twenty-Two

When I woke up, the first thing I became aware of was the searing pain all over my body. The next thing I noticed was how much it hurt to breath. Oh, God. I opened my eyes. It was dark, but I was able to recognise that I was in my own bedroom. That was good at least. But then, memories came flooding back to me — Doro, strangling me, cutting me, beating me... Tears burned my eyes.

A noise from the other room startled me back to reality. I sat up. Mistake. My stomach burned, and my left hip screamed. Looking down at myself, I was pleased to see that I was still wearing my clothes, but the front of my shirt was covered with dried blood, so thick that it looked black in the semi-darkness. Another noise re-focused my attention; someone else was in the flat.

Before I could bring myself to move again, the bedroom door cracked open. I winced at the light, and my heart slammed into my ribs, expecting Doro to come charging in. But instead, Dimitri appeared at my side.

'Lay back down,' he instructed gently.

I breathed a sigh of relief as he helped me ease myself back onto the pillows. 'What...' I tried to speak, but stopped when my voice didn't come out properly. It was croaky and scratchy, and my throat burned.

Dimitri sat down carefully on the mattress beside me. He met my gaze, and answered my unspoken questions.

'Doro's gone. I took care of him,' Dimitri said, his voice low and soft. He must have caught the look in my eyes, because he clarified, 'I didn't kill him. I came close, but I didn't. I can't kill another of Mikhail's men, especially not because of you. I called Mikhail, and he sent some guys to pick up Doro. They'll deal with him.'

I blinked up at Dimitri. More tears threatened to

overflow, but I wouldn't let myself cry in front of him.

'I heard you scream,' Dimitri continued. 'I heard stuff smashing. I knew something was wrong. Had to break in your door. I'll fix it for you.'

Opening my mouth, I tried to speak again. 'Thank you.' My words came out, but it didn't sound like my voice.

'I cleaned up your face,' Dimitri told me. 'Don't touch the dressing. You're lucky—your nose isn't broken, but you will have some nasty bruising. It's coming up already.'

I closed my eyes. First, Tony ripped out my hair and left me with a bald patch, then Doro messed up my face. I wasn't a vain person, but these injuries made me angry.

'You have bruising on your neck, too,' Dimitri continued. 'Probably elsewhere over your body, too. I didn't want to check while you were unconscious.'

I nodded, slowly. Reaching to the nightstand, Dimitri handed me some painkillers, and helped me drink some water. My throat resisted, but I managed to swallow.

'Sleep,' Dimitri commanded gently. 'I'll be on the sofa. I'm not leaving.'

Again, I nodded, and let my heavy eyelids drift shut.

***

I don't know how long I slept for, but when I woke up again, light filtered through the bedroom blinds. It took only seconds until the pain set in, and I groaned. Struggling into an upright position, I was just able to swing my legs over the side of the bed. My stomach ached like I'd just done an intense ab workout, only worse, and I felt pain through my ribs, too. Slowly, I raised to my feet, bracing myself against the wall as more pain radiated through me.

Shuffling to the door, I emerged into the lounge and was welcomed by the smell of fresh coffee. Through the kitchen doorway, I could see Dimitri standing at the stove, shirtless, with his back to me.

He must have heard me, because he turned, and our eyes met. Setting aside a pan of whatever he was cooking, Dimitri crossed the room quickly to be at my side. He helped me to the bathroom, out of my bloody clothes and into the shower, which turned out to be more painful than I could have ever imagined. Every inch of me hurt, inside and out. My face stung, my throat burned, my nose ached. I wished I had a bathtub, but Dimitri stood under the hot water with me, gently using a cloth to rinse the remaining blood off of my skin. He used his fingers to detangle my hair, and left a trail of the barest kisses across my shoulders. I relaxed into him, and let myself find comfort in his gentle arms.

After my shower, I finally forced myself to look into the mirror, and flinched at my reflection. Bruising spread over my stomach and right hip, and around my neck in an ugly dark ring. My nose was bruised, too, the purple shadows billowing out underneath my eyes, and my lip was split. By the far the worst thing, though, was the damp dressing over my left cheek. I ripped it off, against Dimitri's protests, and saw a long, red slice through my raw skin. It was thin and clean, but I knew that I would be left with a scar, and once more had to force back tears. I would be reminded of this every day for the rest of my life.

Pulling myself away from the mirror, I let Dimitri gently towel me dry, and help me into a pair of shorts and a camisole. Settling me onto the couch, Dimitri headed back to the kitchen, returning quickly with a bowl of hot soup. He must have gone to the store down the street, because my fridge had been empty. I appreciated the gesture.

'Drink it slow,' he told me, 'You won't be able to eat properly for a little while.'

I nodded, and winced as the warm liquid burned my throat, but I was so hungry that I had to persevere. Dimitri watched me, and I watched him back. I couldn't quite process the image of him here in my apartment, tracksuit bottoms slung low on his hips, helping me in the shower and cooking me lunch. This was just so different to the memories I had of him as Mikhail's right hand man, shooting a kid in the head, beating Tony unconscious outside the club... And it was moments like this that continued to make it harder for me to remind myself of those images. Because I knew that this was the *real* Dimitri. A few days ago, I had never wanted to see him again, and now he was the only thing holding me together.

'Thank you,' I croaked, using my voice for the first time. 'For everything.'

Dimitri took a seat opposite me on the coffee table. 'Mikhail wanted to come over and talk to you. I told him no.'

'Why?' I asked, my stomach fluttering. Of course Mikhail would want to know why Doro hurt me so badly, but I had no idea what to tell him.

Dimitri paused, rubbing a hand over the light stubble on his jaw. 'Why did Doro do this?' he asked the unanswerable.

'I... I can't tell you.' My gaze dropped to the floor.

Dimitri's hands brushed up my bare thighs. 'I don't have to tell Mikhail.'

I shook my head, still unable to look at him. 'I'm sorry.' It hurt to talk.

His hands pulled away, and I felt him stand, walk away. A crash from the kitchen made me jump, and I looked up to see Dimitri tossing plates into the sink so hard that they probably smashed. When he turned back towards me, his face had taken on that careful blankness that he usually displayed. It made me feel cold inside, because it meant that he was closed off again.

I stood, stepping towards him, but he shook his head, halting me in my tracks. He didn't want me to be near him. The stab of hurt I felt in my chest was irrational, but real. Still, I knew better than to push Dimitri when he clearly wanted space, so I turned and retreated into my bedroom.

***

The next morning, I woke early, while it was still dark, but couldn't fall back asleep, so I dragged my heavy body out of bed. In the lounge, I was startled to see the light on, and Dimitri working on the front door. A tool kit lay open on the floor next to him, and I realised he was repairing whatever damage he'd done when he broke in to save me from Doro.

'What time is it?' I croaked.

He didn't turn to look at me. 'After five.'

'You're fixing the door at five in the morning?' I brushed sleep out of my eyes, confused.

'Yeah.' He shrugged one shoulder, his back still facing me.

'Why?'

He paused, but answered. 'Couldn't leave you on your own. Couldn't sleep. Needed to do something.'

My stomach pinched. I walked carefully across the room to him, reaching a hand up to brush over his back, feeling the carved muscles through his thin T-shirt. He froze, his hands stilling in their work, and I wrapped my arms gently around his body, allowing my hands to trail over his stomach. I couldn't rest my face on his back, due to my injuries, but I was close enough to breathe in the familiar scent of him. I felt him exhale, and he dropped whatever tool he'd been holding onto the floor.

'Help me back to bed?' I whispered into his T-shirt.

He turned, carefully so as not to hurt me, and I looked up to meet his gaze. His expression was indecipherable, but I could see the heat behind his eyes. Minutes later, we were back in the bedroom, Dimitri holding me together as only he could. Afterwards, we were both finally able to sleep. The only time I ever really slept well anymore was when he was next to me.

Chapter Twenty-Three

When we woke again, the sun had risen, and Dimitri's phone was vibrating violently on the nightstand. He answered it, listened for barely thirty seconds, then hung up without a word.

Turning to me, his jaw set, he spoke in an empty tone, 'Mikhail's coming over. Now.'

Groaning, I pulled myself out of bed and dressed in a pair of leggings and a loose sweater. Dimitri and I waited together on the couch, silent tension clouding the room. I was frantically trying to come up with a convincing lie to tell the scariest man I'd ever met, while Dimitri seemed to be purposefully ignoring me.

Until finally, he spoke. 'Have you figured out what to tell Mikhail yet?'

I shook my head, and sighed. I couldn't think of anything believable. I was starting to freak out; if I didn't come up with something pretty damn quickly, Mikhail would be well on the way to figuring out that something was going on.

Dimitri exhaled sharply. 'Doro was mad at you, about you stopping him from pounding on that bartender kid. He isn't happy that you and I are together. Doro has always had a bit of a problem with me.' He signed, thinking. 'Doro and I argued, and he hurt you as a way of getting to me.'

I stared over at Dimitri. He was going to lie to Mikhail for me. Again. But wait. 'You want to tell Mikhail that you and I are together?'

Dimitri met my gaze, raising an eyebrow. 'Unless you can come up with a better story about why Doro did this, or you decide to tell the truth, I don't see another option.'

I swallowed thickly, an unfamiliar emotion twisting my stomach. 'You're gonna lie to Mikhail, to cover for me?' My voice sounded strange, and not just because of the damage to my vocal cords.

Dimitri nodded, holding my gaze, as if ensuring that I believed him. He reached up, brushing a strand of hair away from my face.

I felt guilty. Dimitri knew I wasn't telling the truth, not even to him, and yet he was willing to lie to Mikhail for me. He'd already covered for me when I couldn't go through with my initiation, and he'd been there for me when I needed him, almost since the first moment I met him. Yet, ultimately, I was going to turn Dimitri over to the police. I had no choice; that was my job.

My dangerous thoughts were interrupted by a hard knock at the door. I went to answer it, and had barely opened the door before Mikhail stormed inside. Dimitri rose to his feet, and the two men faced one another. Apparently, neither of them wanted to be the first to take a seat, but since my body still ached all over, I decided to ignore their power play and return to the couch.

Mikhail folded his arms across his broad chest, leaning back against the wall opposite me, and regarding me with a distinctly displeased expression. He was very intimidating. 'Are you going to tell me what happened?'

'Doro hasn't said anything?' I asked, just to be clear before I told my fabricated version of events.

'Not one word,' Mikhail replied, the angry edge to his voice slicing through the room. 'So you better start talking, Mari.'

'It was personal,' I began. 'It had nothing to do with the business. Doro was angry at me because I stopped him from beating up Tad.'

'Who is Tad?' Mikhail demanded, before recalling, 'That bartender from *Arrows*?'

The harshness of his tone almost made me flinch. 'Yeah.'

'Doro has a problem with me, too,' Dimitri interjected, mirroring Mikhail's power stance from across the room. 'He always has — you know that. I told him to back off, leave Mari alone. Guess he didn't like it, because next thing I know I'm coming home to hear him beating the crap out of her.'

'You're saying he beat Mari to punish you?' Mikhail asked, raising an incredulous eyebrow.

Dimitri shrugged.

Mikhail regarded Dimitri and I, flicking his hard gaze between us, deciding whether to believe our story. 'You two seem to be causing me a lot of problems recently,' he warned.

My heartbeat quickened, and I glanced over at Dimitri, who looked calm, bored even. I tried to mirror his expression.

'Both of you, stay away from Doro,' Mikhail ordered, harshly. 'I'll give him the same instruction.' He pushed away from the wall and started towards the door. 'You two need to get it together, now. Or I'll do it for you.' With that, he left, slamming to the door behind him so hard I feared it might break again. Luckily, Dimitri's handiwork was solid.

I let out a deep breath, running my hands over my hair. I didn't like the feeling of being in Mikhail's bad books. When I looked over to Dimitri, he gave me a small nod, calming the butterflies in my stomach.

'I owe you,' I told him.

He regarded me, looking so appealing and at home leaning against the wall where just hours earlier I'd been struggling to breathe. He said nothing.

***

That night, Dimitri had to work, and I called in sick to the bar again. I couldn't show my face like this. I hadn't expected Dimitri to come back to mine again when he finished his job, but he did, arriving a little after midnight.

'What's up?' I asked when I let him in. I'd been in bed, but not asleep.

He regarded me, his face blank. 'I need to ask you something.'

I frowned, lowering myself carefully onto the sofa. Dimitri remained standing. Something was obviously wrong, and my stomach stirred nervously.

'What?' I asked.

'Are you sleeping with Doro?'

I blanched. 'What?' I choked. 'Are you serious?'

Dimitri raised his eyebrows. He *was* serious.

'Oh, my God. No.' I stood up. 'Dimitri, are you insane? Why would you think that?'

'Doro introduced me to you. You've obviously known him for a while. It would explain why he attacked you, if he knew you and I were banging, too.'

I flinched at his description of our intimacy, hurt by both the harshness of his words and the accusation itself. 'I've known him for a long time, that's true, but nothing has ever happened between him and me. Did he say something to you?'

Dimitri lifted his chin, which I took as confirmation. Damn Doro — beating me to a pulp obviously hadn't been enough, so now I guessed he was trying to do whatever he could to hurt me from the distance that Mikhail had enforced between us. The fact that he'd known to target my relationship with Dimitri in order to upset me wasn't a good sign... and neither was the fact that it had apparently worked.

'Well, whatever he told you, don't believe it. He's lost

his way, he's in a bad place,' I said, speaking the truth for once.

Dimitri said nothing still, and my hurt started to bubble into anger.

'Look, if you really think I'd sleep with Doro, then I guess you don't know me at all,' I said, a harsh snap to my voice. 'And honestly, I'm offended. How could you accuse me of that? I'm with you. I guess whatever is going on between us means a lot more to me than it does to you.'

Rage flared in Dimitri's eyes. 'You don't get to say that.' His voice was low, verging on dangerous. 'You have no idea what I've done for you.'

A stab of guilt pierced my chest. 'No, of course I know. You've done a lot for me, more than I deserve.'

Dimitri held my gaze.

I took a step forward. 'Believe me, I know just how much I owe you. Dimitri, there is honestly nothing going on with Doro and me, there *never* has been.'

'Then why did he try to kill you?' Dimitri demanded. 'You really gotta tell me something, Mari. I lied for you.'

'I know! I appreciate that, more than you realise,' I desperately tried to implore him with my eyes, to make him understand that I wasn't just being deceptive for the hell of it. 'But I can't tell you. It's not that I don't want to — if I could, I would.'

'Bullshit!' Dimitri's voice exploded, and I shrank back against the loud anger.

My head span, panic edging into my mind. I couldn't keep lying to him, I was running out of excuses. If I told him the truth, there was no way he wouldn't tell Mikhail, and I'd end up dead. But if I didn't tell him, I knew I was going to lose him, and not only would that be catastrophic for the purposes of my job here, but for me personally. Dimitri was genuinely the only reason I was still standing here, both because he'd saved my life, and because he was keeping me sane.

'Doro and I used to work together,' I said, trying to take as much from the truth as I could. 'That's how I know him. He hurt me because he thinks I betrayed him. Which I kind of did, but only for his own good.'

Dimitri frowned, his perfect face contorted by confusion and anger. 'Work where?'

'Does that matter?' I asked, hearing the alarm in my own voice.

'Why don't you trust me?' Dimitri demanded, throwing his hands up. 'I lied for you, I killed for you. I told you my most painful experiences, things about my job that could get me killed. Hell, I haven't even slept next to anyone since Izzy died. I haven't trusted anyone enough not to kill me or steal all my goddamn money while my eyes were shut! You're the first person, Mari. I *trusted* you. And I don't even know you!'

I blinked, and sank down onto the sofa again, my legs refusing to hold me up any longer. Dimitri's outburst caught me completely off guard—this was so out of character for him, to show any emotion. He must be really pissed off at me. And of course, he had every right to be. He really had risked a lot for me, lying to Mikhail just to keep me safe, trusting me with everything he had.

'I'm sorry,' I said, my voice shaking with the pressure of the situation. 'It's complicated. I wish I could tell you, I just...' I broke off, closing my eyes against the tears that threatened to fall. It was official, I was in far too deep with my relationship with Dimitri.

'Then we're done.' His voice was hard, cold, and emotionless. It sliced through me like Doro's knife had cut through my skin.

I squeezed my eyes shut, hating how pathetic I must look. I wanted to beg him to stay, to tell him the truth, but of course I couldn't. I wouldn't. When I finally opened my eyes, he was gone.

Chapter Twenty-Four

For days, I hid out in my apartment wallowing in self-pity. I screened calls from Jono, and was pretty sure that I had lost my bar job by that point, and ignored the few texts I received from Nina, too. No one else contacted me, and that was fine with me. At first, all I wanted to do was get drunk and sleep all day, but leaving the house to buy alcohol was too much effort for my aching body, so I resorted to just the latter part of that idea.

It didn't take long for the weekend to roll around, and I was eating leftover takeout pizza on the couch and watching reality TV when my phone rang. I glanced at the screen with no intention of answering, until I saw that it was Fabio, and realised it was likely about a job. As much as my body hurt, and as heavy as my chest felt, I knew I couldn't forget the reason that I was here in the first place.

'Hey.' My voice sounded croaky when I answered the call, and I guessed it was probably because I hadn't used it in days.

'Mari, hey!' I could hear the smile in Fabio's voice, and it made me feel a little better. He asked me to meet him at a diner downtown in an hour. Apparently there was a big job coming up that required a face-to-face briefing. So after I hung up, I dragged my reluctant body to the shower, got myself dressed in a pair of leggings and a hooded sweater. Daring to look in the mirror before I left, I cringed. My bruises were a colourful array of purple and green, while the cut on my cheek had now scabbed over, making it look ragged and angry. I debated trying to cover some of the damage with makeup, but I knew that not only would that hurt, I would probably just make myself look worse; my makeup skills were pretty minimal. Instead, I simply threw my hair up into a ponytail and called it a day.

It was after ten p.m. by the time I started my journey to the diner, so at least the darkness provided some disguise over my disfigured face. When I reached the diner, I wasn't surprised by its back alley location or grimy interior. Automatically scanning the room, I saw that there were a couple of older working women at the bar drinking Irish coffees, and a trucker tucking into a burger in the corner. Besides them, Fabio was the only other patron, waiting for me in a booth at the back of the room, hunched over a steaming mug.

I slid over the cracked vinyl seat opposite him. 'Hey.'

He glanced up with an automatic smile, but his expression faltered, and he did a double take when he saw my face. 'What the hell, Mari?'

I shrugged off his concern, and gestured to his face, noticing that he too was sporting a killer black eye. 'Looks like we've both been in the wars.'

'Yeah, and you look like you definitely lost the battle.'

'Thanks,' I replied dryly. Reaching over the table, I took Fabio's coffee, the warm liquid sliding down my still-delicate throat. 'So, what's going on?' I asked.

'Mikhail wanted me to fill you in for the job tonight. Or tomorrow morning, I guess. It's a three a.m. gig.'

I groaned inwardly. 'Go on then, explain.'

'We've got a big shipment coming in from Ireland — guns, ammo, hard-core shit. But the coppers have been all over our warehouses recently, so we're borrowing space from the Thais in exchange for a reduced sale.'

I leaned forward. This sounded intriguing. 'What do you need me for?'

'We need all the man power we've got. You're just gonna need to keep watch, okay? Look out for police, or anyone else coming too close. The warehouse is on the industrial estate nearby, so I'll show you, okay? Give you the logistics, escape routes, you know.'

I nodded, finishing up the last of Fabio's coffee before following him out of the diner. We walked for less than five minutes through the estate until we reached our borrowed warehouse. It looked abandoned. Maybe that was the point.

I made a mental note of the street and location — not only so that I would find it when I returned in the early hours, but also because this was it. I was done tip-toeing around, trying to gain trust and favour. Dimitri calling time on whatever we'd had felt a little too much like heartbreak for my own good, but maybe it had knocked some sense back into me. I had a goal here, and I was going to achieve it. And I was starting to realise that the sooner I did, the better for everyone. Especially me.

So this was it. My chance to catch a whole bunch of Mikhail's men in receiving an illegally smuggled shipment of stolen artillery. That was a jail sentence in itself, and I knew for a fact that most of the men who'd be involved would have outstanding arrest warrants or be suspects in other crimes, too — it would be a sweep.

Once Fabio had given me a tour of the surrounding alley ways to highlight the possible ways we might be compromised, and also the best ways to escape, he walked me back to my neighbourhood. When we passed *Arrows*, I threw my hood up and kept my head down. I didn't have time for the drama that would occur if Jono caught sight of me, especially looking like this.

Fabio noticed my behaviour. 'You gonna tell me how your face got all messed up?'

I shot him a look. 'Someone beat me, cut me, and slammed my face into a door frame.'

He gave a low whistle. 'Damn. On the job? I've had a couple dicey deals recently, apparently our product quality is on the decline. Did someone kick off?'

'Nah, it was personal.' I was being deliberately evasive. If Fabio didn't already know who had done this to me, then chances were that Mikhail didn't want him to know, and that suited me just fine.

At my building, we said goodbye, and I promised to be at the warehouse on time, at promptly three a.m. Delightful. Once inside, I went straight for my hidden work phone and dialled Taylor. He picked up quickly, despite the hour.

He answered immediately. 'Hello.'

'We're getting a huge shipment of illegal artillery into a warehouse downtown at 3am,' I blurted before I could change my mind. 'There's gonna be stolen goods, illegally smuggled into the country. Lots of Mikhail's men, carrying weapons, maybe drugs.'

Taylor hesitated, and I worried for a second that I'd been wrong about this goldmine, but then he exhaled heavily. 'This is great!' The excitement in his voice fuelled my own adrenaline. 'I'll make the arrangements for officers at the scene. They won't know you, so prepare to get arrested if you're caught. We'll have to keep you overnight to make it look realistic.'

'Don't worry. I won't be caught.' I gave him the address, and hung up.

Lying back on my bed, my thoughts turned to Dimitri. I imagined seeing him in handcuffs, in the back of a police car, being taken to a prison he'd never be released from. I sat up. I couldn't do this. I had to warn him. My legs jumped into action, and I'd climbed the stairs to Dimitri's front door before I even realised I was moving.

I knocked, and he answered quickly. Immediately I noticed that he was shirtless, his hair was ruffled, and his pupils were blown wide; his eyebrows shot up and his nostrils flared when he saw me. He looked more than a little crazy. I'd never seen him look so agitated.

'Uh. Hey.' I said, shaken back to reality by Dimitri's appearance, and the fact that this was the first time I'd seen him since he walked away from me.

'What are you doing here?' His voice was empty, but weirdly, the familiarity of his cold tone was reassuring.

'Are you on for the warehouse job in the morning?' I asked.

'Yeah.' Dimitri frowned, folding his arms across his bare chest in a way that drew my eyes to his biceps. 'Why? Are you?'

'Yeah. Look…' I wanted to warn him, but I didn't know how to without giving myself away entirely. 'We need to talk.'

Dimitri opened his mouth to reply, but was interrupted by a soft, female voice cooing from inside his apartment. 'Who's at the door, D?'

I froze, staring up at Dimitri's hooded eyes. The hot talons of jealousy raked my stomach. Of course, I knew how irrational I was being, but I still couldn't quell the churn of anger inside me. Squaring my jaw, I bit down the snarky remark I wanted to snap, and instead managed to speak calmly, 'I'll wait for you. We'll walk to the warehouse together. I need to talk to you. It's not about us. OK?'

Dimitri nodded, mutely.

'Baby?' The mystery girl called from inside again. 'Who is it?'

'No one, I'll be right there,' Dimitri called over his shoulder. For a second, he looked me right in the eye, a million unspoken words pouring between us. Then, he turned away, and closed the door in my face.

Chapter Twenty-Five

The hours passed quickly, during which time I paced the entire length of my apartment at least fifty times, steeled my nerves with a little alcohol, and changed into what I now considered to be my *work clothes*; black jeans, boots, sweater, jacket. I slipped my hands into a pair of thin leather gloves and slicked my hair back into a ponytail. There was nothing to be done about my face, and I hoped that maybe displaying my bruises proudly would earn me acceptance among Mikhail's men.

Lastly, I tucked the gun Mikhail had given me into the band of my jeans. Then I was really ready. At two thirty, I stepped out of my apartment and waited in the stairwell for Dimitri, since I wasn't totally convinced he would've knocked on my door, despite his silent agreement earlier. He appeared a few minutes later, nodding at me in a silent greeting.

I was totally pumped with both adrenaline and whiskey, but I still didn't have it in me to discuss the girl in Dimitri's apartment. I was angry, of course, but I'd managed to talk myself into some semblance of reasonable thought; it was none of my business if Dimitri was sleeping with someone else. It's not like we were ever really a couple, and he'd ended things days ago. Besides, whatever I felt for Dimitri was pointless and stupid and probably some variation of Stockholm syndrome — a symptom of living a lie.

Outside, the temperature had dropped further, so I picked up my speed as we walked. Dimitri kept up easily, remaining silent. I still wanted to warn him about the police that would be showing up at the warehouse, because even though I hated him right in that moment, I still couldn't handle the image of him getting caught. But despite my hours of thinking of nothing but this, I still didn't know how to bring it up.

'Dimitri,' I began, and he looked over at me as we continued to walk. 'If the police show up tonight, promise you'll get out of there as quickly as you can. I know you have loyalty to Mikhail and the other men, but if you get arrested for this, you'll be put away for a very long time.'

'The police won't come,' Dimitri replied, off hand.

'They will,' I argued.

Dimitri came to a sudden stop, and I had to turn around to look back at him.

'How do you know the police will show up?' Dimitri asked, suspicion laced in his cold voice.

'Because we're doing something illegal?' I tried to feign innocence. 'There's gonna be a lot of people at a random warehouse at 3am — don't you think that will raise a little suspicion if anyone sees us?'

Dimitri frowned, clearly uncertain of my explanation. 'You know very well that I can't just run away if the cops do show up.'

I took a step towards him, meeting his gaze earnestly. 'I'm asking you to. I can't watch you get arrested.'

'Why?' Dimitri challenged, a harsh edge to his voice.

'You know why,' I struggled to keep my own voice unaffected.

Dimitri exhaled sharply, lurching into movement as he brushed past me and continued along the dark street. I had to hurry to keep up with his angry stride. He clearly didn't think that the police busting their operation was a likely possibility, and there was no way that I could tell him the truth, but it killed me to stay quiet. Still, the fact that I really *would* be killed if I did spill the beans prevented me from doing so.

We moved through the streets in silence towards the industrial district, neither of us having anything more to say. My heartbeat spiked with anticipation the nearer we got, but my conscience nagged at the back of my mind. It reminded me how welcoming Val had been to me, and how Fabio had been a real friend, and that Dimitri and I shared some kind of bond, no matter how wrong or twisted it was. And these were the people who were walking unwittingly into a police raid, where they'd be arrested and sentenced to prison for the majority of their prime years. And all that was because of me.

Of course, that was the whole purpose of me being here.

My mind span, and I didn't know what to make of my conflicting emotions. I was forced to push my inner turmoil aside when we reached the industrial district and the warehouse came into view.

I caught Dimitri's arm as we reached the top of the alleyway. He tensed, and turned to look at me, although he didn't pull his arm away. I met his gaze, trying to implore him with my own. 'Dimitri, I'm not kidding. I just have this really strong feeling that this is going to go bad.'

'It won't.'

'But if it does,' I insisted, 'you have to get out of there. Get Val, since I know you won't leave him, and get out. Promise me.'

Dimitri's expression shifted almost imperceptibly. 'Mari…'

I let my hand trail down from where I gripped his arm, over the soft material of his sweater, until my hand touched his. I wished I wasn't wearing gloves so that I could feel his skin, but even through the fabric, the familiar shape of his fingers threading through mine did wonders to soothe my overwrought nerves.

For a few seconds, we stood there in the dark alleyway, holding onto each other. Memories fluttered behind my eyes; Dimitri's peaceful face as he slept, his rare laughter, the feel of his hair under my fingers, the addictive roughness of his hands on my face. I blinked, and Dimitri looked away, and the moment was gone.

He pulled his hand away from mine and stalked ahead. I took a deep breath, taking the time to pull myself together before I, too, headed towards the warehouse. Dimitri disappeared inside while I noticed Fabio standing outside with a cigarette between his lips. He smiled when he saw me approaching.

'Hey.' He offered me a drag of his cigarette, and I declined. 'You ready for this?'

I shrugged. 'I have no idea. I'll let you know afterwards.'

Fabio laughed. Behind us, a car pulled up, and two of Mikhail's men climbed out. Beside it, three other cars were parked up. From inside the warehouse, the faint hum of quiet chatter told me that most of the men had arrived already. My heart thumped. Glancing back to Fabio, I was struck by the sudden youthfulness of his face. He had beautiful, clear, caramel skin, his eyes glittering with humour, and his white teeth always on display. He was no younger than I was, but he had this indescribable innocence surrounding him. I could tell that he was just lost, stuck in a life of crime because he didn't think he had any other options. Obviously, he broke the law, a lot, but I was starting to think that that didn't necessarily make a person bad.

Reaching up, I locked my arms around Fabio's shoulders, pulling him into a hug.

His arms enveloped me, so easily accepting of affection. So different to Dimitri. 'Everything okay?' Fabio asked, his breath warm on my neck.

'I just want you to know how much your friendship means to me.'

I felt Fabio smile, and he planted the lightest of kisses beneath my earlobe. 'Me, too.'

Pulling away, I forced myself to walk away and into the warehouse, leaving him to finish his cigarette in peace. Inside, there were over a dozen men, most of whom I only vaguely recognised. Mikhail stood in the centre, attention focused on the mobile phone in his hands. I surveyed the area quickly; crates were stacked along the far wall of the warehouse, which would give some shelter, and there was a back door as well as a side exit. When my roaming eyes saw Dimitri, however, they caught. He was leaning very casually against an empty crate, one hand in the pocket of his jeans. Beside him, Val was speaking, moving his hands animatedly, but even from this distance I could tell that Dimitri was barely listening. His dark eyes were focussed on me, and I knew that he'd been watching me from the second I walked into the warehouse.

The sound of a truck pulling up outside drew my attention. A large man dressed all in black barrelled into the warehouse, commanding the room. Mikhail greeted him with an informal handshake. Behind him, more men appeared, carrying boxes and metal tubing — innocent looking items that could be placed on any cargo truck, but which I knew contained enough illegal weaponry to warrant a 25-year sentence.

Mikhail began shouting orders; he sent his strongest men, including Dimitri, to unload the trucks that were rolling up outside. Others were on assembly duty, so that the guns would be ready for immediate delivery tonight; Mikhail wouldn't hold onto these weapons for any longer than he had too—the faster the turnover, the faster he was in the clear, and holding the cash in his hands.

As for me, I was sent to be a lookout at the back door of the warehouse. It was not an ideal situation, since I was pretty much out of the action. Beside me, my lookout partner — Jag, a thickset man in his fifties with whom I'd worked previously — shifted on his feet impatiently. My understanding was that he desperately wanted to be in on the action, but Mikhail had stuck him on the boring lookout duty instead. I wondered if Jag had done something to anger Mikhail, or if he'd just drawn the short straw for the evening. But Jag was a silent type of guy, so he wasn't sharing the information, and to be honest, at that particular moment, I was glad of the quiet.

I stared out into the dark yard; concentrated on filtering out the noise of the men unloading and unpacking the guns in the warehouse behind me in favour of the distant hum of traffic on the nearby road. I knew that the police wouldn't use sirens, but I waited for the sound of several slow approaching vehicles, which I would take as confirmation of their arrival.

Time ticked by, and my heart beat accelerated with each passing minute. It was almost four a.m., and I was starting to lose hope of the police turning up at all, but then I heard the commotion I'd been waiting for.

'Cops!' A voice boomed from inside the warehouse.

Jag sprang into action, running into the warehouse, gun drawn. I stayed where I was for a second, listening, until I heard the faint roll of tyres over gravel. I exhaled in relief; they were approaching from this side, too. Meaning that most of the men inside wouldn't be able to escape.

I took a breath, focussing myself. Now I knew that this was really happening, I had to pull myself together, and act as panicked as the rest of Mikhail's employees. Whirling on my heel, I raced into the warehouse.

'They're back here, too!' I yelled.

Around me, chaos had erupted; men were frantically grabbing boxes and weapons scattered across the floor.

The side door was uncovered by police, so they were loading out that way.

'Get the stuff out! Get it to the buyers no matter what!' Mikhail bellowed.

My eyes darted around until I found Dimitri, hurrying out of the side door with an armful of automatic rifles. Val followed close on his heels. My heart pounded.

'Mari!' Mikhail's voice commanded my attention, and I turned to see him heading towards the back entrance. 'With me, now!'

He tossed a backpack at me. I didn't have time to think, and I caught it automatically. It was heavy and awkwardly shaped; full of weapons, or at least, parts of them. I swung it quickly over my shoulders before following Mikhail out into the rear yard.

Two police cars hurtled towards us, and Mikhail cursed. Quickly, he ducked behind a stack of discarded crates, and I followed blindly. We crouched down to run along behind them until we were almost out of the yard. Mikhail paused, watching as the police exited their cars and headed into the warehouse, weapons drawn.

Mikhail stood up straight, thinking that he would be out of sight now. But I knew police procedure, and I knew there would be another car waiting in the shadows just outside of the warehouse yard — backup. I grabbed Mikhail's arm, and pulled him back down.

'There's another car out there,' I nodded toward the rear exit. Sure enough, the silhouette of a vehicle could be seen. I could've let Mikhail get arrested, but I knew that the arrest wouldn't be permanent; he had no weapons on him—he'd given the backpack to me for a reason. And letting him get arrested for this wasn't the plan; we were playing the long game. Besides, protecting him would cement his trust in me.

'Shit,' Mikhail hissed, realising that his planned exit

route was now no longer a viable option. He looked around, and his gaze settled on the tall wire fence behind us. It encaged the whole yard, save for the front and rear exits. I eyed the fence; Mikhail was right, it was our only way out of here now, but I seriously doubted my ability to climb it, especially with this bag on my back.

Luckily, that wasn't what Mikhail had in mind; instead, he drew out a long knife from beneath the leg of his jeans, cutting deftly through the flimsy wire. He created a slit through which we could squeeze, although the bulky bag on my back didn't make it easy. Once we were through, Mikhail led the way down a side alley which brought us around to the front of the warehouse. We peered out of the alleyway, with a limited view of the front yard. The trucks had gone, which meant that most of the guns had been successfully removed. Damn — that meant most of the evidence was gone. A few cars remained, though, so not everyone had managed to get away. Mikhail's car was still there, too, of course, although to get to it, we'd have to run straight across the front yard of the warehouse. I could hear police yelling inside; they were close, and there was no way that they wouldn't see us running past.

'Duck down low, and move fast,' Mikhail hissed at me, before making a break for it.

I cursed under my breath, and ran for it. I was across to the other side of the yard in a matter of seconds, so I didn't get a good look inside the warehouse, but there were definitely arrests being made. By a stroke of dumb luck, Mikhail and I made it to his car unseen, and he yanked the passenger door open.

'You drive, I'll shoot,' he instructed me.

I shot him a wide-eyed glance, but my adrenaline acted for me, and I threw myself into the driver's side before I even realised I was moving, finding the keys already in the ignition.

'Reverse!' Mikhail commanded.

I did so, giving him a perfect shot into the warehouse through his cracked window. Gun fire exploded through the air. Mikhail ducked low, and I felt the impact of bullets hitting the car in return to his attack. Screw this — I hit the accelerator, and we peeled away. As I raced down the alley, ignoring Mikhail's yelling, I noticed the slumped silhouette of bodies on the ground, beside a damaged police vehicle. Two bodies. If one was Dimitri, I couldn't tell.

Chapter Twenty-Six

Once he'd finished screaming at me about "running away too early" — because apparently he'd wanted to stay there and get shot at some more — Mikhail directed me onto the highway and North, not to the Beach as I'd expected. He made several calls while I drove in stunned silence, telling each responder to head up to the cabins, wherever that was.

'Did you see who was arrested?' I asked when he was apparently done with this phone calls. I didn't even care this time when my voice shook.

'Vlad, Benny, Fabio, at least two others.' Mikhail cursed violently, slamming his fist into the already dented dashboard. 'That's nearly half the goddamn crew I had on tonight! How the hell did the cops get wind of this?'

His question was rhetorical, and I stayed silent. Fabio had been arrested. My heart sank under the weight of crushing guilt. And yet, I couldn't help but feel relieved that Mikhail hadn't seen Dimitri being arrested in the warehouse. Of course, he admitted that he hadn't been able to identify everyone in there, but I was sure that he'd have noticed his right-hand man. However, the image of those bodies on the ground of that dirty alleyway wouldn't disappear. Dimitri could be dead. I had no idea. I felt like I was going to be sick.

Forcing myself to hold it together, I drove for over half an hour until Mikhail directed me off at an exit. Very quickly after that, I found myself weaving through country roads, heading up towards the Nature Reserve. We were far out of the City now, and I finally found a voice to ask Mikhail exactly where we were going.

'I have a cabin at the lakes. Not in my name, so it's safe. We'll meet everyone there.'

'Okay.' I'd managed to get a handle on the shake in

my voice, but my hands were unsteady, an after effect of the adrenaline I'd burnt at the warehouse, and I had to grip the wheel hard to hide it.

'Mari,' Mikhail said, in a much calmer voice. I glanced over at him, and he gave me a small nod of approval. 'You were valuable tonight.'

I nodded in return, but still all I could think of were those bodies. I don't know how much longer we travelled for until we finally arrived at the lakes, and Mikhail directed me up to a secluded cabin. I pulled up outside and opened my door, glad to be out of the vehicle and to finally take the backpack off my shoulders, dropping it into the footwell of the passenger seat. Before me was a large, old-fashioned wooden cabin. When Mikhail led me inside, I saw that there was a real fireplace and taxidermy deer heads on the walls. The large living space was filled with worn out, old furniture, and lit by dim wall lamps. Only two men had arrived already: Jag and Alexander.

'Did Dimitri get out?' I asked them, my heart pounding.

Jag shook his head. 'No idea, hon. Sorry.'

I covered my face with my icy hands. Behind me, I felt a hand on my shoulder. I turned to see Mikhail, and the strange, calm expression on his face made me feel colder than I'd ever felt in my entire life.

'There were bodies on the ground,' I told Mikhail, struggling to keep my voice level.

He nodded. 'I didn't see who.'

'Me neither.' I felt my heart against my ribs, and took a deep breath. I couldn't show any emotion around these men. I headed over to the sofa, which was printed with the same pattern as my grandmother's curtains had been twenty years ago, pulling my knees up underneath me and staring out the window next to me at the hills adorned with fir trees. I should have told Dimitri the truth, then he would have believed me about the police showing up, and he would have been able to get out of there faster. This was all my fault. I'd sentenced Fabio to spend the rest of his young life in prison, and Dimitri could be dead. I should have told him.

Hell, I shouldn't have even agreed to this undercover job in the first place. I should have known that I couldn't handle it. Because I wasn't handling it. I wasn't even remotely close to handling it. It also occurred to me that a cabin full of Mikhail's men was the worst place to realise this.

I don't know how long I sat there. When the door opened, I looked up eagerly, but it was just some more guys. A few minutes later, Valentin arrived, and at least some of my nerves were calmed, because he smiled at me, which was not an expression I'd expect from someone whose best friend had just died. He sat down beside me, and gathered me into a hug. I let him, forgetting momentarily about the image I wanted to project in front of Mikhail.

When Val pulled away, he met my eyes with his own gentle gaze. 'He's on his way.'

I blinked. 'He's okay?'

Val nodded. 'He delivered the guns. Called me few minutes ago. He'll be here soon.'

A long breath escaped my lips.

Mikhail sat across the room at a mahogany table, pouring a glass of dark liquid, watching the exchange between Valentin and me. 'Dimitri is my best man. He will always be okay.'

I nodded. I accepted a glass of the whiskey when it was passed to me and took a long sip. I sat with my arm touching Val's, waiting, trying to get my thoughts together. All I could think was, what would I have done if Dimitri had been dead?

Some of the men tried to find reception on the fuzzy old TV, while others chatted as if nothing had happened. Mikhail stood by the window, speaking on his phone in a hushed voice. I couldn't make out what he was saying, but even if I had been able to, I doubt the words would have sunk into my memory. I didn't feel like I was really there.

Jag had just managed to find a TV channel that worked, which, at 7a.m., was showing some kind of kids' cartoon, when I saw headlights flash though the window. A car rumbled up to the cabin, and the engine cut out. Seconds later, the door flew open, revealing Dimitri. His eyes immediately scanned the room, and when they found me, I was anchored back into the real world. Val stood, making space on the sofa beside me, which Dimitri instantly filled. He enveloped me into his arms, burying his face in my hair. I took a deep breath, feeling as though it was the first time I'd got any oxygen since we'd left the warehouse. The familiar scent of him warmed me, and everything hurt a little less now that he was holding me.

'I thought you might be dead,' I whispered to him.

Mikhail cleared his throat, commanding the attention of the room. Jag turned off the TV, and Dimitri pulled away from me. There were now eight of us in the room, including Mikhail and myself.

'How did it go?' Mikhail asked Dimitri.

'I took as many guns as we could get out of the warehouse, delivered them to the Thais, but we are down on a lot of the automatics. They're not happy.' Dimitri's voice was deep. 'Did you manage to negotiate?'

Mikhail shook his head. 'They want the rest of the order by Tuesday.'

'It's Sunday,' one of the men at the table pointed out, entirely unnecessarily.

Mikhail shot him a glare. 'I have spoken with Carlos Hernandez. He is willing to sit down with us today.'

I knew from my prep training that Carlos was a local guy with connections to South American gangs, likely the only person Mikhail was in good contact with and who kept a supply of unclaimed guns within the country; there would be no time for an overseas shipment if we needed to deliver by Tuesday.

'His guns are all spliced, repurposed pieces of dangerous shit,' Jag said, almost dismissively, as if he knew Mikhail wouldn't go for this plan.

But I guessed that this was an unusual situation, because Mikhail spat back, 'We do not have the option to be fussy. This is what we are doing.'

Low murmurs echoed around the room. I looked to my left at Dimitri's face, but his jaw was set, he gave nothing away.

Mikhail continued, gesturing to the three men who I didn't know by name. 'You three, take the SUV back to the City. See if you can find out what's happening with those who got arrested. And arrange a meet with the Thais on Tuesday. Val, Jag, check on the clubs and the girls. I'll need you to take over the day to day businesses for the next forty-eight hours. Dimitri, take one of the cars and go deal with Carlos. He's expecting you this afternoon.'

Dimitri nodded mutely.

'And Mari,' Mikhail met my gaze. 'You go with him. You were valuable to me, and this will be a valuable lesson to you.' He paused, smirked, then added, 'And also, you are just Carlos's type.'

I felt Dimitri tense up beside me. 'There are plenty of girls at the club who are Carlos's type.'

'I have asked Mari to go with you,' Mikhail said, his voice low in response to having been challenged on an order.

It seemed that that was the final word, as the room hurried into motion. I followed Dimitri outside to a beat up black car I hadn't seen before. I was barely in the passenger seat when he started the engine and sped angrily away from the cabin.

'You okay?' I ventured to ask.

He didn't reply.

We drove in silence back towards the City. Forty-five minutes later, we were nearly back at the club, but before we reached it, Dimitri took a sharp turn. He drove us down a few unfamiliar side streets, until we reached an empty car park at the beach front. The ocean was dark and still under the rising sun.

'What are we doing here?' I asked, turning to look out the passenger side window for any clues.

I heard a click behind me, and then felt cold metal press into the base of my skull. My breathing stopped. He had a gun to my head.

Slowly, I turned to look at him, turning my palms so they faced upwards where they rested on my thighs, to show I wasn't going to try anything. Instead of racing, my heart seemed to have dropped right into my stomach, and time had slowed. I met Dimitri's gaze. His eyes were cold, empty. He kept the gun pointed right at me, touching my forehead now. He didn't falter. This was not the man I shared a connection with. This was Mikhail's right hand man.

I swallowed. 'What are you doing?' My voice was a murmur.

'You knew the police were coming.'

He knew. I'd given myself away by warning him. I stared at him, not knowing what to say.

Dimitri let out a sharp breath. 'You're not going to deny it?'

'Deny what?' I asked. Beads of sweat formed at my temples. I'd been shot at before, but I'd never had a gun pressed right against my head.

'You're a goddamn cop!' Dimitri yelled, and I jumped.

'No, I...'

He pushed the gun harder into my skin, shoving my head back. 'You knew the police were coming. You're undercover.' I had never heard him sound so dangerous. He was barely contained.

There was no point trying to argue with him. I had no argument. I said nothing.

We were silent for a minute, neither of us moving a muscle. Then Dimitri spoke again. 'How can you even stand to be around me? You must have known exactly who I was before you met me, and all the things I've done. I must repulse you. And yet you were willing to sleep with me, just to get your information. You must be dedicated to your job.'

His insinuation sparked my anger, and I had to reply. 'Sleeping with you was never part of the job. It wasn't like that.'

Dimitri's mouth hardened into a stern line. 'So it's true.'

I held his gaze, trying to keep my expression strong.

He sighed, dropping his head, and finally breaking eye contact. The gun didn't move. 'I believed you. I trusted you. I thought it was real.' He shook his head. He broke my heart.

'It is real, what you and I have. It's real,' I told him, my voice surprisingly steady.

Now he looked up at me again. 'You're good at this. Even now I know you're lying, I still want to believe you.'

'I'm not lying. You're the only thing that's keeping

me sane here.' I sighed. 'I know you won't believe me, but that's the truth.'

His eyes flashed, and I could see that he was torn. But still, he held that gun to my head.

I sighed again. This was it. It was over. I closed my eyes. 'I know you have to kill me. And I'd rather you do it than Mikhail.'

I'd failed. And I was going to die. I'd known weeks ago that Dimitri was going to be my downfall, because I'd let him in, fallen for him. And even now, as I sat there, waiting for him to shoot me, I didn't feel any shame or regret. The clarity of mind that came to me then, waiting for my death, was incredible. I saw everything as it really was. I'd been denying my feelings — telling myself that I was working to the best of my ability, but I'd been distracted, I'd forgotten why I was there. I should have just got in, done my job, and got out. Except that it was too late now. I thought of Dimitri's face — his real face, not his blank mask — and breathed deeply. I was glad that he was the one to kill me.

I waited. I don't know how long for. But then I felt the gun move away from my skin, and heard the safety click into place. I opened my eyes. Dimitri was staring at me with an expression I couldn't decipher, the gun in his lap.

I didn't dare move, or say a word. I just stared right back at him, as his expression gradually softened into his real face.

He reached up to touch my face with a gentle hand, and I didn't flinch. His voice was quiet. 'I'm not going to kill you.'

'You have to,' I told him. 'I'm not stupid. I know what happens to people like me, when we're bad at our jobs and get caught out.'

'You weren't bad at your job. I never suspected you, not until you warned me about the police. And you would never have done that, if we weren't…'

'No, I wouldn't.' I agreed. 'And even though it meant that you figured me out, I'm glad I warned you. If you'd been killed, I wouldn't have been able to live with myself.'

Dimitri frowned, and dropped his hand. 'You'd rather die yourself, than let me get shot down by the police.' It wasn't a question.

I held his gaze. I didn't know how to respond. I leaned across the centre console, slowly, and Dimitri didn't move away. I pressed my lips against his. It took a few seconds, but then he kissed me back, and everything was momentarily OK.

Chapter Twenty-Seven

Dimitri's mouth was hot and demanding, desperate for the comfort provided by human contact. He pulled me on top of him, his hands tangling into my hair. His deft fingers found the zipper on my jacket, and my stomach twisted with anticipation. I unbuckled his jeans quickly, before either of us could think about this and change our minds. He pulled at my waistband, and we undressed just enough to do what we needed to do. It was quick, and raw, and stupid, but it was exactly what we needed.

Afterwards, he held me on his lap, running his hand up and down my back while I buried my face into his neck.

In a way, now that someone had discovered me, I felt real. My life was more at risk, and that made everything one thousand times more real. I could no longer run back to Taylor if things got messy, because if I disappeared, Dimitri would be bound to tell Mikhail about me, and wherever I was, I had no doubt that he'd find a way to get to me. I was compromised, but the only way I could see forward, was to keep playing along until it somehow came to an end. What that end would be, I had no idea, and it was no longer entirely in my control.

I considered the fact that maybe, I couldn't be saved. I breathed in Dimitri. I suddenly understood — really understood — how he felt.

'I'm not going to tell Mikhail.'

Dimitri's voice startled me from my thoughts. I pulled back slightly so that I could see his face. 'Why not?' I asked.

His eyes burned into mine. 'You know why. I guess it's the same reason that I'm not behind bars right now, given all you've seen me do in the past few months.'

I clumsily moved back over into the passenger seat, tugging my clothes back into place. 'So what do we do now?'

Dimitri buttoned his jeans. 'I don't know.' He paused, then said, 'Priority has got to be this meeting with Carlos today. I have to be there, and so do you, if you don't want Mikhail asking questions.'

I frowned. Was he really suggesting we just continue as if he never found out?

'Just, go home, okay? I'll come to your place around 3.'

I sat there for a moment, before realising that Dimitri was waiting for me to get out of the car, which I did without a word. I didn't know what to say. I shut the door, and he drove away.

I had no idea where I was, but I managed to find a train station and get back to my flat, despite the fact that I felt as if I was in some kind of dream. Or nightmare. Dimitri knew who I was. He was going to shoot me, and then he didn't. And now he wanted me to meet with another local gang contact in a few hours. I was confused.

But I was also tired. As soon as my head hit my pillow, I was out.

***

Dimitri knocked at my door a little before 3, and I was ready. I opened the door expecting to head straight out, but instead, Dimitri stepped inside.

He closed the door behind him, and turned to look at me. 'I'm not the target, am I? It's Mikhail. You're building a case against him — you set everything up so he'd want to hire you, and now he trusts you.'

I blinked. Clearly while I'd been sleeping, he'd been figuring it all out.

'You haven't actually seen him do anything yet,' Dimitri continued. 'Sure, he calls the shots, he's got illegal firearms, whatever. But it's not enough to really stick.'

I kept my mouth shut. I still didn't know where I stood.

'Max is not your dad. And Doro, he found out too, didn't he? That's why he tried to kill you, and why he said that shit to me, so I'd call things off with you.'

I said nothing. Dimitri could draw his own conclusions about Doro; exposing myself was one thing, but I could not expose a colleague, even if he had apparently gone rogue.

Dimitri ran a hand over his hair, a movement that had become achingly familiar. 'You planned everything. Working at *Arrows*, and becoming friends with Nina, to get to me, to get to Mikhail.'

He seemed to be waiting for me to confirm his guesses, so I gave a single nod.

'What are you going to do?' I asked.

Dimitri sighed. 'I can't kill you. I can't tell Mikhail, because he'll do worse than kill you. But I can't let you do this. These men might be monsters to you, but this life is all I have.'

'I know,' I replied.

'Can you just… leave?'

'No.' My voice was strong; I was certain about this. Admitting my failure to Taylor, and the rest of the unit, and the whole damn world, was not an option. I took a deep breath. 'Look, I have no interest in doing anything to hurt you, or Val, or Nina. But I don't have that loyalty to Mikhail. I need to stay. You don't even have to talk to me.'

He thought about this. 'So I just stay quiet.'

I nodded.

'Okay. But I am not having any part of this. The only reason I'm agreeing is because you don't deserve to die.'

'I'm glad you think so.'

'What about Doro?'

'Doro won't say anything,' I assured him.

Dimitri frowned at me, but he didn't ask any further questions. He cleared his throat, and the tone of conversation changed. 'Okay. We better go.'

'You really don't care if I come along?'

'Don't give a shit if you take down Carlos.'

Chapter Twenty-Eight

When we reached the Angel Rooms, someone was waiting outside for us. Even in the late afternoon shadows, it took me only seconds to recognize Doro.

'What the hell is he doing here?' I demanded as we approached.

'I could ask the same question about you,' Doro sneered.

'Doro has dealt a lot with Carlos and specifically his Columbian contacts. He knows how to handle them, and they trust him — or at least, they make time for him,' Dimitri explained, his tone guarded. 'He knows that he's a dead man if he lays one finger on you.'

I frowned, not happy about this, but having no choice but to agree. The two men led the way to a nearby truck, and I climbed into the back. We drove south, into an area on the outskirts of the City that I'd never been to before. It looked rundown, full of broken windows and graffiti, and poorly dressed children playing in muddy front yards. I took in the surroundings, and we were pretty much out of the City when Dimitri pulled off the road and onto a large gravel pit, driving up to a building that was apparently a mechanics garage.

The three of us vacated the vehicle, and I surveyed the area. Two mechanics worked on cars nearby, and a couple of scary-looking dogs were chained to a link fence, growling at us. Besides them, there didn't seem to be anyone else here. But apparently, Dimitri knew where the action was, as he headed around the back of the garage and towards a temporary building that rested on disintegrating breezeblocks.

Doro knocked on the chipped plastic door, and when it swung open, I was faced with a heavily tattooed man, wearing gang tags on his ripped denim jacket. His thick dark hair was slicked back, and a dark smatter of stubble dirtied his face. Gold rings glittered from his ear lobes, and more thick-banded jewellery adorned his knuckles; he was intimidating by his own design.

'Boys,' he greeted us, clearly ignoring the fact that I was not actually a man. 'Get in here.'

We stepped into the makeshift office, which smelt strongly of sweat, alcohol and cigarettes. Inside, two other men leaned against the far wall, arms folded across their chests, intimidatingly. I mimicked the position, propping a hip against the opposite wall, while Dimitri and Doro took seats at a metal desk in the centre of the small room. Knowing that Dimitri liked to be in control of a room, I guessed that sitting while others stood was probably killing him inside. The man who had greeted us took his seat on the other side of the desk, leaning far back in his chair, and I knew immediately that he was the boss.

'Doro, it's been too long,' he said in his accented grumble of a voice, lighting a cigarette between his chapped lips.

'Carlos,' Doro replied in greeting. 'Good to see you.'

'You need guns,' Carlos cut right to the chase, blowing smoke across the desk.

'AKs,' Doro responded with a nod. 'We were raided by the cops last night, took half our gear. We were meant to deliver to the Thais, they aren't impressed, want the rest of their order by Tuesday.'

'How many?'

'Twenty.'

Carlos let out a low whistle. 'By Tuesday?' He glanced over at his two men. 'They don't ask for much, ay?' Turning back to Doro and Dimitri, Carlos cracked a smile. 'I might be able to help you out, my brothers. What's in it for me?'

'Cash. Give us a number,' Doro said, with a shrug, like it was no big deal.

'Yes, good,' Carlos seemed to agree. Then, his eyes rolled to me, and I froze. 'You, girl. You are here as part of the payment?'

I looked at him, keeping my arms folded across my chest, and Doro answered for me. 'Mari is here for whatever you need. She is very accommodating.' Doro smiled as he spoke, and I knew he was enjoying this. I wanted to smash his smug face right into that metal desk.

Carlos nodded, looking me up and down. I gritted my teeth, and let him do it. He smiled. 'I tell you what boys. We will come to your club tonight, you will have the money waiting. I will let you know the amount. Then, we will have drinks, and you — Mari, was it? Will be there, making sure we have fun.'

'I don't work at the club,' I told him, anger hardening my voice.

'Tonight, you do,' Carlos challenged.

Dimitri shot me a dangerous glance, and I swallowed my retort in favour of a tense nod. That seemed to satisfy Carlos, and our deal was made.

***

Back at the Beach, Doro, Dimitri and I headed into the *Angel Rooms* to make arrangements for that night. While Dimitri went to Mikhail's office to fill him in, Doro took me through to another backroom, sparsely decorated with wardrobes and mirrors. Two girls sat on the floor, applying makeup, and I guessed that this was where Mikhail's dancers got ready.

'Casey, Bee, this is Mari,' Doro introduced us. 'She needs an outfit for tonight.'

With that, he left the room, and I was faced with two

half-naked dancers, eyeing me like I was the new toy in the box.

'You're the bitch who works for Mikhail, right? You work with the men. Too good for the clubs, are you?' Bee — a petite brunette — sneered, looking me over and curling her lips as if what she saw disgusted her. She couldn't have been much older than twenty-one, but her expert makeup and angry snarl aged her.

'Look, I don't want to be here, just as much as you don't want me here. So let's just get it over with, shall we?' I asked, giving her a stern look.

The other girl, Casey, stood and opened a nearby wardrobe. 'What do you want, honey? Come have a look.' She had a distinctive City accent, and long blonde extensions. Her outfit of choice was a black mini skirt, a sparkly pink bikini top, fishnets, and stilettos.

Approaching the wardrobe, I saw that there wasn't much variation in the outfit choices, aside from the differing colours. Apparently seeing my dismay at the contents of the wardrobe, Casey laughed, not altogether pleasantly, and asked, 'Who are you trying to impress tonight?'

'Carlos,' I told her. I knew that she'd know him.

She raised her eyebrows, and I was irrationally pleased that this information had impressed her. Casey reached into the wardrobe and plucked out a black satin bikini top, and a pair of denim shorts. 'Shoe size?' she asked me. I told her, and she grabbed a pair of black stiletto ankle boots from the bottom of the wardrobe.

Taking the items of clothing from her, I held back a grimace. 'Thanks.'

Behind me, I heard the door open, and turned to see Dimitri stepping into the room. Both girls immediately altered their attitudes, and Casey sidled up to him.

'Hey, D,' she cooed in greeting.

I frowned. I recognised that voice, those words. My brain clicked, and I realised that she had been the girl inside Dimitri's apartment yesterday. I glanced between them, surprised. In all that had been going on, I'd forgotten about that, and the memory stung. She was so peppy. And blonde. And the exact opposite of me. That hurt, though I didn't know why.

My face must have given me away, because Dimitri's eyes flashed with something resembling panic. Ignoring Casey entirely, he grabbed my arm and pulled me out of the room. Back in the main area of the club, he led me to the closest corner.

'She's cute.'

'Look, I didn't know you'd be working with her,' he told me. 'Hell, no one else would even know it was her. Do you have crazy cop hearing or something?'

'Sh!' I exclaimed. 'Are you insane?'

He gave me a look. 'Look, all you have to do tonight is keep Carlos happy. A girl on his lap and a drink in his hand. I won't let anyone hurt you. Trust me.'

Uneasiness stirred in my stomach, and I wanted to argue, but I couldn't forget that he could turn me over to Mikhail at the slightest wrong step. 'I'm fine. It's fine,' I mumbled, staring down at the alarmingly small pile of clothes I still held in my arms. At least it was mostly black. If Casey had tried to dress me in something neon, we would've had a problem. My stomach pinched at the thought of Casey and the way she spoke to Dimitri, the image of them together. I closed my eyes, and chased it away; acting like a jealous teenager wasn't cool at any time, least of all when I was in the middle of a very dangerous game.

'Hey.' Dimitri's soft voice brought me back to the present, and I opened my eyes to see him looking at me with a new expression. 'If it helps, I'm not sleeping with her.'

I raised an eyebrow in disbelief. I did not want to hear about this, but also, I wanted him to convince me.

'Some guys came over, they brought some of the girls, and she was all over me,' Dimitri shrugged. 'I had too many drinks, I did a little coke, and yeah, I wanted to sleep with her. Anything to get you out of my head. But then you show up at my door, and I'm right back there.'

My eyes felt wide. I hadn't expected that. My mouth felt dry. I wanted to say something, but I didn't know what, and before I could think, Casey stuck her head around the door, looking for us.

'Hey, Mari, we need to get you ready.'

I looked over my shoulder at her. She had a face on, and I knew she didn't like me being out here with Dimitri. This night was going to be hard enough as it was without pissing off the girls I needed to work with, so I nodded, following her back into the dressing room with one last long glance at Dimitri. I was glad that he hadn't slept with Casey, and I knew that he felt something for me. But I also knew why he wouldn't say it; what was the point? However this played out, there was no scenario in which we would be together. And besides that, he didn't trust me anymore.

It was over. And soon, everything else would be over, too. Maybe including my life. I'd just have to wait and see.

Chapter Twenty-Nine

Bee curled my hair, pointing out my bald spot, although some hair had finally started to regrow. She was a little too gleeful about it, and a little too messy with the curling iron — my scalp was burned in at least two places, and at least one of those was purposeful. Casey attempted to work on my face, applying makeup confidently, finishing with a deep red gloss over my lips.

When she was finished, she sat back to look at me, and pursed her lips. 'Hon, I'm sorry, but that bruising is not easy to cover. And that slice down your face, I don't wanna make it look worse.'

I glanced in the mirror. The makeup felt like a lot, considering I didn't usually wear much, but she'd done a fair job — better than I would've been able to do. 'Don't worry about it.'

'That happen on the job?' she asked, feigning disinterest by packing her makeup back into her bag.

'Yeah.' I wasn't giving away any more than that.

She looked up at me, and gave a small smile. She understood my unwillingness to share. 'So, you and D are friends?' she changed the topic in a not-so-subtle way.

I replied with a shrug. 'I guess. You know, we work together.'

'Oh, that's cool,' Casey smiled, seemingly placated. I felt a little bad for her, and now that I knew nothing had happened between them, I could afford to spare her feelings. I'd get no benefit from upsetting her, or making her jealous, and I certainly wouldn't get any joy, considering that I'd just felt that exact way when I'd seen her with Dimitri.

As we prepared ourselves, a steady stream of other girls filtered into the dressing room, until there were a total of eight of us. I reluctantly changed into my chosen costume at the last minute, feeling self-conscious and a little ridiculous. The other girls carried their looks off with cool confidence, while I awkwardly regarded myself in the mirror. Bruises still adorned my neck and stomach, despite Casey's half-hearted attempts to cover them with makeup, and my face wasn't much better. But I did like the boots.

One girl revealed a bottle of vodka from her handbag, and I was happy to partake in the apparent tradition of taking shots before work. The slight buzz I felt after three knock-backs gave me the confidence boost I needed, and when the club doors opened, we headed out together into the main room. Taking direction from Casey, I spent the first hour of my night working as a waitress, delivering trays of drinks to tables of leering men. One of the bartenders seemed to take pity on me, and would occasionally load my tray with one or two extra tumblers of vodka, to ease my nerves. I appreciated that.

As the night went on, the club got busier and busier, and I got more and more anxious. I'd managed to avoid seeing anyone I knew pretty successfully, until Doro approached me, and caught hold of my arm to pull me to aside

'Don't touch me,' I snapped at him, yanking my arm away.

He smirked. 'Yeah, I can still see the damage from the last time.' He looked pointedly at the bruises around my neck.

'Did you need something?' I spat.

'Yeah. Show time sweetheart. Carlos just arrived.'

I followed Doro's gaze to see Carlos and a group of his men at the bar.

'You need a condom, or are you prepared?' Doro asked, a smug smile on his face. He was loving this.

'Bite me,' I snapped. 'I'll play along, I'll keep Carlos

drunk and flattered all night, but that's all. As long as he leaves happy, I don't think Mikhail will care how I do it.'

Doro opened his mouth to a loud stream of expletives, but I didn't stick around to hear him. I knew I was right — Mikhail was about results, not about making me humiliate myself because of some double-crossing personal bullshit grudge.

I waved to Carlos and his two friends, who had settled into some seats with a good view of the main podium, and stopped to pick up a tray of drinks on my way over. As I approached, Dimitri, Val, Jag, and a couple more of Mikhail's men emerged from his office, and made their way straight over to Carlos. Crap. It was harder to keep this act up in front of them. One of them, especially.

I forced my feet to keep walking. In my bikini top and shorts, I suddenly felt very exposed. My heart beat nervously, as too many pairs of eyes turned their attention my way. I was greeted with various whistles and comments as I lowered the tray onto the table in front of Carlos. I made a mental note of who said what, so I could exact a suitable revenge at a later date.

Carlos picked up a bottle of spirit from the tray, and simultaneously snaked an arm around my waist, pulling me down next to him.

'I knew you'd make an exception for me,' he said, his breath hot and warm on my cheek.

I laughed. 'What makes you think I'm doing this for you?'

His grip on me tightened painfully, but he smiled. 'I like a challenge.'

He used his free hand to pull a little bag of white powder from his pocket. He passed it to one of his associates, and I was reminded of the incident with Jag and an indebted customer, refusing to pay due to the quality of our product. Recently, on a couple of deliveries

I'd completed alone, several people had complained about the quality, too; whoever Mikhail was getting supply from was cutting it so thin that we were basically selling baking soda. An idea crept into my mind.

I looked Carlos in the eye. 'So do I. How about a deal?'

Carlos's smile widened. 'What do you want?'

'I have a business proposition for you.'

'So what's the deal?'

'Hear me out, and I'll stay by your side all night.' I shuffled closer to him to emphasise my point.

Carlos laughed. 'All I get from this deal is the pleasure of your company? I don't think so. Sex.'

I swallowed my anger, and counter offered, 'A private dance.'

'Done.' Carlos reached up to cup my cheek with his rough hand. 'This will be a fun night.'

I hoped so.

Several other girls were called over to entertain the rest of the men, but Carlos held firmly onto me. Doro joined us, as did a few more of Mikhail's men, who I knew only by sight. Everyone pretty much ignored me. My only job right then was to sit there quietly, looking appealing, and resisting the urge to break Carlos's fingers every time they brushed over my skin.

Casey had apparently lost her bikini top at some point during the night, and I could do nothing but watch when she decided to drape her mostly naked body all over Dimitri. Jealousy twisted my stomach, and I attempted to refocus my attention on the glass of vodka in my hand, and on the action of refilling it. Again.

Noticing Casey, and apparently feeling inspired by her lack of clothing, Carlos plucked at the straps of my own bra. 'Does this thing come off?' he asked in a low voice, his alcoholic breath wafting over me.

'No.' I replied, taking a long sip of my drink.

Carlos slid a finger underneath the string of the halter strap. He trailed his thumb along the hem of the fabric, and down over the curve of my breast. My stomach knotted with anger. My hand twitched around the glass I held, resisting the urge to slam it into his face. When Carlos's other hand found my bare thigh, it took all my will power to stay still. This went against all my natural instincts. I shut my eyes, and gritted my teeth, trying to calm myself, and ignore the bitter anger in my belly as Carlos's hands roamed my skin.

I knew everyone was watching. I knew they'd never respect me now. Unless my deal worked out.

'What do you say we take this somewhere a little more private and work on our deal?' Carlos whispered into my ear.

He stood, and pulled me to my feet. We walked towards the private section of the club. Behind the curtain, most of the booths were in use already, but Carlos found us a free one. He pushed me inside, and drew the fabric across behind us. A terrifying sense of déjà-vu washed over me; this was not the first time a man had shoved me into one of these booths against my will, with every intention of hurting me.

Carlos wasted no time. His mouth crushed mine, his body pinning me against the red painted wall.

I shoved him. 'Hey! What the hell? We had a deal.'

He rolled his eyes, but he sat down on the leather bench. 'Fine. Dance.'

'Business first.'

Carlos's eyes glinted with something sinister. 'How about the same time?'

'You want me to dance, while outlining my business proposition?' I asked, frowning.

He said nothing, but gestured for me to begin. I

sighed. If this was the only way he'd listen, I guessed I'd just have to roll with it.

So, I swung my hips and started some semblance of a dance. 'You know Mikhail needs guns. And I know we are paying you for those. But I've got a better offer.'

'And what's that?'

'Cocaine. We're looking for another supplier. I know you have access to good product, correct?' From his Colombian gang connections.

'I sell my own supply. Turn around.'

I did as he said, shaking my hips in time with the music. 'But we've got the clientele. Do you know how much product we move in a week? In a month? You just don't have access to that resource, or customers with that kind of money.'

That was an educated guess based on what I knew about his operation, but when I turned around to see his face, I knew I'd guessed right.

'Come here,' he instructed.

I took a deep breath, pushing my emotions down, and straddled him on the bench.

'Fifteen percent of everything we sell,' I said, trying to keep the focus as his hands gripped my hips. 'Bigger profit, more product moved.'

'Thirty percent.' Carlos's hands reached for the tie on my bikini top.

I grabbed his wrists and pinned them over his head against the wall. 'Twenty.'

His chest rose and he licked his lips. 'OK. Let me talk to my boss.'

'Forty-eight hours to decide.'

'You drive a hard bargain, Mari.'

'I told you I like a challenge.' My heart was pounding. I hoped he couldn't feel it.

Carlos pulled his arms out of my grip, and held my

face with both of his hands. 'Three days.'

'And the guns.'

'Yes.'

I nodded. 'Deal.'

Carlos reached into his pocket and produced another baggy of white powder. He pushed it into the back pocket of my shorts. 'A sample.'

For one second, I felt elated, and I let myself smile. But then Carlos stopped playing nice. He pushed me sideways onto the bench, crushing me under the weight of his body.

'Hey, stop!' I yelled.

He laughed, his breath hot on my face. 'Come on Mari, that was all foreplay. Time to get serious.'

'Carlos stop!'

I slapped at his face with both hands. There was little power behind my blows due to the angle, but he hadn't been expecting it, and lost his balance on the bench. He rolled sideways onto the floor, but he pulled me down on top of him. Now, he looked pissed. Pissed, and excited. The gleam in his eyes made me sick.

'You want to play?' he asked me, wrapping his arms around me in an ironclad grip.

He rolled us again, so he was back on top, and I was face down on the floor. He twisted my arms painfully behind my back. I struggled, but this time, he wasn't going to let me get away. He was too strong. His whole weight pressed down on my back and I gasped for air. I heard him unzip his jeans, and his fingers tugged on the waistband of my shorts. I was beyond panicked. I couldn't get away. I screamed, louder than I have ever screamed before.

Then, chaos erupted. The sounds of shouting and banging assaulted my already overloaded senses, loud enough to drown out the music. Carlos sat back, and I could breathe properly again. I gulped in air. He stood, and pulled back the curtain, stepping out of the booth to see what was going on. Seconds later, Dimitri appeared.

'Dimitri, what the hell is happening?' Carlos demanded, fastening his trousers as I pushed myself up off the floor with shaking arms.

'Police,' Dimitri replied. 'We gotta go. Come with me, there's a fire exit back here.'

I sat up. Adrenaline rushed my brain, and I didn't understand what was happening. I couldn't process what Dimitri was saying.

But then Dimitri turned his gaze to me, and it felt like a cold bucket of water being poured over my head. He held out his hand. I started to reach out for it, but I stopped myself. As my awareness returned, I realised that Dimitri had let Carlos take me to the private section. He'd sat there drinking while anything could have been happening to me. And it almost did.

I knew that Dimitri had no reason to care about me now, especially not since he found out the truth about who I was, but to be willing to let me get attacked in that way? That was unforgivable.

Fuelled by my newly realised anger, I shot to my feet and pushed past him, hurrying after Carlos, who was following a small crowd back through the private section, through a door that I hadn't noticed before, because it had been hidden behind a curtain. It took us through to a room very much like Mikhail's office, but which was currently being used as storage for the bar, and where there was indeed a fire exit. Outside, I found myself in a dark back alley, littered with industrial bins and abandoned furniture. People were going in all directions, and my fuzzy brain couldn't figure out which way would take me back to somewhere I recognised. I saw Carlos running off to the right, and decided that left was the more appealing direction.

I began to run, partially because everyone else was, but mostly because I needed to get as far away from that place as possible. At the end of the alley was an unfamiliar street. I had no idea where I was, but I kept running, taking random corners, with no route in mind. The other club-goers peeled off in different directions, but I didn't care. It couldn't have been more than a few minutes, but I felt like I'd been running for hours when I saw the gleam of the ocean in front of me.

I loved the sea. I headed straight for it, hopping the railing easily on my adrenaline high, and landing on the sand below. My stiletto heels sank into it, and I couldn't run anymore, but I didn't need to. I dropped to my knees, and the cold, smooth grains under my skin anchored me back to reality. It was almost high tide, so the waves lapped just a few metres away from me. In the distance, a lone seagull cawed. I closed my eyes and focused on the familiar beach-side sounds, forcing myself to take deep breaths. I'd nearly lost it back there.

Chapter Thirty

Only when I felt the water lap on my knees did I open my eyes. I don't know how long I'd been there, but I was starting to feel a little more like myself again. I stared out at the black ocean. How did I get myself into this?

Movement in my peripheral vision caught my attention, and I span my head to look. There was someone there, sitting a few feet to my left. For a second, I was afraid. But then he spoke.

'It's okay, it's only me.'

Dimitri.

I stood, caught off guard by how unstable my legs felt. 'Leave me alone.' My voice was hoarse, and a little shaky.

Dimitri stood, too, and took a step towards me. I could only just make out his features in the moonlight, but his expression was as unreadable as always. 'You okay?' he asked.

'What do you think?' I snapped, pleased to hear a little more bite in my voice this time.

'Mari, please,' Dimitri continued to approach me.

I took a step back. 'Stay the hell away from me,' I growled. 'Seriously. Just go.'

He didn't listen; in two steps, he closed the distance between us, placing his hands on either side of my face so that I was forced to meet his eyes. His shone dangerously. 'Tell me what happened.'

I pushed his hands away. I couldn't bear the familiarity of his touch. 'Why? You want to hear the details? Would that make you happy?'

Dimitri's jaw tensed. 'Don't. Just tell me.'

Rage burned inside me. 'We talked. But then he pinned me down. I couldn't get away. You saw, I was on the floor. I was powerless.' Angry tears burned my eyes.

I'd got my business proposition across, but I'd been stupid to think Carlos would stick to his side of the bargain. 'You let him take me to the private section.'

'You think that was easy for me?'

'Well it didn't seem like you found it particularly difficult.' Turning on my heel, I started back towards the railing. The beach wasn't so relaxing anymore.

Dimitri grabbed my wrist, and I span. Staring down at his hand clamped around my arm, I was flooded with the remnants of panic. I felt Carlos's hands grabbing me, his arms locking around me… My heart raced, and adrenaline burned my veins. I yanked my arm away impulsively.

'Don't touch me.' I spat. The venom in my tone was marred by the break in my voice.

Dimitri froze, understanding my reaction. He held his hands up palm forward, letting me know that he wouldn't touch me uninvited again.

'I know you don't owe me anything,' I said, quietly.

Dimitri hesitated before he spoke. 'Mari, listen to me. I thought the police would have arrived sooner. I was never going to let him hurt you.'

I frowned. '*You* called the police?'

Dimitri rubbed a hand over his jaw, shrugging. 'As far as they're aware, it was an anonymous caller, tipping them off to the drugs being dealt in the club tonight.'

I blinked. Again, there seemed to be too much information, and I just couldn't process what I was hearing. I was so angry. Everything was so messed up, and it was becoming increasingly possible that I wasn't going to make it out. So much had happened since I'd arrived here — hell, so much had happened in the last 24 hours — and my head seemed to be perpetually spinning. I kept trying to make sense of it, but maybe there was no sense to be made. This was the situation, and I just had to accept it. Maybe I needed to stop thinking about doing my job — especially since I'd already apparently failed at that. I needed to focus instead on just surviving.

I looked at Dimitri. He was watching me, waiting for my response, but I had no words.

Luckily, he seemed to understand this, and began to explain. 'I needed to get you out of there without getting myself or Mikhail into shit with Carlos and his guys. So I called the police, to create a distraction, and a reason to interrupt. There was no risk. Mikhail is still at the cabins laying low, and I knew that I was gonna get Carlos out of there. Any drugs being sold at the club aren't ours, I made sure that our guys weren't dealing on the premises.'

I thought about that for a moment. 'What about Mikhail's office? Won't they search it?' My inner policewoman wouldn't quit.

Dimitri shrugged. 'I removed his personal stash earlier, his laptop, guns, excessive cash. There's nothing incriminating, only legitimate business paperwork. And I'll put it all back before he comes out of hiding.'

I frowned. I guessed that Mikhail's illegitimate business dealings didn't exactly require a lot of paperwork. It surprised me that Dimitri had called the police just to get me out of there, but like he'd explained, there had been no real risk to Mikhail's business. And I couldn't help but think that Dimitri's plan almost hadn't worked.

'What if the police didn't show, or if they'd arrived too late?' I asked. 'A minute later, and it *would* have been too late, he...' I stopped. I just couldn't say it.

'It got that far?' Dimitri's voice was incredibly low.

I nodded, and Dimitri cursed.

'I had to find a way of protecting you, without screwing everything up! I didn't have a whole lot of options, Mari.'

I closed my eyes. 'I know.'

I felt Dimitri step towards me, and very slowly reach his arms out. Gently, he brought me into a hug, and his familiar scent enveloped me. I allowed myself to sink into him, resting the lesser-damaged side of my face against his hard chest, closing my eyes, and taking a deep breath. Dimitri trailed a hand through my hair, resting his chin on my head.

'I'm so sorry,' he whispered, so quietly that I barely heard him.

But I did hear, and that's all it took for the last of my fading strength to crumble. I let myself cry, and he held me for a long time.

Chapter Thirty-One

After that night, I stayed in bed for two days, after which time I was disturbed only by my phone buzzing with a text from Mikhail, notifying me of a meeting at the club that evening. The last thing I wanted to do was drag my body out of bed and face reality again, but I knew I had no choice. I crawled to the shower, hoping the hot water would help me pull myself together, but it was cut short by a knock at the door.

Throwing a towel around myself, I shuffled to the door and pull it back to see Dimitri. He looked me up and down, quickly, but I noticed it. Then he frowned at me.

'Get ready. We need to get to the Beach.'

I indicated to the towel. 'What does it look like I'm doing? Give me five minutes.'

Dimitri followed me inside the apartment, closing the door behind him, though he stopped short of trailing me into the bedroom.

'We have a situation,' Dimitri said from the lounge, while I tried to find some clean clothes.

I rolled my eyes, although he couldn't see me. 'There's always a *situation*.'

I threw on some jeans and a T-shirt, grabbing the small pouch of cocaine from my nightstand and slipping it into my pocket before returning to the living room.

'So, what's going on?' I asked.

Dimitri simply sighed. 'You'll find out. Let's go.'

Twenty minutes later, the two of us entered the *Angel Rooms*, where Dimitri led me straight through to Mikhail's office. He didn't knock, and inside I saw that half a dozen men were already gathered. Mikhail sat behind his desk, while the others leaned against either the wall or the various pieces of furniture dotted around the room. I noticed that Val was present, as was Jag, and quickly realised that Mikhail had assembled the crew who'd been part of the gun delivery last week. Aside from those who had been arrested at the scene, obviously.

I shut the door behind me, and Mikhail immediately began to speak.

'As you all know, Carlos came through and sold us the guns we needed. These were successfully delivered yesterday, and our business is settled.' Mikhail looked at me. 'The police were here on Sunday night, and while they found nothing to incriminate any of us, I believe I know why they came.'

I was standing next to Val in the far corner of the room, while Dimitri had positioned himself close to Mikhail, and now my eyes met his across the room. He ignored my questioning gaze. His calmness reassured me that Mikhail did not, in fact, know why the police had raided the club that night.

'I believe,' Mikhail said, 'That one of the men who was apprehended at the warehouse is talking.'

'Who?' demanded one man — Nick, primarily a dealer, partial to blonde dancers. His outraged expression was mirrored around the room.

'Fabio.'

My head snapped to look at Mikhail with wide eyes, taken completely off guard by his revelation. I didn't believe it. I'd interviewed many suspects, and from what I knew of Fabio, I did not see him as the talking type. He'd rather spend his life in prison than turn on Mikhail.

'You're wrong.' I didn't realise I'd spoken out loud until Mikhail fixed a glare on me.

'You know this how?' he asked, a deadly edge to his voice.

'Uh…' I swallowed. 'I just don't think Fabio would do that. He's too loyal. He's a good guy.'

Mikhail sneered at me. 'Well, I'm sure he's good at a

number of things, Mari, of which you may have more knowledge than me...' Snickers rumbled around the room, and I felt myself blush. 'But my source is reliable, and Fabio is young, easily scared by the idea of prison,' Mikhail said, matter-of-factly. 'He is our weak link. So we must take action.'

'Kill him,' said one man, so flippant and unaware of the effect his words had on me; my blood ran cold. It was my fault that Fabio had been arrested. I could've warned him. He wasn't a bad guy, and he was a lot less guilty than most of the men in this room. I couldn't let him die.

Luckily, Mikhail shook his head at the suggestion. But my relief was short lived when he revealed his plan.

'We just need to remind him to keep his mouth shut. If he keeps quiet, he'll be in prison for years, no longer our problem. We just need leverage,' the gleam in Mikhail's eyes made me feel sick. He continued, 'I will take care of it. As for the rest of you, the usual rules apply; if you are questioned by police, you know nothing, yes?'

When he was satisfied that everyone understood, Mikhail nodded once, and I guessed this signalled the end of the apparent meeting, as the men began to trickle out of the room. Their mood was elated, as they talked on their way out, and it sickened me. Of course, I realised that Mikhail's 'leverage' would likely involve threatening Fabio's family until he did what they asked. I hated myself for letting Fabio get into this position, and it felt even worse that there was absolutely nothing I could do to help.

I started to follow the rest of the men out of the office, but Mikhail stood and caught my arm as I walked by his desk. Turning to face him, I saw that Dimitri stood beside him, and that we were the only three left in the room.

'Carlos spoke well of you,' Mikhail told me. 'Although I understand that you have unfinished business.'

'My business with Carlos is definitely finished,' I replied, my voice harsher than I'd intended. 'But yours isn't.'

Mikhail raised his eyebrows in surprise, a dangerous edge in his glare. 'Oh?'

I took the pouch of white powder from my pocket and tossed it over the desk to Mikhail. 'You know there's been issues with our supply. It's basically baking powder, and people are starting to notice. Carlos has better product, and he's local. He should be our supplier.'

Mikhail leaned forward, his hands resting in fists on the desk, and fixed me with a menacing glare. 'Do you think this is any of your business?'

I glanced at Dimitri, who had a face like thunder, but I ignored this.

'Try it,' I told Mikhail. 'It's good stuff. And either we take control of his supply, or we lose business to it.'

Mikhail looked the angriest I had ever seen him, but he picked up the bag, using a key from his pocket to scoop a small amount of powder, which he snorted expertly, before rubbing the remnants into his gums with his finger. I held my breath while he considered. Eventually, Mikhail nodded.

'Very well. Tell Carlos the deal is on. I'll be in touch with him.'

I couldn't help the triumphant smile that rose to my lips. I'd done something that would not only make Mikhail trust me, but would mean that when we brought him down, Carlos's gang would also be implicated, or at least interrupted. The more criminals we could intercept as part of this operation, the better.

'But, Mari,' Mikhail continued, his voice low. 'I do not like you conducting my business affairs for me, without my knowledge. I make the decisions, is that clear? Or do I need to remind you?'

I wasn't smiling anymore. 'No, I understand.'

'Hmm. Just to be safe, here's a direct order for you.' A sickening smirk spread over Mikhail's face. 'You will do whatever is necessary to take care of this problem with Fabio.'

Mikhail regarded me smugly, as my heart dropped into my stomach. He knew how to punish me.

I looked up at Dimitri, who gave me a very stern glare. He was warning me, and I wasn't stupid enough to test Mikhail twice in so many minutes. I nodded again in response to Mikhail's request, and he looked pleased. Hopefully, Fabio would respond to whatever threats Mikhail made and I wouldn't have to do anything to harm him further. The thought did little to make me feel better.

Chapter Thirty-Two

A few days passed, during which time I heard from Carlos, and I completed our first pick-up of the new supply. It took a lot of effort for me not to smash his smug face into the wall, but I reminded myself of the bigger picture. I also seemed to be taking on a lot more delivery jobs for Mikhail in Fabio's absence, but I didn't mind. It kept me busy, and it was useful; I made a mental note of the names and addresses of some of the more indebted customers. The more money they owed, the easier it would be to obtain their testimony in exchange for protection or immunity.

I had a renewed sense of determination to get the job done, so I made the effort to meet Nina for a drink, and smooth things over with her. I'd been ignoring her for a little while, but she understood when she saw my face; while most of the damage from Doro's assault was fading nicely, the bruises were still noticeable, and the slice down my cheek was now the most defining feature of my face.

Dimitri text me once, asking if I was okay, to which I replied with a simple 'yes', and that was the extent of our contact.

Saturday night, I was in my apartment, since I no longer had a job at *Arrow's* to go to. There was a pouch of pills on my coffee table. I had gone to deliver them last night, but the guy couldn't pay up, so I'd withheld the goods. They kept catching my attention. I was glad when a knock at the door distracted me, and I answered it immediately.

To my surprise, I saw Jag standing in the hallway. He looked out of place.

'Hey,' I said. 'What are you doing here?'

'Hey, kid. We've got to move on this Fabio situation.'

Jag's voice was a low rumble. 'He hasn't responded to our threats, so we gotta take action.'

'What does that mean?'

Jag raised an eyebrow. 'You know what it means, sweetheart. Let's go.'

Swallowing the sickness that crept into my stomach, I took the time to change into jeans, a sweater and boots, throwing on a jacket to hide the bulge of the handgun at my waist, before following Jag out into the cool night air. He began to walk, and I had no choice but to follow.

'Where are we going?' I asked.

'A bar,' Jag replied vaguely. 'The target is there.'

'The target?' I repeated, as understanding crashed over me. 'You're gonna kill someone? Someone that Fabio cares about?'

Jag looked at me as if I were an idiot. 'Yes.'

'Who is it?' I demanded, hurrying to keep up with Jag's long strides.

'I don't know,' Jag replied, irritation clear in his voice. 'We go to the bar, Mikhail tells us who, and when, and we do it. Okay? I don't know why he made me bring you along, I think he's trying to make a point, but you better not get in my way.'

I frowned. I knew what Mikhail's point was; he was in charge, and I was his pawn. But could I stand there and watch Jag kill an innocent person? A person who Fabio loved?

It didn't take long for me to recognise the neighbourhood, and I began to feel nervous. When we stopped outside *Arrow's* bar, my suspicions were confirmed. Taking a deep breath, I followed Jag through the door. The bar was fairly busy at this time on a Saturday, and I didn't immediately recognise anyone in the crowd.

'What now?' I asked Jag.

He shrugged, and began to make his way towards the bar. 'We get a drink, and we wait. You want one?'

I nodded, hopping up onto the only free barstool. When I looked down the length of the bar, I was surprised to see Tad serving drinks. He was on his own, but seemed to be managing well. I guessed that Jono had convinced Tad to come back to work, after he realised that I wasn't coming back. I hoped Jono didn't see me while I was here, though I knew that was unlikely; he never came down from his office during opening hours.

Jag and I waited our turn, and when Tad finally reached us, he did a double take. 'Mari? What the hell happened to your face?'

Charming. 'Uh, hey. How you doing?' I asked.

Tad ignored me, worry clouding his usually pleasant features. 'Where have you been? You just disappeared; we couldn't get hold of you. I thought something had happened. Are you okay?'

I waved away his concern. 'I'm fine. You came back to work. That's good.'

Tad noticed Jag beside me, and his frown deepened. Looking back to me, he leaned forwards, dropping his voice. 'Mari, are you okay?'

I nodded. 'Yes. Could I get a double vodka lemonade please? And a vodka on the rocks for my colleague.'

Jag smirked at my description of him, and Tad hesitated, but completed the order. When we had our drinks, Jag and I turned to look for seating away from the bar; Tad's questions weren't fun for either of us. As we surveyed the room, I noticed the familiar inhabitants of the corner booth, Nina, Val and Dimitri.

Jag saw them, too. 'Why don't we join them, while we wait?' he suggested.

I hesitated, but nodded, and we approached their table. Nina saw us first, and her face lit up in a beautiful smile.

Following her gaze, Dimitri spotted me next. His expression was a lot less welcoming; his eyes clouded over with suspicion as he glanced between Jag and me.

'What are you two doing here?' Valentin asked with a smile. He was always so cheerful and accepting, and that struck me as strangely naïve for a man of his profession.

'We're waiting on instruction from Mikhail,' Jag replied, dragging a chair from a nearby table to the end of the booth. This gave me no other choice than to slide onto the vinyl bench beside Dimitri, with Nina and Val on the other side of the table. 'Figured we might as well get a drink while we wait.'

I admired Jag's response; truthful yet vague. Exactly how Dimitri would have done it.

'Well, the more the merrier!' Val replied.

Nina took my hand across the table. She smiled at me warmly, and I felt a little better.

Val, Nina and Jag held the conversation for the next twenty minutes or so, while I surveyed the room. I didn't know Fabio well enough to know about his family or friends, so I was sure I wouldn't recognise our potential target, even if he was stood right in front of me. I doubted that Jag knew either, so we were really just waiting on Mikhail. When Jag received a text, I tried to catch a glimpse of his phone, but he kept the screen angled away from me while I he tapped out a reply. I managed to catch his gaze, but he gave nothing away.

A few minutes later, Jag touched my arm. 'Anyone for a smoke?'

I looked at him. 'I don't smoke.'

'Come anyway.'

We stood, and Nina followed suit. 'Ooh, yes, I'll join you!' She fished a cigarette from her handbag, and skipped after us towards the door. I wished she wouldn't have come, because I wanted to ask Jag about the text he'd received, but I couldn't exactly tell her that.

Outside, we turned the corner into the alley, out of the way of the few other patrons who'd chosen to get some air. Nina and Jag lit up, while I stood upwind. I wasn't impressed with being dragged outside for no good reason. The two of them chatted easily about nothing in particular, until Jag dropped his cigarette butt and stamped it out with his boot. I began to head back towards the bar, when a muffled yelp caught my attention.

Turning back, I saw Jag pinning Nina up against the dirty brick wall. He had one hand over her mouth, holding her still with his body weight, while his other hand grabbed inside his jacket. I felt the ground fall out from beneath me. I turned with the intention of running inside, getting help, but a metallic click froze me in place. Jag's gun was pointed at my head.

'Get over here, princess,' he growled.

I held my hands up, palms forward, indicating that I wasn't going to run. Slowly, I approached him. Nina looked at me, fear plain in her wide eyes. Satisfied with my movement, Jag turned the gun away from me, and pressed it to Nina's throat. I suddenly understood; Nina was the target.

'Jag, don't do this,' I begged.

'Mikhail's instructions were clear,' Jag replied. 'Fabio didn't withdraw his statement, so we gotta show him we're serious.'

'Nina is really the person he cares about most?' I asked, incredulous. I'd known about their history, but I'd assumed he had other people in his life. The fact that Nina was still Fabio's most loved person, years after they'd separated, was heart breaking.

'Yeah,' Jag confirmed, 'Apart from their kid, of course.'

Nina squeaked against Jag's hand, and tears streamed from her eyes as she fought to break free, to no avail.

'Their baby was given up for adoption,' I argued. 'You don't know where the kid is. If you kill Nina, you've got no leverage left to use against Fabio!'

Jag glanced sideways at me. 'Of course we know where he is. He's cute. Doing well in school.'

Nina made more muffled noises, and it killed me to see her struggle. I had to do something.

'Jag, please, I'm begging you. Don't do this. This can't be what Mikhail wants, he needs Nina! For when Olivier visits. He can't kill her. Please.' I could hear the break in my voice, as I became desperate.

'His instructions were clear,' Jag repeated. He pushed the gun into Nina's neck, under her chin, and she wailed behind his hand.

'Wait!' I yelled, frantic. 'Kill me instead! Fabio cares about me, you know that. Please.'

Jag frowned at me, unable to comprehend why I would offer myself up in place of Nina. 'Mikhail's instructions were clear,' he repeated, the dead tone of his voice sending cold waves over my skin.

I couldn't let this happen. There was nothing left to say; I had to act. I lunged for the gun, throwing all my weight at Jag, hoping to knock him off target. My body hit his, and a shot rang out. My ears rang, my head span, and I hit the floor. For a moment, everything blurred, and I felt pain erupt over my hip as it met the pavement.

I blinked rapidly, trying to clear my vision. I was flat on the ground. All I could see were feet running around me. Pushing myself to my knees, I caught sight of Valentin. His face was twisted in agony. I couldn't hear anything properly. I forced myself to stand, and suddenly, time caught up. If everything had been slow before, it was now too fast. I looked around frantically. People were running, obviously scared by the sound of a gunshot. I saw Jag turn the corner, and he was gone. Then, I saw Nina. She was on the floor. Valentin was at her side, howling; I'd never heard so much pain. There was blood on the pavement, blood on Val, blood on Nina. It spread over her neck, down her chest, a black river.

She was dead. I hadn't been able to stop it. She was dead. I screamed. Nina was dead. I couldn't breathe.

Arms encircled me, pulling me away. I tried to push them away. I couldn't just leave her there, on the ground. But I was being dragged away. I yelled, and I fought, but Nina's body was getting smaller, further away, until I could no longer see her at all. And I knew that I'd never see her again.

Chapter Thirty-Three

Nina is dead.

'You did this!'

Nina is dead.

'I don't give a damn! You did this!'

Nina. Is. Dead.

'Go to hell!'

I looked up. Dimitri was there. He threw something across the room, with a wordless yell. His phone. It smashed against the wall. He sank to his knees, his face in his hands. I was in his apartment — how did I get here?

Nina was dead. Jag shot her, and she died, because Fabio still loved her. Pain ripped through me. I tipped forward, off of the sofa, onto the floor. I moved across the floor somehow, until I reached Dimitri. I was on my knees, and he was on his. His strong arms enveloped me, holding on so tightly I could barely breathe. But I didn't need to breathe. He buried his face in my neck, and I felt the warmth of his silent tears. My own fell, and I sobbed, letting the pain overwhelm me.

***

I gripped the gun in my hand until my knuckles turned white. Crimson rage burned inside me, it was all I could see.

'What the hell are you doing?' Dimitri demanded, returning from the kitchen with a bottle of clear liquor and two tumblers.

I took a deep breath, and placed the gun down on the coffee table, replacing it with the large vodka which Dimitri handed me.

'She's dead, Dimitri.' My voice didn't sound like my

voice. I took a sip of my drink, but it didn't help. 'How can you sit here and let Mikhail get away with this?'

'He won't,' Dimitri promised, his voice low.

He sat down beside me, his hand reached up to cup my face, his thumb running lightly over my wounded cheek. I turned my face into his hand, feeling the roughness of his palm over my lips, and letting the familiar scent of his skin calm me. My eyes closed and, without thinking, I kissed his palm.

When his hand dropped away from my face, I cringed. I'd crossed a line. But then, Dimitri's mouth was on mine, hot and demanding. The desperation behind his kiss drove me, and I pushed back. I needed the physical contact, and I knew that he did too. We didn't move to the bedroom, probably because if we paused to think, we would've realised what we were doing. The sofa was small and awkward, the fabric rough on my bare skin, but I lost myself in Dimitri, and that was all that mattered.

Afterwards, we lay side by side on the floor, looking up at the ceiling. Tears dried on my cheeks.

When Dimitri spoke, his voice was so quiet I barely heard. 'I'll help you.'

I turned my head to look at him. 'Help me?' I sounded breathless.

He met my gaze. 'I'll help you bring down Mikhail.'

I sat up, too quickly. Looking down at Dimitri, I searched his expression. He looked serious, but he couldn't be. 'What are you talking about?' He was Mikhail's right-hand man. Dimitri's whole life was the gang, and the work he did for it, and he was endlessly loyal to them. Except, maybe he wasn't anymore.

'He trusts me. If anyone can get damning evidence on him, it's gonna be me. And I will get it. We'll take him down, Mari.' He reached up, trailing a hand over my bare shoulder and down my arm. Goosebumps erupted over my skin.

'You're serious?' I asked. I had to check.

'He killed Nina.'

My heart hurt. It didn't seem real that Nina could actually be dead. 'I should have done something. I should've saved her.'

Now, Dimitri sat up, too. He took my face in both hands. 'Don't. Don't do that. It'll drive you mad. There was nothing you could've done. Even if you'd got her away from Jag, Mikhail would've sent someone else. He wanted her gone, and there's nothing we could've done.'

I looked at him. 'I know what you think of me, but I loved Nina. You know that, don't you?'

'Yes.'

My eyes began to sting, but there was no way I was letting myself cry again. Not now. I stood, and headed for the shower. I took a long time in the hot water, pulling myself together, focusing on what I had to do now. I trusted Dimitri, I knew that he meant what he said; he was going to help me gather evidence on Mikhail, and that would be invaluable. There was just one thing I didn't understand.

Shutting off the shower and grabbing the first towel I found, I exited the bathroom. Dimitri was no longer in the lounge, although his clothes remained on the floor, along with my own. I found him in the bedroom, laying across the bed, naked, eyes closed. My stomach dipped at the sight. With the towel knotted around my chest, I lowered myself onto the mattress beside him, my hand trailing over his stomach and tracing the ink over his chest. He made a contented sound, his eyes still shut. How could moments like this exist just hours after I'd witnessed the death of a friend?

'I have a question.'

'Hmm.'

'What happens when Mikhail is gone?' I asked, resting my un-scarred cheek on Dimitri's warm shoulder.

He hesitated for so long that I didn't think he'd answer, but he did. 'It all comes to me.' He wrapped an arm around me, and sighed. 'Not that I want to take over Mikhail's position. A few months ago, sure, it would've been the natural next step. But now, it's not what I want.'

'What do you want?' I asked, my voice barely a whisper.

'Something I can't have.' His was even quieter.

And I knew what he meant. I wanted the same thing. There was nothing left to say. We fell asleep like that.

Chapter Thirty-Four

'Can't you just record his conversations?' Dimitri asked.

'Technically yes but it's not enough on its own. Plus, he's usually vague enough that he could dispute the meaning of his words.' I sighed. 'We also need people to come forward — someone who has acted under Mikhail's instructions, but is willing to turn on him.'

'You mean, like me?'

I stopped pacing, turning to stare at Dimitri. 'Not you.'

'Why not? I know everything. I've killed a lot of people under his instruction.'

'Well, that's the problem. You'd be perfect, but you've committed so many crimes that even with your help and your testimony, you're still looking at life. And we both know that Mikhail has guys in prison who'd kill you, no questions asked.' I held his gaze. 'I'm not letting that happen. We've got to find another way.'

Dimitri rubbed a hand over his hair. 'This is gonna take too long.'

'Yeah, well, like I said, it's been three years already.' I shrugged. 'Maybe there's nothing we can do, except continue to observe, tip off police when we can. You know, *build a case*.'

Dimitri frowned at me. 'You haven't been here for three years. Are you saying there are other undercover cops in the gang already?'

I shrugged. 'But don't ask me who, it's unlikely that I even know.'

'They don't tell you who the other undercovers are?' Dimitri asked, seemingly disbelieving.

I sipped my coffee. 'Have you spoken to Mikhail? I mean, since you yelled at him on the phone yesterday?'

Dimitri shook his head. 'He's giving me time to cool off. He thinks if he leaves me a few days, I'll come to see the necessity of the situation.'

'Does he really know where Nina and Fabio's son is?'

'I don't know.'

I shook my head. 'He can't kill a child.'

Dimitri pulled a face. 'He can. Hopefully it won't come to that. I'm willing to bet that Fabio has already backed down. He won't be saying another word to anyone.'

'Yeah,' I agreed. The heavy weight of my guilt settled in my chest. Fabio was looking at years in prison, Nina was dead, and I still had no sure-fire way to make sure Mikhail paid for his crimes. I felt more than a little useless. But at least I had Dimitri now, whose insider knowledge was invaluable.

I sighed, placing my empty mug into the sink. 'I need to get dressed; I've got to pick up from Carlos in an hour.'

'Need company?'

I smiled. 'No.'

Dimitri shrugged. 'Fine. I've got a car downstairs, take the keys and just drop it back to Mikhail when you're done with it.'

'Thanks.'

This wasn't the first time I'd been to Carlos's place alone, as I'd done the same the first time I'd picked up from him, so I wasn't worried. Despite Carlos's force with me at the club that night, he hadn't tried anything since, I guessed because he was now forced to see me as a legitimate business contact, rather than a girl in a bikini who he could overpower. That was progress. And, although Mikhail had been pissed that I'd set the arrangement up behind his back, he did seem impressed by the increase in our sales. He was also apparently impressed by the quality of the product, if his personal use was anything to go by.

As instructed, I drove the car back to the *Angel Rooms*, and went inside to return the keys. Mikhail was in his office with Doro. My heart sped up when Doro smiled at me. It wasn't a pleasant expression.

I tossed the keys to Mikhail. 'Car is outside, the product is inside.'

Mikhail nodded. He would now have his men check and cut the bricks into small, deliverable amounts before distribution. 'Carlos is still happy with our arrangement?'

'Why wouldn't he be? He's making more money in a month than he's seen all year.'

Mikhail laughed. 'So feisty, sometimes.'

'I'm glad I amuse you.'

Doro stood. 'Come on Mari, I was just leaving, I'll walk out with you.'

I narrowed my eyes, but said nothing.

As we left, Mikhail warned us to 'play nice', but there was amusement in his tone. Clearly he was in a good mood today, something that was becoming less and less frequent. In fact, his moods in general were noticeably more changeable and volatile. I wondered if it was down to his increased use of drugs, or if it was just his psychopathic personality. Probably both.

Doro waited until we were outside, the setting sun casting shadows of his harsh features, making him more intimidating than normal, before hissing, 'I don't appreciate you pushing your way into business with Carlos.'

I rolled my eyes. 'Why? You jealous, because he used to be your best friend, and now he's mine?'

Doro growled. 'Mikhail may have warned me to stay away from you, but don't push me, bitch.'

I sighed. 'Look, I don't know what you're playing at here, but you must know that this can't continue. What do you think will happen when this all ends?'

'You mean, when justice is served?' Doro laughed, humourlessly. 'You are so naive. They keep telling us their building a case, but it will never be enough. This will never end. Mikhail has too many friends in powerful places, he's untouchable, and you're a fool if you believe otherwise.'

'What friends?' I asked, suspicious.

Doro ignored me. 'Just stay out of my way. This is my life now, and I'm embracing it. If you piss me off again, I might just tell Mikhail that there's a rat in our midst...'

'Don't threaten me,' I warned.

Doro smirked, as he started to walk away. 'Or what? You'll set your boyfriend on me?'

I watched him leave, anger bubbling in my chest. How dare he threaten me? I hadn't considered that he would ever tell Mikhail about me, but now he'd said it, I wondered how I could have been so ignorant. His loyalties had changed, and I knew that he was serious about his threat. I just didn't know what to do about it.

Chapter Thirty-Five

Nina's funeral was the hardest day of my life. I attended with Val and Dimitri. Val was inconsolable. I couldn't bear to look at the obvious heartbreak in his eyes. I felt pain, and I felt guilt. I should have known as soon as we walked into *Arrow's* that Nina was the target, and I should have saved her. And if I wasn't here, the police would never have known about the guns at the warehouse, Fabio wouldn't have been arrested, and Nina would still be alive. There was no way in which this was not my fault.

I managed to hold it together for most of the day, but when I saw Jag among a group of Mikhail's men, I nearly lost it. Dimitri must have seen it in my face, because his hand grabbed mine.

'How dare he be here,' I hissed.

'I know.' Dimitri pulled me into him and held me tightly. I didn't know if he was trying to comfort me or stop me from storming over there.

There was a wake at one of Mikhail's clubs, but I couldn't bring myself to attend. Mikhail's men didn't care that Nina was dead. I knew if I was there, I wouldn't be able to stop myself saying something stupid, so instead I went home and cried and drank until I fell asleep.

***

A few weeks passed, during which I completed some delivery and collection jobs for Mikhail, as well as covering some bar work at a few of his clubs throughout the City. I'd told him I needed the money, but really I just wanted to scope out his other establishments, get to know the staff, the girls, and so on. Also to distract myself, because spending time alone in my apartment with a readily available supply of substances, and Dimitri living above me, was becoming more challenging.

It was after one of these bar shifts, when I was walking home, seemingly swimming upstream against the current of office workers heading to their day jobs, when I saw the newspaper. A vendor was setting up his cart on the corner, commenting to a customer about the headline that day, and my blood ran cold.

I grabbed a paper from the stack, and found myself looking at a mugshot of Fabio.

Career criminal to be tried over international weapons smuggling operation.

I knew this meant he'd confessed. He looked so young in his photograph, his eyes wide, disbelieving of what was happening to him. I felt like I couldn't breathe.

'You gonna pay for that?' the stall vendor asked me.

I shook my head, throwing the paper down and hurrying away. I swiped at the angry tears on my cheeks as I tore up the stairs to my apartment and went straight for the secret compartment where my phone was stored.

I'd spoken to Taylor a few times recently, updating him about the new relationship between Mikhail and Carlos, and informing him of Nina's death, though I'd had to leave out a lot of the details, since I was still concealing my direct involvement with the gang. As far as Taylor knew, I was still working at *Arrow's*, gathering information from the side-lines.

'Hello?' Taylor answered the phone.

'Fabio Marin. He's going down for the international gun trade. That's why Nina was killed. It's not true. He's innocent and you need to do something.'

Taylor paused. 'I doubt he is innocent, Harper.'

'Of this crime, he is. I'm telling you. He's a drug dealer, that's all. Don't let him take the fall for this.'

'That's all? Dealing is still a crime, you know.' Taylor

hesitated, then asked, 'Are you alright?'

I took a breath. 'I'm fine. I'm just asking you to help Fabio, please. He is not guilty and it is not justice to give him life in prison for something that we know Mikhail is responsible for.'

'Do you think he would respond to an offer?'

He meant; would Fabio give evidence against Mikhail as part of our investigation.

'I'm not sure,' I replied. 'They killed Nina to force his hand. They're threatening his child.'

'Where is the child?'

'I don't know. Apparently he was adopted as a baby, but Mikhail's men claim to know where he is.'

'Okay. Leave it with me.'

'Promise you'll do something about this.'

'Yes.'

I hung up.

***

That weekend, I was called to the *Angel Rooms* because the Thai gang were coming in for business discussions with Mikhail, and apparently they'd appreciated my company last time. My heart ached, because last time, Fabio had been with me. But I had no choice other than to push my feelings down, and focus.

The boss, Tanet, arrived with several of his men a little after midnight, and I set them up at a podium and brought over a tray of drinks. I sat down with them, starting up a casual conversation with one of the men as I poured his drink. Mikhail came over to greet them, inviting Tanet and Ram into his office.

To my surprise, Mikhail also called my name. 'Mari. Come.'

I followed the three men into the office, where Doro,

Jag and Dimitri waited for us. They looked surprised to see me. I understood. I shared the feeling.

Tanet and Ram took the two seats in front of Mikhail's desk, and Mikhail settled in his own chair. The rest of us stood.

'I understand you have heard of our deal with Carlos and the Colombians,' Mikhail began.

'Yes,' Tanet confirmed. He was an intimidating man, with a gruff voice. 'I am a little disappointed, Mikhail. If you were looking for a new supplier, why did you not speak with us? You know we have regular imports from Thailand, which is of course famous for its substances.'

'The deal with Carlos was one of opportunity. We were not looking for a new supplier, but rather Mari used her *position* with Carlos to our advantage,' Mikhail explained.

I gritted my teeth at his insinuation, biting my tongue as Ram and Tanet both glanced over at me with what can only be described as disdain.

'Now you let girls do your business for you?' Ram asked.

'Mari is tougher than she looks,' Dimitri spoke up. 'And the deal has worked out well for us.'

I shot him a look, trying to convey my appreciation with my eyes but not my face. He met my gaze.

'Be that as it may,' Mikhail reclaimed the conversation, 'It should not be perceived as anything against you, my friend.'

Tanet huffed, unimpressed. Ram glanced back towards me and winked, before asking Mikhail, 'How do I get into a more beneficial relationship with your girl?'

I couldn't hold it in that time. 'What is it you're after?' I asked him, stepping forward, my arms crossed over my chest. They would not speak about me as if I wasn't there.

Ram opened his mouth, no doubt to make some crude comment, but Tanet interrupted, 'We want you to sell our product, too. You have the customers, we have the supply.'

'We've got a supplier.' Mikhail told him. It sounded like he was losing patience with the conversation.

'What products do you have, other than cocaine?' I asked.

'Ecstasy, hallucinogens, weed.'

'We can't take your cocaine, but perhaps we could make arrangements for your other products,' I suggested. Every person in the room stared at me, most with some degree of irritation, but I stood my ground. I met Mikhail's gaze. 'Of course, this is not my decision,' I said.

'You got that right,' Doro scoffed from across the room.

Mikhail rubbed a hand over his stubbled jaw, considering. Then he nodded. 'Mari, give Ram your telephone number.'

I stepped forward and took Ram's phone from his outstretched hand, keying in my number and handing it back.

'We will offer you 30% on your product, excluding coke,' Mikhail told Tanet. 'Think about that, and let Mari know your answer.'

Tanet nodded, once, and the two men stood. Both nodded to me on their way out of the office.

As soon as the door was closed behind them, Doro exploded. 'Who the hell do you think you are?' he bellowed at me, crossing the room in seconds and pushing me back into the wall.

I shoved him back. He snarled, raised an arm and backhanded me across the face. It stung, knocking my head to the side, but I wouldn't let him exert control over me like this, not in front of Mikhail. He obviously hadn't expected me to retaliate, so when I struck, my blow landed solidly to his jaw. He swore and lunged for me, but then Dimitri was between us.

'Back off,' he commanded, in his most threatening voice.

'I should beat your ass, too,' Doro spat.

'Try it.' Dimitri was calm, but the danger in his tone was clear, and made my skin cold. I'd seen Dimitri in "work mode" before, but each time it was a shocking reminder of who he was, and the powerful position he held within the hierarchy.

Doro glowered, but retreated to the other side of the room. Dimitri followed him, and I was left to defend myself against Mikhail's glare.

'Doro has a point. Who do you think you are?' Mikhail growled. 'You fancy yourself my business advisor?'

Being on the receiving end of Mikhail's displeasure was never easy, but I ignored the quickening of my heartbeat, and focused on mirroring Dimitri's careful, calm expression. 'Why not? I'd be a good one. I'm making you money, aren't I?' I asked, sounding a lot more confident than I felt.

'Yes, but you are also on thin ice, Mari.' Mikhail regarded me for a minute, before continuing, 'I do not think I'm clear on your motives, here.'

'*You* pursued me, you didn't give me a choice but to work for you,' I pointed out. I didn't like where the conversation was heading.

'Yes, for simple delivery jobs, club jobs. Not making business deals with rival organisations! Remember your place, little girl!' Mikhail bellowed, shooting to his feet, his chair scraping the floor behind him.

I resisted the urge to shrink back against the wall as

his anger filled the room. I guessed he didn't like me arguing back, no matter how valid my point was.

'I told you already that I need money, that's why I'm doing bar shifts at your other clubs,' I reminded him. 'Isn't that what motivates us all?' I gestured to the others in the room. 'Money.'

He stared at me. 'You are responsible for this arrangement with Tanet. But understand me, if one thing goes wrong, it's on you. And the punishment will be final. Are we clear?'

The threat in his voice was unmistakable. I nodded.

'Good.' He sat down. 'Now get out, all of you.'

The four of us filed out of the room, and I could feel all of their eyes on me as we went. I started to head back into the main club room, but Dimitri grabbed my arm, steering me into a private booth and drawing the curtain across behind us. I'd been in the private booth enough times to know that nothing good was about to happen.

'What the hell is wrong with you?' he whispered urgently. 'Why would you do that?'

'I'm sick of being the butt of Mikhail's jokes, he needs to take me seriously.'

Dimitri raised his eyebrows. 'Are you serious?'

I shrugged. 'Well, what do you suggest I do?'

'Keep your damn head down,' Dimitri said, as if it should have been obvious. I suppose it should have been.

I shook my head. 'Look, I'm here, OK? This is where we are. And it's my fault that a lot of bad things have happened, so I need to make this count, otherwise it was all for nothing.'

I watched his chest rise and fall, heavily, and he seemed to have exhaled his anger. Dimitri took my face in his hands, holding my gaze intensely. 'Nina is not your fault.'

I pushed his hands away, and left the booth.

I didn't go back to the Thai men, deciding that they'd probably had enough of me, and I'd rather go home anyway. But I didn't get very far; Doro was waiting for me outside. I'd barely stepped out onto the pavement before he'd grabbed my arm and dragged me towards him.

'What do you think you're playing at? Did you not hear my warning?' he demanded, blowing cigarette smoke in my face.

'You mean when you threatened to tell Mikhail about me?'

'Oh, so you did hear me. You must just be stupid.'

I rolled my eyes, yanking my arm out of his grip. 'No, you are. If you tell Mikhail about me, don't you think I'd return the favour?'

Doro scoffed. 'Who do you think he'd believe, you or me?'

I shrugged. 'Who's earning him the most money right now, you or me?'

'Ha,' Doro snorted. 'You think because you've just grown some balls that suddenly you're valuable? You entertain him, like a naughty kitten. But if you bite too hard, he'll stamp on you.' He dropped his cigarette butt and squashed it beneath his boot. Subtle.

Now I laughed, but there was no humour. I couldn't believe this man had been my friend, even my mentor. What had the City done to him?

'You know, Steve,' I said, using his real name to make a point. 'It really seems like you're jealous. Is it because you want Mikhail to yourself...?'

'If anyone's slipping it to Mikhail, it's you,' Doro spat, clearly not finding my joke funny. 'That's how you get your information, isn't it? And it explains why he's letting his new pet get away with so much at the moment.'

Why did people always think my appearance was all I had going for me?

'No, it's because I'm good at my job,' I replied. 'Now leave me alone.'

I tried to walk away, but he grabbed my arm again, hard enough to bruise. 'I'm not done talking to you.'

'Yes you are,' I told him.

Doro snarled, 'If you're gonna be like that, I'll just march back inside and tell Mikhail about the little rat in his crew.'

'What's going on?' Dimitri stepped into view. I didn't know how long he'd been there; neither of us had heard him exit the club. Underneath the streetlight, his face was thunder.

Doro let go of my arm, but he was smiling, and that wasn't good. 'Or maybe I'll just tell lover boy, instead.' He turned to Dimitri. 'Do you know who she really is?'

'Doro,' I warned. This could only end badly.

'Tell me, Dimitri,' Doro continued, 'what's the normal reaction to finding out you've got a rat in your midst?'

Dimitri said nothing.

'You'd kill them right?' Doro went on, taking a step towards Dimitri. 'But here's the twist. What if the rat turns out to be your girlfriend?'

I gasped. I couldn't believe he'd actually just turned me in. If it had been anyone other than Dimitri to walk out of the club at that minute, I'd have been in big trouble. As far as Doro knew, he'd just sentenced me to death.

'How could you?' I cried. 'What has gone so wrong in your tiny pathetic brain that you don't even remember who you are anymore? This isn't your life! Why are you acting like it is?'

'This *is* my life!' Doro roared. 'But it's not yours. Not anymore.'

The burn of angry tears stung my eyes. 'Do you really hate me so much that you want me to die?'

Doro simply shrugged. 'This is where my loyalties lie now. I warned you.'

'Who else have you told?' Dimitri asked, his voice level.

'No one, yet.' Doro replied. He was enjoying this, the sick bastard. 'I thought you'd like to be the first to know.'

'I appreciate that.'

Then, before I even knew what was coming next, Dimitri pulled a gun and shot Doro in the head.

Chapter Thirty-Six

The body hit the ground.

'No!' I screamed. I dropped to my knees, pulling on Steve's collar, trying to get a reaction, but he'd died instantly. 'No, no, no, no!'

I looked up at Dimitri, who was watching me with a conflicted expression. 'Why did you do that?' I sobbed.

'Because he was a cop.'

I stood, slowly, and took a step towards him. I didn't know what I was going to say, but I didn't have time to figure it out, because he pulled out his phone instead. Whoever he called must have picked up instantly, and Dimitri said, 'Come out front. Bring someone.'

Moments later, Mikhail and Jag exited the club, the heavy bassline of the music pouring out into the street until the door shut behind them. At least no one inside had heard the gunshot. I swiped at my tears, trying to regain my composure.

Mikhail took in the scene before him, his eyes blazing, and turned to Dimitri for an explanation.

'He was an undercover police officer,' Dimitri told him.

My breathing was too fast. I felt like I might fall. I tried to focus on Dimitri's story; I needed to go along with it convincingly.

'Bullshit,' Jag protested.

'I overheard him trying to persuade Mari to turn on you,' Dimitri told Mikhail.

Mikhail considered this, then looked at me. 'Mari?'

I blinked, my thoughts racing. Then I nodded. I had no choice but to play along. 'He told me he'd put me in witness protection. I told him no.' I couldn't hide the shake in my words.

'Why should I believe you?' Mikhail asked. His voice

gave nothing away.

I took a deep breath. This was so wrong, but Steve was dead already, and if I wasn't convincing enough, I'd meet the same fate. 'He told me his real name. Steven Blackwood.'

'Jag, call our contact, check it out,' Mikhail instructed.

Jag nodded, pulling his phone from his pocket and stepping away to make the call. I wanted to follow him. Who was their contact? Someone in the police department? The 'friend' in a high place that Steve had referred to previously? But my attention was pulled back to Mikhail, when he came to my side and wrapped an arm around me. He smelled of expensive aftershave, and expensive alcohol. I tensed, but didn't move away. It wasn't a gesture of comfort; it was one of control.

'If you two are right about this,' Mikhail spoke softly to me, 'I'll need you to tell me exactly what he said to you, and exactly what you said back.'

I nodded mutely.

It didn't take Jag long. 'It's confirmed. DS Steve Blackwood, no cases for the last few years, fits with an undercover job.'

Mikhail swore. His arm was still around me. 'Okay, Mari. I'm gonna need you to come with me.' He started to lead me back into the club. 'Dimitri, Jag, clean this up.'

I glanced back over my shoulder at Dimitri. He gave me an almost imperceptible nod. He was telling me to be strong, to go along with it, and it would be fine. But he was wrong. Nothing about this was fine.

***

In Mikhail's office, I sat opposite him at the desk, watching him pour vodka into a couple of crystal tumblers. He slid one across the mahogany towards me. I picked it up with shaking hands and drained the contents in two quick gulps. Mikhail reached across to pour me some more.

'Are you alright?' he surprised me by asking, in an almost gentle tone.

I nodded, emptying my glass once more.

'Have you ever seen someone shot like that before? Right before your eyes?' he asked.

I stared at my hands on the desk. They were very pale. 'Once. Nina.'

'I don't imagine that it will ever get easier to see, not for someone like you.'

Now I looked up, frowning. Mikhail met my eyes with his own piercing blue gaze. 'Why are you being nice to me?' I asked.

'You look quite traumatised,' Mikhail told me.

I let out a single, harsh bark of laughter. 'You think?'

'I need you to tell me what he said to you. Word for word. Walk me through it.'

I took a deep breath, and prepared to lie to save my life.

'He was waiting outside for me,' I began. 'He asked me why I was getting myself more and more involved with your business, asked me if I needed help or protection. I asked what he meant, and he said, "witness protection". I guessed then that he was police, and he said he was, and he told me his real name, so that I knew he wasn't lying. He told me that if I provided evidence and testified against you, that he would protect me.'

Mikhail's face was blank. 'And what did you say?'

'I said no. I said that if I turned on you, you'd kill me.'

'Correct.'

'He was trying to convince me that I'd be safe, and then Dimitri came outside, and he must have overheard the conversation, because he just shot Doro.' I sighed, dropping my head into my hands. I felt awful for lying about Steve to save myself. I didn't know who he'd become, but I knew who he used to be, my friend. How did I end up here?

I heard Mikhail moving, and when I lifted my head, he was sat in the chair next to me. 'Mari, you know that I have become fond of you. I think it is because, if I had a daughter, I imagine she'd be quite like you.'

I blinked. That was out of the blue.

'You handle yourself better than almost any woman I've ever met, and you are bright, and seemingly not afraid of much,' he continued. 'Hear me now. Your loyalty will not go unrewarded.'

'What does that mean?'

'If there's anything you need, you let me know.'

I nodded.

Seriously, *how* did I end up here?

***

On my way home, I stopped by the 24 hour off licence, cracking the bottle of spirit open before I was even out of the store. By the time I got to my apartment, I was buzzed. By the time Dimitri knocked on my door, I was absolutely blackout drunk. There was music blaring that I didn't remember putting on — Stevie Nicks. Random choice. The neighbour downstairs was using something to hit her ceiling — maybe a broom? Which was bumping the floor underneath my spine. I'd taken off my clothes, since they'd been subject to blood spatter, and was lying on the cold lino floor in my underwear, and my slippers, because my feet felt cold.

I guess when I didn't answer the door, Dimitri let himself in. He shut off the music. I sat up, and the room span.

'Heyyyy,' I protested weakly. 'My music.'

'The neighbours are about to storm this place. It's 5am.'

Even in my inebriated state, I noticed he'd changed his clothes. He was no longer wearing jeans and a cashmere sweater, but jogging bottoms and a t-shirt. I preferred this look on him. He looked cosy. I felt cold.

'Can I have your t-shirt?'

He frowned at me. 'No, but I will find you some clothes.'

I lay down again, and rolled onto my belly. The chill of the floor gave me goose bumps, which tickled and made me laugh.

Dimitri went into my bedroom, and returned with a hoodie and some pyjama trousers. He helped me stand up. I was very wobbly. He was very warm. I leaned into him, breathing in his clean scent. He'd showered. I guessed moving a body was the kind of work that would cause one to break a sweat. Steve's body. Stevie Nicks. Had I done that on purpose? I reached for the speakers again, but Dimitri stopped me.

'Come on, get dressed,' he said. I appreciated how gentle he was being.

'Mikhail was gentle with me, too,' I told him.

He frowned at me. 'I'm going to assume that you didn't mean that how it sounded.'

I considered. 'Well, he's not *un*attractive.'

What was I saying? My mouth was no longer connected to my brain.

Dimitri arched his brows, but he looked amused. 'Oh, really? Do I need to be worried about the competition?'

Dimitri sat me down on the couch, and knelt in front of me to help me into the pyjamas. His hands brushed my thighs as he pulled the trousers up to my waist. I shivered involuntarily.

'There's no competition,' I sighed, contentedly. 'You know I love you.'

Dimitri's eyes snapped up to meet mine, his hands stilled on my hips. He didn't look amused anymore. Oh, God, why did I say that? I inwardly cursed my stupid disobedient mouth. Why wasn't it listening to my brain?

'I just killed your friend, right in front of you.'

I blinked at him. Why was he talking about that? I didn't want to talk about that. 'Yeah.'

'I am a murderer,' he told me.

I nodded. 'I know that already.'

Dimitri stood up, suddenly, and paced across the room. When he turned back to look at me, he stared at me, like I'd turned green or something. I pushed myself to my feet, and shuffled over to him. I placed my hands on his chest, feeling the pure muscle under the fabric. His heartbeat was fast.

'I'm very drunk,' I told him, as if to justify myself.

He sighed, and his arms encircled me. 'I know.'

'Can we go to bed?' I asked. I had no shame. My sober self was going to be embarrassed about that tomorrow.

'As you've just pointed out, you're very drunk,' Dimitri replied.

I pouted. 'That's a no, isn't it?'

He sighed, his arms dropping away from me as he took a step back. 'It's never been a good idea, the two of us being together like that.'

What was he saying? My brain scrambled to understand, and reached the wrong conclusion. 'Are you mad because I said I love you?'

Dimitri swore, and turned away from me. 'Stop saying that!'

'Why?' I demanded.

He spun to face me again, his eyes blazing. 'Because it isn't true.'

I frowned. That was a mean thing to say. It made me angry. 'I'm not a liar.'

'You don't know how you feel.'

Again, that made me angry. 'I'm not a child.'

'I killed your friend!' Dimitri yelled. 'You should be mad at me; you should be disgusted by who I am and what I do every single day!'

'I am.'

Dimitri threw his arms up, apparently exasperated by me. 'Then you can't possibly love me.'

I shook my head. Even when I stopped, the room kept moving.

'I am going to bed,' I announced, before shuffling into the bedroom.

I fell onto the bed and sighed. My body ached. Bed felt good. Better than the floor had felt. I don't know whether I fell asleep, or passed out. The last thing I remember thinking about was Steve, lying in a pool of his own blood, his eyes empty and lifeless. Another death on my conscience.

Chapter Thirty-Seven

Memory loss was never something I'd had trouble with, no matter how much I drank. I'd always appreciated that, until I woke up mid-afternoon with a pounding head and perfect recall of the conversation I'd had with Dimitri just a few hours earlier. I also had the image of Steve, dead, imprinted on my eyes. I knew that I'd never shake that from my memory, even if I drank every single day.

I needed to call Taylor. I reached for my hidden phone, but I couldn't pick it up. How was I meant to tell my boss that I'd seen one of our own killed last night? Or that the reason he'd been shot was because he'd told Mikhail's right-hand man that I was a police officer? And that Mikhail's right-hand man already knew that, and shot Steve to protect me, because we'd been sleeping together for months, and I might even have been in love with him?

I had no way to cope with this. I'd come so close to being killed myself last night. If anyone other than Dimitri had walked out of the club at that moment, I would be dead already. That made me want to thank Dimitri — actually *thank* him — for killing Steve, because he'd saved my life. But to do that, he'd shot Steve. What was I meant to do?

***

I tried all afternoon to pull myself together, but I couldn't even bring myself to get out of bed until a knock at my door forced my movement. I didn't know what time it was, but it was dark, which was probably a good thing, given that I was a hungover, unwashed, tear-stained mess.

'Oh.' I hadn't expected it to be Valentin at my door. I

was glad I'd taken the time to pull on a T-shirt.

'Hey,' he said, giving me a sympathetic look over the two paper coffee cups he held.

I held the door open, inviting him inside. Val and I had never spent much time together just the two of us, and I had barely seen him at all since Nina died. She was the only reason that Val and I ever saw one another, and it felt as if she should be walking through the door alongside him. But he was painfully alone.

I switched on the lamp in the lounge, hoping it would be a little more forgiving than the overhead light. We sat together on the sofa, and Val handed me one of the coffees he'd brought.

'Figured you might need it, after last night,' Val said. I'd never seen him on my couch before. Again, I felt the lack of Nina's presence.

'Thank you,' I was more grateful for the caffeine than he knew. 'You heard about Doro, then?'

'Dimitri called me this morning. How are you holding up?'

'I'm fine.'

Val looked at me. He didn't believe me. 'Come on, Mari. You've lost a lot of people recently. Nina, now Doro, and Fabio's in prison. You're not working at *Arrow's* anymore. You're dealing with the Colombians, and now the Thais. Are you really fine?'

I don't know if it was the hangover, or hearing Val list it all out like that, but I suddenly felt like there was no gravity anymore, and I was spinning out into the atmosphere, alone and untethered. Val nodded, like he understood what I was feeling, and reached his arm out. We leaned back together into the sofa. I rested my cheek on his chest. He smelled a little like Nina, and I wondered if he'd been staying at her place.

'I spent the day with Dimitri,' Val told me. 'He's a

mess about this whole thing, too.'

'I bet he's not as much of a mess as I am.'

Val chuckled softly. 'He shows it differently, that much is true. But he's not the stone cold man that he pretends to be.'

'I know,' I said. And I did know that. I just didn't know why Val was telling me. 'I missed you, you know.'

I felt Val sigh. 'Me, too. It's just hard without her.'

'Yeah.' I agreed. 'How have you been?' It was an inadequate question.

Val hesitated before answering, then said, 'I don't know. I'm not sure who I am without her. I'm just trying to figure it out.'

I felt my heart break all over again.

***

The next morning, I got in the shower and washed my hair and got dressed. I needed routine and I needed to feel normal. I even put a little makeup on to disguise the dark circles that seemed to be permanently etched beneath my eyes. Then, I headed upstairs to Dimitri's.

It wasn't early, but he answered the door rubbing sleep from his eyes, dressed in nothing but a pair of shorts. 'Hey.' His first word of the day was always husky, and it made my stomach dip.

'Hey. Can I come in? I need to talk to you.'

Dimitri led the way inside to the kitchen, where he set about making coffee.

'So, what's up?' he asked, pulling two mugs from the cupboard.

'I need to know where Steve's body is.'

Dimitri turned to meet my gaze, surprise evident in his expression. It occurred to me then that he might have assumed I wanted to talk about something else that had recently happened between us. Now that we were only talking about the police officer he recently murdered, Dimitri seemed more relaxed.

'I need to call my boss,' I explained. 'I haven't told him what happened yet, and he'll need to know where Steve is, so they can retrieve the body.'

Dimitri turned away from me. 'Yeah, I expected as much, so I buried him rather than… anything else. In the woods, behind the graveyard where we went once. Not very far in, and not very deep. It will be easy to find.'

I swallowed the lump in my throat. 'Thank you. And don't worry, I won't mention your name.'

Now, he turned around, running a hand over his ruffled hair. 'I'm not worried about that. We've got a bigger problem.'

I almost laughed. Almost. 'Really?'

'Doro introduced me to you, and you told me that you and he had known each other for years. If he told Mikhail the same thing, which I'm assuming he did, then you're going to need to come up with an explanation.'

I groaned. 'Of course. God, everything really is messed up, isn't it?'

Dimitri's expression softened. 'Yeah. We just need to get a story straight, okay?'

I considered this for a minute. 'Didn't he tell you once that he and I were together?'

Dimitri nodded.

'Well, can't we just say that? He told you, so he might have told other people. It would also explain the vague or differing reasons that people might have heard. It could have ended badly.'

'I guess that would explain the awkwardness, and why he hated you so much,' Dimitri said, and I flinched at the word *hate*.

'Steve was undercover for years,' I explained, 'So we

could say this happened a year or so ago, before I met Mikhail. I could have encountered him at *Arrow's*.' I sighed, shaking my head. 'I don't like this. It feels disrespectful to Steve. And I don't really want to encourage the idea that I just sleep with everyone. But that's the most believable option, isn't it?'

'More believable than the truth.'

I hesitated before saying, 'Valentin came over last night. He seemed to think that you might be having a bit of a rough time, too. Are you okay?'

Dimitri looked at me, his expression careful. 'Yes.'

'I mean, obviously nothing is okay right now,' I continued, apparently losing control of my words again. 'Everything is falling apart. It's just, I know that you've done that a lot, what you did to Steve, and I guess it didn't occur to me that it would really bother you. You and Steve didn't get along anyway. And you did it to protect me. Not that that makes it any better, I guess. I'm actually grateful to you, but then I feel guilty, because I shouldn't think that. You saved my life. But I can't tell my boss that. I just have to tell him that Steve is dead.'

I sighed, giving into myself and wrapping my arms around Dimitri. He was very still. 'I'm sorry that you're in this position because of me,' I said, resting my forehead on his bare chest.

I listened to him breathing for a minute, then his arms encircled me, and he murmured into my hair, 'You must know by now that I'd do anything for you.'

My heart skipped. I couldn't help it. My fingers traced the muscles in his back, and over the lines where I knew his tattoos were, even though I couldn't see them. I knew every inch of his body. And he knew mine, too, evidenced when he touched just the right place on my collar bone to make me tilt my head back almost involuntarily.

He kissed me. He was gentle, even as we responded to one another, and he walked me backwards to the kitchen counter, lifting me carefully up onto the surface top. I wrapped my legs around his waist, enjoying the fact that he was already mostly naked. He was so, so beautiful.

Dimitri undressed me slowly, his fingers lingering on my skin, his eyes seeming to take in every part of me as if it were the last time he would see me. He kissed my neck, down over my chest, my stomach, to the inside of my thighs. It was tender and sweet. And amazing. As it always was. Afterwards, he held me tightly, our damp bodies rising and falling together as we caught our breath. Dimitri buried his face in my neck, and I almost didn't hear him when he whispered into my skin.

'I love you, too.'

Chapter Thirty-Eight

I called Taylor that evening. I told him that Steve had been killed by one of Mikhail's men, but I said that I didn't know who was responsible. I also left out the fact that it had happened right in front of me, choosing instead to let Taylor believe that I'd heard about it from someone else. If I told him I'd seen it first-hand, he'd pull me out with immediate effect.

Taylor responded professionally, but I knew him well enough to hear the masked devastation in his voice. I told him where Steve was buried, which is when my own voice broke, but I managed to hold myself together. Just barely.

'Do you need me to get you out of there?' Taylor asked me.

'No. I'm so close now. I don't want to waste all of the work that we've done. I don't want to waste Steve's life.'

'Promise me that you are safe. There's nothing you're not telling me.'

'I promise.'

Oh, boy, was I going to be in trouble when Taylor found out the truth.

'There is something though,' I said. 'Mikhail has a contact in the police department, I think.'

Pause. 'What makes you think that?'

'Steve insinuated it. And apparently, they called this person to find out whether Steve was undercover or not, and whoever they spoke to confirmed it.'

Taylor swore. 'So they must have access to our records.'

'Yeah. Any ideas who it could be?'

He sighed. 'No. But I can't imagine anyone in this office betraying us like this. I need to look into this.'

'Be careful,' I warned. 'They won't want to be found.'

***

Dimitri had been right; Mikhail called me to his office on Saturday evening, before the club was due to open. I found him sat behind his desk, part way through a bottle of whiskey, a glass of which he poured for me when I entered.

'How are you?' he asked me.

I sat down opposite him and took the glass he offered. 'How do you think I am?'

'I need to talk to you about Doro. Or, Steve, as we now know him.'

I said nothing, waiting for him to ask the question I knew was coming.

'I need you to explain to me how you first met him, and the truth about your relationship. You and Doro and Dimitri — your complicated personal lives — have caused me a lot of trouble. And now we know who Doro really was, I must admit I have some suspicions,' Mikhail said, his voice level. He leaned back in his chair, lacing his hands behind his head and showing the impressive size of his upper body. I swallowed my nerves.

'Okay,' I replied, preparing my rehearsed story. 'I met Doro eighteen months ago at *Arrow's*. I didn't have a lot in my life at that time, and he was nice to me, he bought me expensive gifts, and we started sleeping together. He introduced me to Dimitri and Nina.'

Mikhail watched me, his expression neutral, unreadable.

I continued, 'After a while, I started seeing Dimitri, so I broke it off with Doro. He obviously took it badly, which is why he assaulted me, and why it's been so awkward between the three of us. I had no idea he was undercover until he told me the other night. I guess he got worried about how involved I'm getting, and I guess he

265

was trying to help me. I don't know.' I shook my head, looking down into my lap, trying to play the part.

I heard Mikhail exhale slowly, considering my story. Then he said, 'Why should I believe this? I have heard many different stories about you and Doro now. How do I know which is the truth?'

I looked up. 'Ask around, I'm sure he told people about us. He was really pissed when I got together with Dimitri.'

'Hm.' Mikhail shrugged. 'Why did you not just tell me this before?'

'You already think I'm sleeping my way through your men, it's not exactly an image I want to encourage.' It physically hurt me to degrade myself by saying the words, but I knew it was the only way to save myself here. And really, who was Mikhail to judge me?

'I am aware that Doro had a certain reputation with women, and that he liked to take advantage of my girls often,' Mikhail said, and I grimaced internally. 'But it does surprise me that *you* would be interested in him.'

I frowned. Was that really Mikhail's main question about my story?

'Well, like I said, I was lonely and broke when I met him.' I shrugged. 'That's why I'm so involved with you, with the business. I'm making money, and I actually feel like I belong somewhere, for once.'

Mikhail looked at me, as if deciding whether to believe me or not.

I couldn't sit in silence and wait for his verdict. 'I honestly had no idea about Doro being undercover. I wouldn't even believe it now, if you hadn't verified it. Do you have a contact in the police department, or something?'

'Yes.' Mikhail sat forward, dismissing my question without giving me any more details. 'Okay, Mari. I believe you. And I know what it is to be lonely. You comfort yourself with men, I comfort myself with this.'

He opened a drawer in his desk and retrieved a box. Tipping a little of the substance inside onto the smooth mahogany tabletop, he used a blade to set up several lines of cocaine, then passed me a rolled bank note. 'Indulge with me, won't you?'

I took the paper in my hand. Was this some kind of test? 'I'm fine, thanks.' I tried to hand the note back to him, but he didn't take it.

'Mari. Come on, now. This is the product that you secured. You should try it at least once,' Mikhail had a glimmer of something in his eyes, and I knew he wasn't really giving me a choice.

I took a deep breath. I'd never taken drugs before, not once, although I'd seen enough people partake to know what I was doing. *Well, down the rabbit hole we go…*

I put the note to the desk, and copied what I'd seen many of Mikhail's men do over the last several months. It stung the back of my nose, and I coughed automatically, squeezing my eyes shut and my teeth together involuntarily.

Mikhail nodded, pleased. He took the rolled note back from me, and finished the lines on the table. Then, he reached for a bottle and filled our glasses with dark liquid. I took a drink to wash the powder down my throat. I guessed we weren't done, so I decided to use the time to my benefit, while I was still thinking clearly.

'How can you feel lonely, with so many loyal people around you?' I asked.

Mikhail took a drink from his own glass. 'My men are loyal, yes. They would do anything I asked them. But as I have got older, I have realised that they are not a substitute for family. They do not have concern for me. They do not contact me if it is not about the business.'

'Do you not have family?' I asked, although I knew the answer from my training.

'I do not. My parents died when I was young, my sister too...' Mikhail finished his drink and nodded for me to do the same, before reaching for the bottle again.

The whiskey burned my throat, and I was starting to feel the caffeine-like burst of energy from the coke. This was not a good combination. But weirdly, Mikhail was actually talking to me. I couldn't pass up this opportunity. I slid my glass towards him for a refill.

'Don't you date?' I asked.

Mikhail shrugged. 'In my line of work, women are always around if I want them.'

I laughed. I don't know why. 'No, I mean, what about a relationship?'

'There have been some. I find it tiresome.'

'It is,' I agreed. 'But sometimes, it's worth it.'

Mikhail shifted in his seat, and smiled at me, knowingly. 'Like with Dimitri?'

I nodded.

This seemed to please him. 'My best man, and my first female man.' Mikhail laughed. 'If you understand my meaning.'

I did. He meant that I was the first woman to work for him in any capacity other than as a bartender, a prostitute or a dancer. I felt weirdly proud. Then I noticed I'd finished my drink — again. I needed to stop, but I felt almost excited, like something really good was about to happen, and drinking was going to make it even better. I was starting to think that getting high should have been part of my undercover training, so I would have been prepared for this moment. Maybe I'd suggest it to Taylor. I laughed out loud at the thought.

Mikhail laughed along with me, even though he had no idea what I'd found so funny.

'I think,' Mikhail mused. 'That when I go, I would like you and Dimitri to run things together.'

I frowned. 'Really? Why? You hardly know me.'

'Dimitri has had a lifetime of training for this, he knows all of our business ventures inside out, all of our contacts. And you, you're smart. You've got the business acumen that my enterprise would otherwise lack. With the exception of myself, of course.'

'Of course,' I agreed.

Mikhail stood, rounded the desk, and pulled me up by my arms. I worried momentarily that they might fall off, but they didn't. He tugged me over to a small leather couch at the back of the room, beneath a bookcase filled with files. I wondered what was in them; given that Dimitri had not removed them when the police raided the club, I guessed that it was probably legitimate business paperwork. Boring.

I settled back into the soft leather, and Mikhail made himself comfortable beside me. This was the closest we'd ever been, but I didn't feel nervous; I just felt dizzy, and like there was a buzzing of some kind behind my eyes. Mikhail smiled contentedly, leaned his head back and took a deep breath. He was at his most comfortable level of intoxicated. I suddenly found him to look his age, for once, weary almost.

'Do you ever get tired of this business?' I asked.

'No,' he answered, lifting his head to meet my gaze. 'It is the rivalry that is tiring. Always looking over your shoulder to protect what you have worked for.'

I considered this. 'Well, you now have connections with Carlos, and Tanet. That's two rival gangs under your leadership, isn't it? I mean, they're depending on income from your sales, right?'

Mikhail nodded, his eyes narrowing with interest.

'They're the two biggest rivals you've got here,' I

continued, my mind surprisingly sharp without warning. My thoughts seemed to come too fast, and I struggled to catch them before they dissipated. I was onto something.

'Yes,' Mikhail mused. 'You are suggesting that I comprise a kind of… merger?'

'Why not? It's already kind of in place,' I replied. 'Oh! A super-mafia!' I laughed at my own joke too hard.

Mikhail grinned at me. 'Mari, my star. All business in this City—for miles around—will be at my order. It is almost that way already, I just need to formalise it.'

He grabbed my face in both of his warm, clammy hands, and planted a kiss on my forehead. 'My protégé!' he announced, a wild flare in his sky-blue eyes.

A knock at the door startled me. Dimitri entered, followed by Nick, Jag and Val. They all did a double take when they saw me sitting with Mikhail on the sofa, his hands still on my face. Did it look like we'd been making out?

'Hey!' I said when I saw Dimitri, only I drew the word out painfully. What was wrong with my voice? Also, why was the room starting to look fuzzy in the corners?

Dimitri's eyes flashed. 'What the hell is wrong with her?' he demanded.

'Relax,' Mikhail replied, releasing me and sinking back into the seat. 'Mari and I have had a nice evening. I think, though, that she may not be used to indulging in our product, only delivering it.'

'She's high?' Dimitri sounded mad. He grabbed my arm and pulled me to my feet. 'I'm taking her home. Catch me up on this tomorrow.' He gestured to the room, presumably referring to whatever business they'd been about to discuss.

Dimitri bundled me into a taxi and practically carried me up the stairs to my apartment. He took me straight to the bathroom, where I was promptly sick. The last thing I remember was lying down on the floor and wondering why I'd never noticed how comfortable my bathmat was until that moment.

Chapter Thirty-Nine

I woke up in my bed. My head was killing me. My stomach churned. Why on earth did people do drugs if this was the after effect? Or was this just the half bottle of whiskey I'd drank? Either way, I was never touching either substance again. I managed to sit up, rubbing my eyes in defence against the sunlight creeping in around the blinds. I knew that Dimitri had brought me home, and that he must have put me to bed, but he wasn't beside me.

Despite my foggy-feeling head, I was able to recall my evening with Mikhail. He'd been talking about getting all of the criminal organisations together. And it had somehow been my idea. Maybe I should take cocaine more often; *this was it!* If I could get evidence of his plans, we could prove conspiracy, the maximum sentence for which was life imprisonment.

Elated, I sprung to my feet and retrieved my secret phone from its hidden compartment. I dialled Taylor, smiling with excitement at the thought of his reaction when I told him my latest discovery, but he didn't answer. There was no voice mail set up — for obvious reasons — so I tried calling him several more times. Still, he didn't pick up. I frowned. That was the first time since I'd been here that he'd not been available for my call.

I put the phone away and was just sliding the drawer shut when I heard the bedroom door open behind me. I turned to see Dimitri step into the room. He was wearing tracksuit bottoms and a T-shirt, so I guessed he'd stayed here.

'You stayed on the sofa?' I guessed, wondering why he hadn't slept in the bed like usual.

'How are you feeling?' he responded, and then I knew why he was avoiding being close to me; he was angry. His voice was cool, his face a mask.

I stood, still fully clothed from last night, and shrugged. 'Not great. But it's so worth it. I got some great information from Mikhail, so now…'

Dimitri interrupted me. 'Oh, right, okay. Well that makes it okay then. You swan around the City, completely off your face, with the most dangerous man around, but you got some *information*.' He huffed, shaking his head in disbelief.

I frowned. 'I don't get why you're mad. Just wait 'til you hear what he told me.'

'It's probably not going to be any great surprise to me,' Dimitri pointed out, dryly.

'No, seriously, listen,' I sat down on the bed, pulling the duvet over my legs. 'So, he wants to coordinate all of his rival criminal organisations into one kind of super-mafia, under his control. He would control all the drugs, all the trafficking, everything. Any crime would be under his order, or at least his knowledge.'

Dimitri's blank expression gave way to a frown. 'He told you that?'

'Yeah!' I couldn't help my grin. 'And that's conspiracy, if I can get evidence of him planning to work in conjunction with other criminal organisations.'

Dimitri stepped further into the room and sank onto the other side of the bed, his anger seemingly forgotten. For now, anyway. 'Evidence? Like what?'

'So obviously there's no paper trail, but all we need to do is prove that Mikhail and one or more other organisational leaders planned and orchestrated some illegal act.'

'Oh, is that all?' Dimitri rolled his eyes.

'All I need is some kind of proof to show that Mikhail and whoever else were somewhere together, and that they were all aware of the plan. CCTV from the club maybe? It wouldn't be too hard to convince a jury that they were in on it together, given the nature of their businesses.'

'There's no CCTV at the club,' Dimitri told me. I wasn't surprised. 'And, not to throw a spanner in the works, but weren't you behind the deals with Carlos and Tanet?'

I hesitated. He was right, technically. 'But, it's still all under Mikhail's order. Just because I gave him the idea, doesn't mean that it isn't his doing. Besides, I got the impression that he's planning something more, from the way he was talking last night.'

Dimitri scoffed. 'You mean, while you were high as a kite?'

And the anger had returned. I threw my arms up in frustration. 'What is your problem? I've seen you high multiple times, but I'm not allowed?'

'I have tolerance. I don't get into a state like that,' Dimitri seethed. 'You put yourself at serious risk.'

'I was fine! Mikhail believed my story about how I met Doro, and he wanted me to "indulge" with him, so I did.' I shrugged. 'He opened up to me, a lot. He told me he is lonely, and that he wants me and you to run the organisation together, when he's dead.'

Dimitri looked like I'd slapped him. '*What?*'

I stood up, tired with his attitude, and suddenly very aware of my clothes sticking to me. 'Look, Dimitri. I appreciate your help, I really do. But I don't need your judgement. I think I'm doing pretty well, given recent events. Even if you don't agree.' I turned away from him to tug my shirt over my head.

'I just don't think you should be putting yourself in situations like that.'

I span around to face him again. He was now on his feet, too. Irritation warmed my cheeks. 'You don't think? Since when did I need your approval?'

'Since you'd be dead without me.' Dimitri shot back.

I gaped at him for a second, unable to believe that he'd throw that in my face. Then my jaw snapped shut. 'Get the hell out of my apartment,' I growled.

Dimitri crossed the room in seconds, and I involuntarily shrank back against the wall. His hands pressed into the plaster board at either side of my head. I kept my chin up, defiant, holding his gaze. This was the first time he'd tried to intimidate me like this, and I wouldn't let him succeed.

But when he spoke, his voice was soft. 'I just couldn't take it if something happened to you. Not after Izzy. Nina. Doro. Not when we…'

I took a breath, and felt my own anger start to dissipate. 'I'm not Izzy. I know what you do, I've always known. I know what I have to do, and now I have a solid lead on how to do it.'

Dimitri leaned further towards me, until our foreheads were touching. 'And then what?'

I closed my eyes. I couldn't answer. If I succeeded, I'd never see Dimitri again.

He planted the barest of kisses on my lips. 'Spend the day with me. No work talk. Just me and you.'

My eyes opened. 'Okay.'

***

Dimitri and I did spend the day together. We made love, we went for dinner, we watched a movie, we relaxed in bed talking about nothing for hours. It was perfect. But it also felt like goodbye. Because it was.

Chapter Forty

Mikhail called me the next morning, shortly after Dimitri left to shower and change his clothes in his own apartment. 'Good morning, Mari,' his low rumbled in my ear. 'You recall our conversation the other night?'

'Of course.' I sat up in bed, the duvet pooling around my waist.

'I'm calling a meeting with Tanet and Carlos. I want you there. Dimitri, too.'

My heart beat hard, but I took a deep breath and kept my voice casual. 'Sure. We'll be there.'

'Be in my office tonight.'

'Wait.' I thought back to the conversation I'd had with Dimitri — I needed proof of conspiracy, but he'd told me there was no CCTV in Mikhail's clubs. I just so happened to know somewhere that not only had CCTV, but was widely believed not to have any such surveillance equipment installed, and as such, was frequented by the exact types of people who wanted to avoid detection.

'We should meet somewhere else,' I said. 'Neutral ground. They will be more willing to negotiate when it's not on your turf.'

Mikhail paused, and I delighted in the fact that he was apparently thinking about it, rather than instantly dismissing my idea, as he would have done a few weeks ago. 'My turf gives me the upper hand.'

'Okay, so let's meet somewhere that we know, but isn't technically yours. How about *Arrow's*? You've done business there before.'

Again, he was silent for a moment, considering. 'Alright. *Arrow's,* tonight, 9pm.'

'See you then.'

I hung up and rolled over, reaching for the phone

hidden in the bedside table. I dialled Taylor but still he didn't answer. A deep, unsettled feeling stirred in my stomach. Something was wrong. But I didn't know who else to contact in the department without potentially breaking cover. A nagging voice reminded me that Mikhail also had an inside man within the force. I couldn't trust anyone and, at this point in the game, it wasn't worth the risk. With a deep sigh, I returned the phone to its hiding place, and slid the drawer shut.

Then, I called Dimitri to brief him.

***

When Dimitri and I walked into *Arrow's* several hours later, we didn't know exactly what to expect. Stepping inside, we saw Mikhail immediately, waiting for us in a booth. And he wasn't alone; he was with Tanet, Carlos and another man who had his back to us, and who I didn't immediately recognise. Nervous anticipation buzzed in my stomach.

It was a Monday night, and it was always quiet early in the week at *Arrow's*, but the distinct lack of customers other than Mikhail's table was unusual. I glanced at the bar and saw Tad, eyes wide, nervously wringing a tea towel in his hands. He noticed Dimitri and I enter, and started mouthing something to me. I couldn't tell what he was trying to say, but the fear in his eyes was clear. I approached him, and he leaned over the bar to whisper to me.

'They came in ten minutes ago and ordered all the customers to leave. They've got guns. Get out of here, and call the cops.'

'We're here to meet them,' I replied quietly. 'Stay calm, don't do anything.'

He looked like he wanted to protest, but he nodded.

'The CCTV is on?' I asked, in a hushed voice. Mikhail wouldn't be in here if he knew it existed.

Again, Tad nodded. The poor guy was white as a sheet.

'Tad, stay calm,' I repeated. 'Trust me, okay? It's fine.'

His eyes flitted between me and Dimitri, but he didn't argue with me. I hoped he wouldn't panic and do something stupid. I wished he wasn't here, but I knew if he left, Mikhail would react.

Dimitri led the way over to Mikhail's table, where the four men were already half-way through a litre of vodka. We pulled chairs from the neighbouring table, upon which sat several abandoned beverages, but before I took a seat, I cleared my throat.

'I just need to use the bathroom. I'll be right back.'

Forcing myself to move casually, I made it into the ladies' room before letting out a breath I wasn't aware I'd been holding. Bracing myself against the cold tiled wall, I focused on inhaling and exhaling, sorting through my racing thoughts. This was literally the endgame. If I could get proof of this conversation, it wouldn't be admissible in court, but in conjunction with the CCTV footage and my testimony, it would hopefully be enough to arrest Mikhail for conspiracy to supply, and Tanet and Carlos, too.

I splashed my face with cold water. I had to get it together. Reaching for my phone, I activated the microphone, and whispered, 'DS Hallowell, covert recording, 12th April, *Arrow's* bar.'

I zipped the phone back into my jacket pocket, microphone still on. Then I steeled myself, and headed back into the bar.

I took the seat next to Dimitri, feeling a renewed determination. But it was rattled when I came face to face with the fourth man at the table — Olivier. The man who spent his visits to the City with Nina. I felt anger bubbling beneath my skin. Dimitri shuffled his chair closer to me, nudging my arm in the process. When I met his gaze, he held a warning in his eyes, clearly knowing what I was thinking.

Mikhail poured us each a tumbler of clear liquid, no ice, while making introductions.

'Gentlemen, you all know Dimitri already, my most trusted comrade.' There was general nodding between the men, then Mikhail gestured to me. 'Most of you know Mari, too. She has joined us relatively recently, but she has proved a valuable asset. Olivier — I do not know if you had the pleasure of meeting Mari on your last visit?'

Olivier regarded me closely from beneath hooded eyes. 'I believe we crossed paths briefly.'

I stared back at him. His gravelly, slightly accented voice immediately conjured images of Nina, and my chest ached, but I kept my mouth shut.

Mikhail either didn't pick up on the tension, or he simply chose to ignore it. 'Excellent.' He placed the bottle in the centre of the table, and turned to me. 'Mari, Olivier is a significant investor in our business.'

'Can we get on with this?' Tanet grumbled, impatiently, leaning back in his seat with his arms crossed over his chest. His purple button-up shirt was rolled up to the elbows, revealing the gaudiest gold watch I'd ever seen.

'So, you will know by now that our businesses are intertwined, our profits dependent on one another's success,' Mikhail looked at each of us in turn. 'However, if there is an interruption to the Columbian supply chain, or the shipments from Thailand, or even to my client base, then we all suffer considerably.'

'So what?' grunted Carlos, emptying his glass for the

third time since I'd arrived.

Even though I was in regular contact with Carlos now, since having established our dealing with him, I couldn't help but flash back to our encounter at the *Angel Rooms*. Every time I saw him, I felt the hot flash of rage. Justice couldn't come fast enough.

'So, my friends,' Mikhail replied, 'I propose we combine our efforts.'

Now, Tanet leaned forward, propping his elbows on the table. He was intrigued. 'What, exactly, does that mean?'

'Well, we are all working to the bone to keep our respective parts of the business running, right? To keep our turf under control, and our customers loyal. I'm saying there could be a benefit to working together.' Mikhail sat back, letting his proposal sink in.

I glanced over my shoulder to check on Tad; he was stood behind the bar staring at our table, chewing nervously on one thumb. But he wasn't reaching for the phone, so that was something. I tried to reassure him with a small smile.

'And we are supposed to trust you?' Carlos scoffed. 'Didn't you have an undercover cop in your crew until very recently?' He meant Steve, of course. I swallowed, hard.

Mikhail cleared his throat, but it sounded more like a growl. From the expression on his face, I surmised that he had hoped that information wouldn't get out. 'The matter was dealt with accordingly. My inside contact is checking out any possible associates as we speak. But rest assured, this is an anomaly, and does not impact my proposal.'

'The hell it doesn't,' Carlos snorted.

Mikhail's fist slammed the table so suddenly, I jumped almost out of my seat. 'I will *not* have you undermine my operation. Without me, you'd still be selling to a few poor crackheads. I have *tripled* your profits, so you will show me some damned respect!' Mikhail barked. Carlos dipped his head, submissive to Mikhail's temper.

Issue dealt with, the men proceeded to talk details, hashing out the hypothetical specifics of Mikhail's proposal. I was listening, but my mind was racing; who was Mikhail's inside contact? Was he looking for other undercover officers? Would I be found out?

Dimitri glanced over at me, again understanding what I was thinking. He casually put his hand on my thigh, silently reassuring me. I appreciated the gesture, but it didn't calm my mind. I tried to focus on the conversation at hand.

'So, let me get this straight,' Tanet said. 'We give up our area of the City to you? And what, you pay us some kind of dividends?' He tutted, clearly unconvinced.

'No, my friend,' Mikhail shook his head. 'You give up nothing, you *gain* everything. In combination, we would have control of the entire City, and beyond. You still work your area, but we expand our operations across the territorial borders, so to speak. For instance, my dealers and your dealers will be one team, working across all areas. Do you understand?'

Tanet nodded, seeming to consider the idea. 'But someone still needs to be in charge. I suppose you're suggesting that should be you?'

'Well, not exactly. Olivier is my chief investor, but not only in terms of money. Olivier supplies many valuable products, many contacts. And this is my idea,' Mikhail explained. He held up his hand for silence when it looked like Tanet and Carlos might argue, and continued in his calm, businessman-like voice, 'However, rather than one boss with individual responsibility, we would operate as a council, of sorts.'

I almost laughed. A council? What next, quarterly

meetings?

'Dimitri and Mari will be my eyes and ears, leading on the day-to-day running of things,' Mikhail continued. 'I suggest you each appoint someone for that position, too. Then the three of us will only operate at the high-level. Increased protection for us, increased responsibility for our best men — oh, and woman,' Mikhail added, with a wink in my direction, 'and overall control of the entire City, region, and eventually, the country.'

Glances were exchanged around the table while all parties considered the implications of what Mikhail was suggesting. After a long, heavy silence, Tanet nodded, once. Carlos downed his drink, pounded the glass on the table, belched, and declared his agreement. Olivier smiled his approval at Mikhail. Mikhail laughed heartily; a sound so wrong when it came from him.

'Barkeep,' Mikhail called over to Tad. 'Another bottle!'

Mikhail was clearly pleased that his plan had been accepted, however when his phone rang, his smile faded as soon as he looked at the screen. He put the phone to his ear.

'You have it?'

Then he hung up. He watched his phone for a few seconds before it chimed. Twice. Then, not only was he not smiling anymore, but his face was twisting in a familiar storm of anger.

Dimitri's hand twitched on my thigh; he saw it too.

When Mikhail looked up, his expression was stone. His eyes focussed on me, and I knew.

He'd found out who I was.

Chapter Forty-One

'Gentlemen, I am sorry to cut our celebrations short,' Mikhail apologised charmingly to the men around the table, 'but I have some urgent business to attend to. Please, take the bottle, and I will catch up with you later.'

Tanet and Carlos exchanged a glance, but stood, taking the fresh bottle of vodka with them. The bar door slammed shut behind them, and my heart slammed into my ribs.

Olivier didn't move; clearly Mikhail's instructions did not apply to him. 'What is wrong?' Olivier asked quietly.

Dimitri shifted in his seat, taking my hand, as if to leave. 'We should be going too.'

'Stay where you are,' Mikhail growled in a voice deeper than I'd ever heard, his charming façade well and truly gone. He turned to Olivier, 'It seems that we have another rat in our midst. Our friend was kind enough to send me a photo. Here.' Mikhail held his phone out for Olivier to see.

Olivier's eyebrows jumped, and his eyes widened, then fixed on me.

It was really happening. I couldn't speak.

Luckily, Dimitri was a lot better in stressful situations than me. 'Mikhail, what's going on?' he asked, as if he didn't already know.

'Why don't we ask Mari?' Mikhail suggested. He downed the last of his drink, slamming the glass down on the table so hard that it split down one side, and I flinched.

Mikhail turned his phone around so that Dimitri and I could see the screen. Sure enough, there was a staff photo of me in uniform. I was younger, my hair was different, and there was no damage to my face, but it was undeniably me.

283

For one long second, nobody moved. I wasn't breathing. And then, all hell broke loose.

To my left, Dimitri was suddenly on his feet, gun pointed at Mikhail. To my right, Mikhail had also pulled a weapon and was aiming it squarely at my head. I stood so quickly that my chair fell back behind me, clattering on the floor. I started to reach for the handgun tucked into the back of my waistband, but Mikhail took a step forward, and I froze.

'You had me fooled,' Mikhail told me, his voice a low rumble, his pistol just inches from my forehead. 'And for that, I will make your death hurt.'

My mind raced; if I died here, this would all have been for nothing. I had to get away. Or, at the very least, I had to get my phone back to Taylor, with the recording evidence intact, even if I wasn't.

'Mikhail, think about this,' Dimitri was saying, his voice incomprehensibly steady. 'Do you really think Mari is with the police? She's proved her loyalty to you. She completed the initiation. She even set up new connections with rival organisations.'

Mikhail kept his eyes on me. 'And yet, I have photographic evidence of the contrary. I must admit, *Mari*, you played a good game.'

'There's no game,' I replied, finally finding my voice. I sounded nervous, but hoped that they would attribute that to having a weapon aimed at my skull. 'I don't know what's going on here. I'm not a police officer. You know me.'

Mikhail laughed, humourlessly. 'No, I do not.'

'You know me, though,' Dimitri said, redirecting Mikhail's gaze to him. 'You know me. And I know her. Your contact is wrong.'

Mikhail scoffed. 'She fooled you, just as she fooled me. More so, perhaps.' He glanced between me and

Dimitri, a frown passing over his brow. 'Or, did you know?'

Dimitri said nothing. My breath caught in my throat. Even if I was caught, I couldn't let Dimitri go down, too.

'You killed Doro,' Mikhail continued, piecing it together. 'You overheard him disclosing his true identity to Mari. Or, so you claimed. But if they were in it together, surely you would have heard that, too?' Mikhail's eyes narrowed. 'You chose to spare her? Why? Because you're banging her?'

'Because she isn't a cop,' Dimitri replied, his voice unbelievably steady, as was his aim, still trained on Mikhail.

Mikhail shook his head, holding Dimitri's gaze. I could tell he didn't want to believe that his right-hand man would have betrayed him, but I also knew that he'd figured it out, and he wouldn't be easily persuaded otherwise.

While he wasn't looking at me, I took the opportunity to make my move. Bending at the knees, I dipped below the aim of Mikhail's pistol, and rushed him. My shoulder hit his stomach, and I heard the breath rush from his lungs. Driving us backward, we hit the wall, and I grabbed Mikhail's right wrist, attempting to knock the weapon out of his grip.

But he was stronger than me, and he twisted free. He grabbed me by the throat with his left hand and spun us, so that he was pressing me into the cold, chipped brick wall. Over his shoulder, I saw Dimitri take aim, but he was tackled by a surprisingly fast-moving Olivier. The two of them tumbled to the floor, exchanging punches, and I flashed back to the first time I saw Dimitri in action, when he beat Tony outside of the *Angel Rooms*. That was a lifetime ago.

Dragging my gaze back to Mikhail, I met his icy blue

stare. 'Okay,' I said, my voice strained against his grip on my neck. 'You got me. Do what you want to me. But Dimitri didn't know.'

Mikhail's lips curled into a snarl. 'I will deal with him later. You first.'

My heartbeat hammered in my ears, but I knew I couldn't let him see my fear. I wanted to beg for my life, but I wouldn't. If I was going to die, at least I could do it with dignity.

'Are there others?' Mikhail asked me, loosening his grip ever so slightly, so as to allow me to answer him.

'No,' I replied. I had no idea if there were other undercover officers.

'You and Doro were working together?'

I let out a humourless chuckle. 'No. He was loyal to you, believe it or not. Probably one of your most loyal, as it happens.'

Over Mikhail's shoulder, Dimitri and Olivier continued to struggle, their grunts of pain escalating. Luckily, Dimitri seemed to have the edge, but then I saw Olivier grab the leg of my fallen chair. He swung his arm back and brought it down on Dimitri, the metal chair frame meeting Dimitri's skull with a sickening *thud.*

'Dimitri knew?' Mikhail asked his next question.

I forced myself to look away from Dimitri's still body, and met Mikhail's gaze boldly. 'No. He heard Doro's side of the conversation, and jumped to conclusions. He never heard anything about me. He knows nothing.'

Mikhail shook his head. He didn't believe me. But I thought he probably wanted to.

Olivier appeared in my peripheral vision. 'We should go,' he told Mikhail.

Mikhail nodded, and pulled me away from the wall towards the door, clearly intending to take me elsewhere to finish our little interview.

The metallic clunk of a shotgun cocking stopped us in our tracks, followed by a new voice. 'Let the girl go.'

We all three turned to see Jono behind the bar, aiming squarely at Mikhail, who actually looked like he'd been taken by surprise, for once. Understandably. I hadn't even seen Jono pull a pint, let alone a gun.

I didn't know what the hell was going on, but I knew an opportunity when I saw it. I drove my knee up into Mikhail's crotch as hard as I could, and he doubled over instantly, grunting in pain. I slammed my fist into the side of his head, and he stumbled over. I stamped first on his wrist, forcing him to let go of his weapon, then on his chest, satisfyingly breaking at least one rib, judging by the crack.

Olivier glanced between me, Jono, and the door. With Mikhail down, he was outnumbered, and he knew it. He made a run for the door. I tried to grab him, but his jacket slipped through my fingers.

'Let him go,' Jono instructed.

As Olivier escaped out into the night, and Mikhail cradled his balls and his broken ribs, I made my way over to Dimitri. Crouching at his side, I shook him by the shoulders, relieved beyond words when his eyelids fluttered. I ran my hand lightly over the side of his head, feeling a sizeable bump beneath his hair, but no blood.

Behind me, I heard movement, and turned to see Mikhail clambering to his feet. His face was red and angrier than I had ever seen it as he started towards me.

'Stop, or I'll shoot,' Jono bellowed, keeping his position behind the bar. Tad was nowhere in sight, and I hoped he was calling the police; I could do with some backup.

Mikhail looked to his left, where his weapon laid on the floor. I dove for it, and he followed suit. I don't know which of us touched it first, but somehow, seconds later,

Mikhail was on top of me. The cold, sticky tile floor was hard against my back, and the barrel of Mikhail's gun was hard against my left temple.

He'd won. He was stronger, and faster, and smarter. And he'd beat me.

His frost blue eyes were the only thing I could see, and it occurred to me that they were the last thing I'd ever see.

A gun shot echoed through the bar. I waited for the pain. But there was none. And then, Mikhail slumped onto me, his weight crushing down on my body. I couldn't breathe. And I was too hot, damp, sticky. My ears rang with a screeching pain.

Then Mikhail was gone, and I scrambled backwards across the floor instinctively. My hand slipped underneath me, and that's when I became aware of the blood. It was on me, around me. I sucked in a breath, but it was metallic. The blood was everywhere.

'Mari.' Dimitri's voice cut through my confusion like a knife.

I blinked, and looked up. He stood over me, pistol in one hand, the other reaching out for me. On the floor at his feet was Mikhail, gasping for breath, holding both hands over an apparent bullet wound in his chest.

'You shot him,' I realised, taking Dimitri's hand and letting him pull me to my feet.

Mikhail made a gurgling noise, through which I just about made out the word, 'Traitor.'

Dimitri squatted down next to him. 'You lost me when you killed Nina. And this death is too good for you.'

I realised then that Dimitri had shot Mikhail in the chest, wounding his lungs and heart, rather than in the temple. Even with Mikhail and I struggling, I had no doubt that Dimitri could've made the shot. But he wanted Mikhail to die more painfully, more slowly.

Part of me — the police officer part — was aware that this meant we would never get to bring Mikhail to justice, but another part of me was more than happy to watch him die.

Dimitri stood again, and pulled me into his chest, regardless of the blood that covered me. I breathed him in.

'Backup is on the way,' Jono announced from across the room. He still held the shotgun, though he'd lowered it.

'It's okay,' I replied. 'I'm a police officer, DS Harper Hallowell. You can stand down.'

'DS James Andrews. Nice to meet you — the real you,' he replied, with a conspiratorial smile.

I blinked. *What*?

Sirens interrupted the shocked silence, and I spun to face Dimitri.

'You have to go!' I told him.

'I'm not leaving you,' he argued, stubbornly unmoveable as I tried to push him towards the rear exit.

'Dimitri, please!' I begged. 'Police are coming, they will arrest you. Go, now!'

He stared at me, clearly conflicted. Then he pulled me into a tight embrace. 'You did it.'

I sighed. 'We did it.'

Pulling back, I took in Dimitri's beautiful face for what I knew was the last time. I wanted to memorise every detail, but there wasn't enough time.

'Get Val, and get out of the City,' I told him. 'Don't come back.'

He took my face in both hands and gave me the most passionate kiss of my life. His love enveloped me, and I felt like my chest was going to burst with the pain of having to say goodbye. I'd known that I'd have to let him go at some point, but I was still not prepared for how much it hurt.

'I love you. And I will never forget you.' Dimitri whispered against my lips.

'I love you, too.'

Then, he was gone. Forever.

Chapter Forty-Two

They put me in a hotel room and stationed officers outside the door.

For the first 24 hours, I was pretty much checked out. But after that, I was aware of the time dragging on, and I felt increasingly trapped with every passing second. There was no mini-bar, and the level to which I craved a drink was more than I needed to know about myself.

I overheard from the officers outside the door that Mikhail had died in the hospital shortly after reinforcement had arrived at the bar. I was gutted that he would never get his comeuppance in the eyes of the law, but I was also grateful that I would never have to face him again. I didn't want to ask about Dimitri for fear of raising suspicion — the official line was that he'd escaped despite my best efforts, and I needed it to stay that way.

Finally, after two days without any contact, I finally had visitors. Jono — or James, as I now knew him — knocked and entered the room, followed by Chief Superintendent Joseph Sawyer. Taylor had been in charge of our undercover unit, but Sawyer was Taylor's boss. I recognised him from a few meetings, but I'd never spoken to him before. The fact that he was here now meant that something was up, and my adrenaline spiked.

Was I in some kind of trouble here? Why had I been kept in this room, while James was apparently free to walk around with senior management?

'What's going on?' I demanded, standing.

Sawyer closed the door behind him, and the two men stood opposite me. I recognised the carefully composed expression on their faces; I'd used it, when I'd had to tell people that their loved ones had died.

'I'm Joseph,' Sawyer introduced himself. 'It's nice to

officially meet you, DS Hallowell.'

'I know who you are. Where's Taylor?' My heart was beating hard, but my voice was level.

'We have to tell you some things, and we need you to listen before you react,' Sawyer said, keeping his tone purposefully gentle, like I was some kind of fragile little girl.

'Just tell me.'

Sawyer and James exchanged a glance, then James stepped forward. 'First, we've lost Dimitri. He fled the scene, and we haven't been able to find him.'

I met his gaze. He knew that I'd told Dimitri to run, and given that he'd been posing as the owner of a bar where I'd spent a lot of time, he likely knew a lot more, too. But his words led me to believe that he also knew how to keep a secret.

'You know I've not had access to a phone, or been let out of this damn room,' I seethed. 'I have no idea where he is, if that's what you're getting at. And while we're on the subject, why *am* I in this room like some kind of prisoner?'

'Harper, please,' Sawyer approached me. 'Just hear us out.'

I bit my tongue. I was pissed, and I wasn't used to hearing my real name, but he was still in charge.

'We think he and Valentin have fled the country,' James continued. 'You don't need to worry about them.'

Sawyer nodded. 'We will know if they return. We wanted you to know you are safe.' Then, he sighed, and I felt my stomach sink. 'There's something else. You might want to sit down.'

'I'm fine,' I replied, bracing myself for whatever was about to come.

Except, I couldn't have prepared for what they said next.

'Taylor is dead.'

***

'The CCTV footage, the bartender's testimony, your phone recording and the texts on Mikhail's phone are enough to go after conspiracy. We've arrested two of the other men who were at the scene, and identified several informants who are willing to exchange details on the interlinking drug operations for their safety, or other such deals.'

'So they'll convict based on this?'

'This, plus everything you've seen? Yes.' Sawyer leaned forward on the table. 'This is why we need to do this now. I need you to walk me through everything that happened from the moment you met Dimitri, the moment you met Mikhail, up until he died.'

I sighed. This was going to be a long day.

***

A week later, I finally got back to my apartment. I hadn't been home for over a year. Everything was exactly as I'd left it; the mug on the draining board, the book on the coffee table, the half-burned candle on the mantelpiece. But it didn't feel like home anymore. I didn't want to be there. So I left.

***

James answered his phone immediately, and he didn't sound surprised to hear from me. I told him the name of the bar where I was, and asked him to meet me there. He arrived ten minutes later, sliding onto a barstool beside me and ordering a whiskey and coke.

'You didn't tell Sawyer about Dimitri.' I meant about my relationship with him, and the fact I let him get away, and James knew it. 'Why?'

'Undercover is a different world. We do what we need to do to survive.' The look in his eyes told me that he knew what he was talking about.

'I should lose my job for what I did.'

James shook his head. 'No. You're the only reason this operation succeeded.'

I scoffed, downing the last of my vodka. It reminded me painfully of Dimitri. 'You think Mikhail dying was a success? It's not exactly the outcome we were going for.'

'Isn't it?' James looked at me. 'We've disrupted not only this gang, but also the Colombian operation, the Thai group, numerous local dealers. If anything, we've done *more* than we set out to do. And that's down to you. The conspiracy charge would never have even been a passing thought without the intel you gained. Without help, I might add.'

'That's not strictly true,' I said, holding James's gaze.

'Dimitri helped you?' he guessed, his voice hushed, but neutral. He wasn't judging me.

I nodded. 'That's why I had to let him go.'

Now James's mouth turned up in a small, almost sad, smile. 'That's the only reason?'

I shrugged, turning my attention to my empty glass.

'I heard something today,' James said, apparently changing the subject. 'About Fabio.'

My head snapped up; my attention thoroughly captured. In all the craziness of the past week, I hadn't had time or space in my head to consider Fabio. 'Tell me.'

'His sentence has been dramatically reduced; 5 years, in exchange for everything he knows about Mikhail. Apparently, they got some evidence a couple of weeks ago that, although Fabio confessed, he wasn't the mastermind behind the gun trade. And it fits with this conspiracy charge, too. We all knew it was Mikhail anyway.'

I breathed a sigh of relief, and guessed Taylor had made good on his promise to help Fabio. My heart broke again that Taylor wasn't here to know that the operation had succeeded.

'There's more.' James paused, hesitating, but then continued, 'I know where his son is. I overheard that guy Jag on the phone one day, giving someone an address. It was just after Nina died. I noted it down. Shortly after, Fabio went down for the gun trade. It didn't take a genius to work it out.'

My heart pounded. I didn't even realise I'd stood up, but I was suddenly moving towards the door. James caught my arm.

'What are you doing?' I demanded. 'We have to go get the kid!'

'It's done,' he told me, keeping his voice calm, so as not to startle me with any loud noises. 'I already told Sawyer, and they picked him up yesterday. He's in child protective services, with added police protection.'

I sat down. I felt heavy. 'They'll change his identity, right? Send him far away from here for adoption.'

James nodded. 'Probably.'

'Does Fabio know?' I asked.

'Doubt it,' James replied. His eyes sparked with mischief, as a smile spread over his face. 'You wanna tell him?'

***

James told me to wait for the call, and when a withheld number appeared on my phone the next day, I answered immediately.

'Hello?'

'It's Fab. Who the hell is this?' His voice was hard and low, not how I was used to hearing it, but it was definitely him.

'It's me.'

Silence.

'Mari?' Fabio breathed.

I felt tears prick my eyes, and blinked furiously to hold them back. 'Yeah. Hi.'

'Shit. Some guy gave me this number this morning, told me to call it, or else. I figured I was about to be threatened or something.' I heard a smile in his voice. It sounded so good. 'This is definitely better than I expected.'

I couldn't help but laugh. 'Yeah? I'm glad.'

'I can't believe I'm hearing from you.'

'I'm sorry I've not been to visit. It's complicated, but I can't. That's why there's all this mystery around getting my number to you.'

'You know calls are recorded, right?'

'Yeah. So we can't talk again after this.'

Fabio sighed. 'Okay. What's going on? Is something wrong?'

'No, nothing's wrong. But I do have something to tell you.'

'What is it?'

'Your son is safe. He's in protective custody with child services. He's safe, Fabio.'

There was a moment of silence, and then Fabio sobbed gently into the phone. His relief was almost enough to patch up the damage to my broken heart. Almost.

***

James had kept my secret about Dimitri. He'd saved Fabio's son, and somehow snuck my number into prison, so that I could tell Fabio the good news myself. So I thought I could trust him. And I knew he was the only one who fell into that category, and the only one who'd be able to help me. So I took the leap of faith, and I told him the secret that had been eating away at me since I'd found out about Taylor.

The secret I hadn't even told Sawyer.

'There's a leak in the police department. Mikhail had a contact, who kept him informed about our operation.'

I'd expected him to be shocked, but James simply nodded. 'I know. That's why it took so long to bring him down. He knew what we were doing, before we knew we were doing it.'

'You know?' I repeated, incredulous. 'Why the hell haven't you said anything to Sawyer?'

'Why haven't you?' James countered.

I said nothing.

'I don't trust Sawyer, either.' James said, confirming my own suspicions.

'I told Taylor about the police leak, and next thing I know, he's dead.' It sounded crazy to say out loud. But again, James just nodded.

'Yep.' He fixed me with an earnest look. 'And there's no way Taylor didn't tell Sawyer. Which means Sawyer's covering something up. So, I guess that means it's down to the two of us to find out what the hell is going on.'

I took a breath, downed my drink, and nodded.

So much for returning to a normal life.

The end.

About the Author

Natasha Head was born and raised in the Cotswolds, England. She grew up reading everything she could get her hands on, and started writing stories from an early age. As a Forensic Psychology graduate, Natasha's interests in storytelling, crime and human behaviour combined to create her first full-length work of fiction, The City.

When she's not writing, Natasha enjoys staying active, spending time with friends, and snuggling up with her cats.

Find out more by following Natasha on social media:

Instagram: @_love.your.shelf

TikTok: @_love.your.shelf

www.blossomspringpublishing.com

Printed in Great Britain
by Amazon